Books by Loren D. Estleman

Kill Zone
Roses Are Dead
Any Man's Death
Motor City Blue
Angel Eyes
The Midnight Man
The Glass Highway
Sugartown
Every Brilliant Eye
Lady Yesterday
Downriver
Silent Thunder
Sweet Women Lie
Never Street
The Witchfinder
The Hours of the Virgin
A Smile on the Face of the Tiger
*City of Widows**
*The High Rocks**
*Billy Gashade**
*Stamping Ground**
*Aces & Eights**
*Journey of the Dead**
*Jitterbug**
*The Rocky Mountain Moving Picture Association**
*The Master Executioner**
*White Desert**
Sinister Heights
*Something Borrowed, Something Black**

*A Forge Book

Poison Blonde

An Amos Walker Novel

Loren D. Estleman

A Tom Doherty Associates Book
New York

This is a work of fiction. All the characters and events portrayed in this novel are either fictitious or are used fictitiously.

POISON BLONDE

This book is printed on acid-free paper.

A Forge Book
Published by Tom Doherty Associates, LLC
175 Fifth Avenue
New York, NY 10010

www.tor.com

Forge® is a registered trademark of Tom Doherty Associates, LLC.

Library of Congress Cataloging-in-Publication Data

Estleman, Loren D.
Poison blonde: an Amos Walker novel / Loren D. Estleman.—1st Forge ed.
p. cm.
ISBN 0-765-30447-3 (acid-free paper)
1. Walker, Amos (Fictitious character)—Fiction. 2. Private investigators—Michigan—Detroit—Fiction. 3. Detroit (Mich.)—Fiction. 4. Illegal aliens—Fiction. 5. Women singers—Fiction. I. Title.

PS3555.S84 P65 2003
813'.54—dc21

2002035242

First Edition: April 2003

Printed in the United States of America

0 9 8 7 6 5 4 3 2 1

With love, for Kevin Williams and Jill Mulkey:
two stories of depth and devotion, bound in striking covers.

Poison Blonde

ONE

The last line of security was a big Basque built like a coke oven. He wore a familiar face behind picador sideburns and a dozen-odd rivets in his eyebrows, nose, and the deep dimple above his lip. In another Detroit, under a different administration, he'd specialized in kneecapping Republicans. When the market went soft in '94, he'd scored work in show business, playing a succession of plumbers, janitors, and building superintendents in Spanish-language soap operas. I couldn't approach him without glancing down at his chest for a subtitle.

"Hello, Benny. I thought you'd be busy opening a supermarket."

He looked at me down the treacherous bends in his nose, one of which I claimed credit for. A caterpillar had taken up residence under his nostrils, which were as big as gunports. Fourteen-karat gold buttons gleamed on his mahogany double-breasted Armani. He looked like a tall chest of drawers. "It's Benito," he said.

"Benito like in Mussolini? I didn't know you were Italian."

"Benito like in Juarez. I'm Chicano."

"You were Colombian back when you smuggled cocaine aboard the old mayor's jet. You must have more passports than a soccer team."

"What you doing here?"

"Working, same as you. And for the same person. She's chilling me a bottle of Tecate right now." I showed him my pass. It contained no words, just a holographic image of Genesius, patron saint of theatrical performers. He looked at it, crossed himself out of habit, and reached behind his back to rap the door.

"*¿Quién es?*" A smooth contralto, deadened slightly by the panels.

"Benito, *señorita. Es un visitador.*"

"Right on time. Hokay."

He worked the doorknob, again without turning. I had to walk around him to get through. On the way, he leaned down and called me a son of a whore in border Spanish. I grinned and patted his big face. It was like slapping a truck tire. His hand jerked toward his left underarm, also out of habit. He remembered where he was and let it drop.

Where he was was Cobo Hall, three hundred thousand square feet of convention arena, exhibition space, and concert facilities on the western end of the Detroit Civic Center, a white marble aircraft carrier of a building with a green granite section tacked on forty years ago and a curving covered promenade that looked like a furnace pipe with windows. Some history had taken place there, including the Republican National Convention of 1980, several decades of auto shows, and a couple of hundred body slams courtesy of the World Wrestling Federation. The incoming traffic plunged straight under the building by way of the John Lodge Expressway and parked on the roof, where the windshields shattered by homegrown vandals and tape-deck thieves tinkled down like fairy dust.

The dressing room I'd entered was one of the largest on the site, reserved in the past for presidential hopefuls, famous fat tenors, and the occasional evangelist and his mistresses. It had been done over more times than the government of Argentina. At present it was dressed in the colors of the flag of the island nation that had given birth to its present occupant, with some Roman Catholic bric-a-brac cast about and a portable bar as big as a pumpwagon, stocked with lethal-looking spirits with foreign labels. One of those gurgling mood recordings that make your bladder ache was playing on a hidden stereo system.

"Your name is Hamos, yes?"

The contralto was stronger without a door standing in front of it. It belonged to a tiny woman in a plum-colored kimono sitting at a Moorish vanity table, inspecting both profiles in a three-way mirror lit from behind. She looked both smaller and darker than she did in concert, but at close range it was the white-gold of her hair that made her caramel skin seem duskier than it was. With the waist-length waves pinned up in braids and no arcs or fills to bring out the glitter, she looked like a well-preserved old lady. I had a bottle of Scotch older than she was, and I can't afford a vintage label.

"Amos," I said. "If it makes you uncomfortable, you can call me Mr. Walker."

She caught my eye in one of the mirrors. Hers were a very deep brown, almost black, but too warm to bridge that gap; but you can get any effect with contacts. Eyes had gone the way of lips, breasts, noses, and hair, as protean as a sandhill. I hadn't bothered to crack *The Big Book of Facial Features* since before I renewed my license.

"*Comprendo*. You don't want your picture took with me. Hokay. You like, let's see, the oldies but the goodies, no? The Platters, the Drifters, the Dave Clark Four?"

"Five. I'm not eighty. Your stuff's fine. It's got a beat and you can dance to it, if you've consulted your physician first. It's your personal protection I don't like. Big Bad Benny's turn-ons include arson and pulling the skin off DEA agents."

"Talk to my manager. He hired him." She smoothed an eyebrow with a little finger. A holy icon was painted on the nail in glittering red and gold. "I'm Gilia, but I guess you know that." She pronounced the name as if it started with *H*.

"I do. I saw you once on MTV when my Kay Kyser tape ran out."

She filled and emptied her celebrated lungs. "I apologize, hokay? In my country you were born either before the coup or after. Is a wide space between. You learn to translate."

I moved a shoulder. It would have taken more than an armed military takeover of her government or mine to draw attention from the Gilia phenomenon. She was Carmen Miranda, Ricky Martin, and the Baja Marimba Band all rolled into one ninety-six-pound package. They were splitting and splicing words in order to pigeonhole her: rock-salsa, Cuban hip-hop, jalapeno pop. She sang and danced in front of back-projected hydrogen bomb explosions in stadiums and concert halls and on military bases, owned a record label and a Hollywood production company, and had signed with United Artists to be the next Bond girl. Two years before, she'd made the rent on her fourth-floor walk-up in East L.A. by dubbing in the voice of a cartoon cat on Little Friskies commercials.

In the meantime she'd broken up half the storied marriages on the West Coast, served six months' probation for illegal possession of a controlled substance, and performed eighty hours of community service for running a red light, broadsiding a Bel Air cop, and spilling his coffee. The only thing the Christian Right and the Politically Correct Left had agreed on in years was the importance of tying a bell around Gilia's neck. That was why the security was so tight at Cobo and I was picking up cigarette money patting down people in line at the entrance for fragmentary grenades.

"I heard someone say you're a private detective. I didn't know they did this kind of work."

"I didn't either, until I bounced a check off Detroit Edison."

"What kind of work do you do when your checks don't bounce?"

"I look for people who went missing. As I recall."

"Oh." Her face fell as far as a face can fall on her side of twenty-five. But before that I caught a golden snap of light in her eye. She was going to do just fine in the movies.

I looked at my watch. I didn't have anyplace to be, but I'd drunk a Thermos full of coffee outside and the gurgling music had begun to have its effect. "If it's my fast draw you wanted to see, I haven't greased my holster since Christmas."

"Are you any good at following people?"

She'd stopped looking at me in the mirror. She'd half twisted my way, resting an elbow on the back of her chair and letting the kimono fall open to expose a caramel thigh. Her bare foot was stuck in a slipper that was just a strip of leather and a pompon. She had a high arch and a pumiced heel. That altered my opinion of her, a little. You can always tell a woman who works on her feet by how well she takes care of them.

"It's one of the things I'm best at," I said.

She studied my face for irony. Her brows were steeply arched as well, undyed black in contrast to her hair, and she had a good straight conquistador nose, a strong chin, and a fragile upper lip; no collagen there to turn it into a slice of liverwurst. The bones were good. Age would not harm her.

She said, "I have a thief in my employ. You can follow her, yes? Find out who she is stealing it for. I will pay you ten percent of the value of what she has stolen so far."

"How much has she stolen?"

"Seventy-five thousand dollars."

"I can follow her, yes," I said.

TWO

You can tell more about an entertainer's career by whether you've ever heard of him than by who he's opening for. If the name is unfamiliar, he's on his way up, sharing a bill with a big star. If you remember him vaguely, he's on his way down with an armload of anvils, warming the stage for a Johnny- or Janie-come-lately who was in diapers when he was headlining in New York and Vegas. Gilia's opener was a country crossover whose first hit had been his last, and whose most recent exposure had been an *Entertainment Tonight* feature on his release from detox and a riches-to-rags spot on *Behind the Music*. The underwear being flung at him by the women at Cobo had plenty of Lycra.

From where I stood, his hip-swivel seemed to have developed a hitch, and he couldn't hit middle C with a shovel; but from backstage even the best acts always look like Open Mike Night at the Pig 'n' Whistle. In any case I wasn't being paid to follow the program. I only had eyes for the wardrobe mistress.

Her name was Caterina Muñoz, and like many women trained to match a three-hundred-dollar scarf to a pair of crocodile pumps, she dressed like a fire in the big top. She was a dumpy sixty with her hair chopped short and dyed bright copper, and she had cut a hole in a painter's drop cloth and stuck her head through it on her way out the door. I watched her using a portable steamer to take the creases out of a dozen of Gilia's costumes hanging from a rack on wheels and wondered what she was spending the money on, since it didn't appear to be clothes.

According to Gilia, the Muñoz had sold a pirate photograph of her employer trying on the gown she'd planned to wear to the Golden Globe Awards in January to a supermarket tabloid, which had run it on the front page. This had forced Gilia to spend another seventy-five grand on a replacement gown. She'd shown me pictures of herself wearing both outfits. I used more material cleaning my revolver, but that wasn't the point. Without quite resorting to a pie chart, she'd convinced me the surprise factor on the red carpet outside the arena was worth a couple of million in good press. No surprise, no sizzle.

"What makes it Caterina?" I'd asked. "Anyone can sneak a picture."

"She was the only one present at the fittings, apart from the designer. *Signor* Garbo makes tons more money keeping his designs secret than he ever would selling the details."

Everything about that made sense, not counting the name *Signor* Garbo. Now the Grammies were in the chute and she wanted me to nail the wardrobe mistress and her contact before history repeated itself. With a tour of Canada on tap after Detroit, she was reasonably certain the next exchange would have to take place locally. That meant a tail job, and with my five-hundred-dollar-a-day rate guaranteed and a payoff of seventy-five hundred if I delivered, I could spend the rest of the winter sopping up the sun on a beach in Cleveland.

Muñoz was busy throughout the concert. The hardest part about keeping an eye on her was staying out of the way of an army of grips and talent wheeling pianos, a harp, banks of lights, and set pieces throughout the wings at Grand Prix speed. The place smelled of perspiration, ozone, animal-friendly cosmetics, marijuana, and all the other indispensable effluvia of show business. I saw a relationship consummated in a stairwell, overheard someone giving someone else complicated directions to the local cocaine connection, and almost tripped over a female backup singer having a full-blown anxiety attack during a cellular telephone conversation with her analyst in Pasadena. There was enough material there to keep an enterprising private detective in business through Thanksgiving. Meanwhile the woman under surveillance recycled the costumes as needed, catching discarded articles of clothing on the fly, handing out changes, and sewing split seams with an arsenal of needles and spools of thread from an emergency basket she carried slung over one shoulder.

I saw Gilia naked many times. She peeled out of her Wonderbras and sweat-soaked bikini panties and rigged up for the next number without bothering to seek cover, while the hundred or so supernumeraries, most of them male, boiled about her showing all the interest of vegetarians at a steak fry. I got tired of looking at it myself, but then the whomping guitars, amplified drums, and laser effects had my head hammering like Sunday morning, and anyway there wasn't a major magazine in the country that hadn't featured every pore of her body at one time or another. It was an athletic body, but without a G-string or a halter top to call attention to the racy parts, it was just a slipcase for her talent.

The scalpers were getting five hundred bucks per ticket, and she gave the victims their money's worth. Her brand of juiced-up Latino music had been burning down the competition from rap and third-generation rock for months, and she showed no signs of coasting. At the climax she climbed into a harness attached to a boom and soared around the auditorium fifty feet above the audience's heads, belting out her chart-topper of the month over a radio headset and flapping a pair of electrified butterfly wings that would have blown every fuse at Tiger Stadium during the 1984 World Series. She had a voice, too; what could be heard of it above the roar from the seats. It chilled spines and tightened every scrotum this side of Windsor.

When the concert finished, a flying wedge of Cobo security guards formed around her with Benito, the born-again Chicano, at the point, and swept her down to the basement and the private exit the Detroit Police had cleared for her escape. The announcer, a squirt in a pompadour with an exposed heart and lungs printed on his T-shirt, gave her fifteen minutes, then announced over the

P.A. system that the butterfly had flown. More security appeared to usher out the fans and prevent the seats from being torn loose of their bolts.

I hung around while Muñoz packed Gilia's costumes into a wheeled trunk, taking note in a memorandum pad as she did so of missing buttons, broken zippers, and ripped linings. Off in an untrafficked corner, yesterday's country-pop powerhouse stood smoking a conventional cigarette with this month's rent written all over his face.

The wardrobe mistress accompanied a pair of grips in the elevator to basement parking and watched while the trunk was locked away in an unmarked van. I went along, attracting less notice than the elevator carpet. I stood between a couple of cars pretending to fish in my pocket for my keys while she chirped open the lock on a rental Toyota and got in. She had a nine-by-twelve manila envelope in one hand.

Gilia had arranged a slot for me near the van. I climbed under the wheel of the venerable Cutlass and tickled the big plant into bubbling life. I'd replaced the carburetor recently, steam-cleaned the engine, and yanked the antipollution equipment I'd had installed to clear my last inspection. The body was battered, the blue finish broken down to powder, and thirty blistering Michigan summers and marrow-freezing lake effect winters had cracked the vinyl top, but I could hose Japan off the road in a head wind.

I gave her until the exit ramp, then pulled out and followed. I wanted a look at what was in the envelope.

Muñoz's megastar employer was staying at the Hyatt Regency in Dearborn, for the very good reason that after three decades of recovery from the riots, Detroit had yet to harbor a hotel where the silverfish didn't have a key to the executive floor. When the Toyota turned west on Fort, I thought that was where she was headed. When she swung north on Grand and made a left on the Dix Highway I was sure of it. Then she made another left onto Vernor and we entered a foreign country.

DelRay—the old Hungarian section southwest of downtown—had been going steadily Mexican since the 1990s. *Carnicerías* and Mexican restaurants had opened in former pastry shops and Gypsy storefronts, and on Cinco de Mayo the streets teemed with pretty *señoritas*, well-kept children in native dress, and mariachis. It was February, and only the Spanish signs and one old woman in a head scarf carrying home a sackful of fresh-slaughtered *pollo* identified the area apart from the many other neighborhoods trying to make the long slow climb from hookshops and crack houses toward lower-middle-class respectability. The current mayor's face smiled out from a ragged poster carrying the legend *Vota ¡Si! por* Detroit.

The Toyota turned down a side street and parked in a lot next to a building with a sign on it warning drivers in Spanish and English that it was for residents only. It was the sort of building that had been new when sharing the same roof with a few dozen other families was considered novel and suspiciously European; its sandstone corners were worn round as loaves of bread and the arched windows near the roof appeared to be holding up their skirts to avoid contact with the three rows of prosaic rectangles beneath their feet. But a decade ago the whole thing had been headed toward demolition, and most of the glass panes had only recently taken the place of weathered plywood.

I drove past, turned around in the driveway of a Queen Anne house with a scaffold in front, and parked across the street from the apartment building. The Toyota was still there. Its driver was not.

It was a clear winter night, no snow, but the moon was as bright as halogen. My breath smoked in the splintery air. On my way to the front door I made a detour and peered through the rental car's windows front and back. There was no sign of the manila envelope on any of the seats.

A Mexican in his forties, built close to the floor but powerfully, opened the gridded-glass door when I thumbed the buzzer marked SUPERINTENDENTE. He had on a navy sweat suit and black work shoes, but his face belonged between a sombrero and crossed bandoliers. It was broad and brown and wore two heavy black bars, one above the eyes, the other under the nose. He combed his thick black hair straight back without a part.

"*¿Habla inglés?*" I asked. I hoped the answer was *sí*. I'd exhausted my high school Spanish.

"A little." It came out flat even with the accent.

I gave him a glimpse of the sheriff's star the county wasn't using anymore. "Caterina Muñoz."

"You don't look like a Caterina Muñoz."

"I'm laughing inside. Sixty, five-two, a hundred and sixty, red hair. She came in a minute ago. Which apartment?"

"You ain't no deputy."

"Neither was Alexander Hamilton." I stretched a bill between my hands.

He looked at it, then at me. "Fourteen C. By the elevator."

I gave him the ten-spot. He folded it into quarters, spat on it, and flicked it at my chest. It bounced off and landed at my feet. "There ain't no fourteen C. There ain't no elevator either."

I stepped back in time to avoid picking glass out of my face.

I stood there sucking a cheek, then picked up the folded bill, wiped it off against the doorframe, and went back to the car. The wave of honesty that had begun to wash over the working class threatened to put me out of business.

Ten minutes later I was still sitting behind the wheel, watching the door, when it opened and half of San Ignacio spilled out into the moonlight. All four men were built like the super, but they looked more like one another in the face than they looked like him, and they were younger by at least fifteen years. They bore a resemblance to someone else as well. I was working on just who when they spotted me. They fanned out like professional gunfighters and came my way, not bothering to look for traffic as they crossed. They wore construction workers' uniforms, heavy-duty overalls over cotton twill shirts, and their heads were sunk between their shoulders in a way no one ever has to teach anyone. I popped open the special compartment I'd had built into the dash, took out the unregistered Luger, got out, and closed the door behind me with the Luger stuck under my belt in front where they could see it.

That stopped them, but only long enough to run the odds. You have to be very good to place four slugs where they need to be placed in the time you need to do it. They decided I wasn't that good. They came on. I drew the pistol and snicked off the safety.

"Pedro! Pablo! Juan! Diego!"

The names rang out in bursts like someone testing a machine gun. The men stopped on the center line. The woman who had shouted at them charged down the front stoop of the apartment house and crossed the street. The four parted to let her through and she closed the distance between us, pumping her arms and slapping the frozen pavement with the thin soles of her slippers. Her black eyes were fierce and her hair sparked bright copper above the ridiculous poncho.

I put away the Luger. I know when I'm outgunned.

THREE

Big Bad Benny put down his prop copy of *Don Quixote* and got up from his chair when I came off the elevator. He'd changed into a windowpane plaid sport coat and brown turtleneck, but he still looked like a massive piece of furniture.

I wasn't in the mood for him. I hit him without missing a step and he tripped over his feet and fell back against the wall, jarring the whole floor. I used the meaty part of my fist on the door to the suite.

The door swung away while I was pounding and I had to check myself to avoid hitting Gilia, not that the idea lacked merit. It was morning at the Hyatt, the drapes were wide-open, and she stood against the light in green-and-silver lounging pajamas with white espadrilles on her feet. Her hair hung free to her waist, casting a white-gold halo. "Mr. Walker," she said.

I lowered my fist and held up the eight-by-ten photograph I had in my other hand. It was a color shot of Gilia in her butterfly wings, with the suspending wires airbrushed out so she appeared to be flying under her own power. Someone had used a black felt-tip pen to write, "*A Pablo, con amore de* Gilia," in the lower right-hand corner.

"Caterina had eight of these in an envelope," I said. "The others were signed to Pedro, Juan, Diego, and four of the lesser apostles. She said you signed them."

Her nose twitched. "Have you been drinking?"

"Mescal. That's what the Muñoz family serves in Mexicantown. We got on like Cisco and Pancho, once we moved past that business of wanting to beat me to death on a public street. But I slept it off, or tried to. You're smelling it on my clothes on account of I couldn't decide what shirt to put on this morning to come down here and throw you out a window. You shouldn't have left the wings at Cobo."

Something tickled me behind the right ear. I knew it was a pistol. "Let's go to the basement." Benny's breath was warm on the back of my neck.

"Thank you, Benito. Mr. Walker and I have some things to talk about."

"I don't think so, *señorita*. He's no good for you."

"Should I call Hector and get his opinion?"

There was a little silence. Then my ear stopped tickling.

"Come in, Mr. Walker. Can I offer you breakfast? They always bring too much." She turned and walked away from the door, leaving me to close it in Benny's face. I wondered who Hector was and why I didn't like the name. Benny hadn't either, the way she drew it like a knife.

The sitting room was as large as most complete hotel rooms, with fat club chairs, a love seat, a twenty-seven-inch TV set on a stand, and a round oak table with four sturdy chairs. The table was covered with dishes containing omelets, rashers of bacon, hash browns, slabs of toast, and a stack of pancakes wallowing in syrup. It all looked and smelled good to someone who hadn't eaten since last night, but all I took was coffee. I put down the picture, poured from a white carafe into an unused cup, and put it away in a lump. It scalded my throat and burned away the last of the mescal. Juan—or maybe it was Diego; all four brothers looked alike—had made a production of fishing the worm out of the bottom of the bottle and swallowing it like a goldfish. He was the family comedian.

"Do you mind if I get dressed while we talk? I'll leave the door open." Gilia spoke from the bedroom.

I set down the cup and went through that door. "Go ahead. Pretend I'm your crew."

She'd taken a dress on a hanger from the closet. Now she thought better of it and hung it back up. Two people alone in a bedroom was not the same as a hundred people backstage. She was either a woman with facets or a woman who wanted me to think she had them. She sat on the upholstered bench at the foot of the king bed, pressed her knees together, and folded her hands in her lap. The room had a good view of Dearborn and the Glass House, where Ford executives sat around long tables like in a *New Yorker* cartoon, chewing Mylanta and arguing about Tokyo and General Motors.

"Caterina Muñoz's nephews and their families live in Detroit," I said. "That slipped your mind. It didn't when you signed a picture for each of them."

"That was months ago, at her request. Before the betrayal."

"I'm not *People* magazine. You can't brass this one out. I had a long talk with the wardrobe lady. Her English isn't so good, but her nephews helped translate. One of *Signor* Garbo's assistants took that shot of you in your Golden Globes dress with a James Bond camera and sold it to the tabloid. The designer fired and blacklisted the party, all *sub rosa*, because the publicity would ruin him and he'd have to go back to calling himself Manny Schwartz. Only he and the assistant and you and Caterina knew about it. She's been with you since your first audition. That doesn't mean so much, maybe, but you pay better than the tabloids."

"She's worth it. I hope you didn't turn her against me."

"That's between the two of you. I'm not the one who rigged the frame. Why's a good place to start."

She looked at me. She looked down at her hands. She looked at the Glass House and got no help there either, so she looked back up at me. At least she'd given up on the pidgin English. That had begun to get old when the job still looked legitimate.

"You don't know what it's like," she said. "Oh, I suppose you've heard the usual celebrity complaint, about privacy and how much you have to spend to have it. I made that trade in the beginning and I never missed it. But you make a little money, okay, a lot of money, and soon everyone you meet has a chisel. It seems I've never hired an orphan or an only child. Everyone has a mother or a brother or a cousin ten times removed who's out of work, and they all wind up on my payroll. When someone told me I had a private detective working security with the experience to help me out, who wouldn't spill the story to *Access Hollywood* for a couple of thousand bucks, I couldn't go on just that. You might be someone's uncle."

"Caterina was a dry run."

She nodded. Then she got up and hugged herself and looked at her reflection in the full-length mirror on the closet door. Her hair made a pale golden fall to her seat. Without help it would be blue-black and full of mystery: Truth in Advertising. Her eyes found mine in the mirror.

"If you're waiting for some kind of apology, you're wasting five hundred dollars a day. I owe it to Caterina, but except for the part that hurt her I'd do it again. There's too much—on the line, is that how you say it? Too much on the line to take anyone's word that you can be trusted. You found me out fast enough, but am I going to have to wait a week and not read about last night in *USA Today* to know I have your confidence?"

"I could give you references," I said. "You may even have heard of some of them. But then they'd have to give you references to vouch for them, and so on. It's a conga line without an end. Somewhere you'll have to take someone on faith. I'm not saying it has to be here, but it would save you a lot of time."

"My name's not Gilia."

That brought me up short. I knew she'd make the decision, and I thought it would be on the side of trust, but I'd expected more of a stretch while she made it. But she'd come a long way in a small space of time; a minute to me was an hour in Gilia years, or whatever name she called them. She'd turned from the mirror and was facing me, still hugging herself, as if there were a draft. If anything the room was overheated, a climate she would find familiar.

I went to the bedroom TV, hit the power button, found a cable news station, and ran up the volume. A woman correspondent in ugly glasses and a head scarf was standing in front of a cave in Afghanistan, describing it for viewers who didn't know what a cave looked like. If Benny or anyone else had his ear pressed to the outside door, that was what he would hear. I shut the bedroom door and the cone of silence was complete.

"My real name wouldn't interest you," said the woman who was not named Gilia. "I left it home for a reason, and, anyway, it doesn't mean anything anywhere else. The woman of that name is wanted by the police."

"Ours or theirs?"

"Theirs. My native soil grows two things very well: coffee and police. Each year the harvest is richer than the year before."

I gave her a helpful nod. I'd seen footage: Peaked caps, Sam Browne belts, truncheons; everything from the SS catalogue, summer 1940. They changed presidents with the sheets but never the uniforms or their tactics. That was a pocket of the world the Greatest Generation had overlooked.

"What charge, enemy of the state?"

"Murder."

"Ah."

She lifted her chin. She knew all her best features. "What's that mean?"

"American for *olé*. Murder's something I know a bit about. For a minute there I was afraid I was going to have to recommend someone."

"We had a revolution five years ago. You might have seen something about it between the sports and weather; that's about how long it lasted. The leader of the rebels, when he wasn't firing his assault rifle and running backwards, shared his tent with two women. Well, one woman and one girl. The woman was killed. Poisoned, they said, by an injection of Stelazine. Do you know it?"

I shook my head.

"I've learned much about it since then. In small doses, it's used to treat depression. In larger doses it causes drowsiness, convulsions, fever, hypotension, and cardiac arrest. All this starts to happen in twenty minutes if taken orally. Immediately when injected. The woman didn't suffer from depression. Quite the opposite." She pulled a face.

I said nothing. I had a picture of bare brown shoulders, flying petticoats, white teeth, and tonsils. I'd seen *The Wild Bunch* a time too many.

"Ordinarily," she said, "a crime of passion wouldn't have made the front section of the newspaper in the capital, but the government saw its opportunity to drive the rebels apart. A federal warrant was issued for the girl's arrest."

"Would there be a trial involved, or would that be untidy?"

"There would be a very public trial. Otherwise there would be no point in issuing the warrant. And the girl would get off."

That prevented me from finishing the story for her. In my version the girl was convicted.

She was watching me. "Ask me on what grounds."

"Okay," I said.

"On grounds of the first law of nature," she said. "No one can be in two places at the same time."

"It's not only a law, it's a good idea. So why wouldn't that come out, or am I getting ahead again? I'm supposed to ask if it came out."

"It's okay. I'm tired of that game. There was no trial. The defendant ran away because her alibi was worse than the crime for which she was charged. Or at least it was in the eyes of the government. Either way she faced execution.

"Someone slipped a needle into that woman's neck while she was passed out on cheap wine," she said. "At the moment that was happening I was three hours away at a small fishing harbor, helping a man down a path to a boat. He had trouble seeing the path. He had only one eye. Someone at the prison had placed a red-hot penny on the other one when he wouldn't tell him who his friends were."

I said, "Ah!" again. The moment seemed worth being redundant.

"They call it the Lincoln Question down there," she said. "I couldn't testify without condemning myself for smuggling political prisoners out of the country; *Señor* Cyclops wasn't my first. And if I *did* testify, the witnesses I named to back me up would go to the gallows.

"One week later I took the same path and got into a boat."

I lit a cigarette. It wasn't a smoking room, but one eye had begun to itch. I needed the distraction.

"What's the blackmailer's name?" I asked.

"You are one smart *hombre*. I'm starting to think I made the right choice." She stopped hugging herself and did the hair-flip. The weight of it must have been pulling against her spine. "The blackmailer's name is Gilia."

FOUR

On TV, a man stood in a parking lot shouting about how many automobiles he had in stock. Why do they always have to yell? Everyone needs cars.

"The blind begin to see," I said, not to the man on TV.

The woman who was living in Gilia's hotel suite hugged herself again. "My country is like eBay. Anything's available if you're willing to bid high enough. A grubby little petty official sold me an original birth certificate, issued to a girl who'd died in infancy within a few months of my own birthdate. I applied for a passport under that name. It was Gilia Cristobal.

"The rest was easy. Not the show business part. Back home, I sang on the radio at sixteen. I knew I had talent, but it took a long time for anyone to see that here. First I had to learn English. Paying for lessons exhausted my—what do you call it, the money you need to escape and establish yourself elsewhere?"

"Disney dollars."

"No." She scowled, deep in thought. "Stake, yes? Stake."

"Getaway stake. Case dough, if your friends call you Fast John. I don't guess the lessons got that far."

"*Sí*, getaway stake. I cleaned houses, stuffed envelopes. For six whole months I telemarketed. I would rather roll cigars. At least you see the faces of the people who scream at you. People say I am an overnight success. Maybe, if you count the nights I slept on the Interurban. Four years is a very long time to wait for your break when they are filled with such nights."

"Some whole lives are filled with such nights."

"I know. I do not complain. I'm just saying, people see I'm young and famous and rich and so they think I am lucky. They say you must have lived to deserve so much. There are twelve-year-old prostitutes walking the streets of the city of my birth, girls whose parents died against walls because they gave food to a rebel. They have fifty-year-old faces. They have lived."

I leaned into the bathroom and flushed my cigarette stub. When I came back out she hadn't moved. "When did Gilia Cristobal come back from the dead the second time?" I asked.

She nodded, in response to nothing. She was still thinking about the child prostitutes. "I said you were one smart *hombre*. The death notice that appeared in the newspaper was inaccurate. She was close to death from infantile paralysis, but she recovered. After her parents separated, she came to America with her mother, using her mother's maiden name. Here she is Jillian Rubio. She wrote me the first time a year ago. She enclosed copies of her birth certificate and immigration papers. Also a newspaper clipping in Spanish with the full particulars of the poisoning of the rebel leader's woman."

"That took detective work."

"As I said, in my country everything is for sale. The official I bribed knew who I was, I could tell. He probably made as much money selling the information to the Rubio woman as I paid him."

"Bad move. He stood to earn a lot more from you for keeping it to himself."

"If he were smart, he'd have been in charge of much more than the office of records. The same cannot be said of Jillian Rubio. I've been paying her five thousand dollars a month for a year for the privilege of using her birth name."

"You could have paid to get her off your neck anytime. Why now?"

"But I am not. I'm offering to pay to get her back on my neck."

The U.S. attorney general was speaking. Someone had tried to hijack a plane with a glue gun, and interior decorators had been added to the profile list. I switched off the set. I'd only turned it on to raise her confidence.

"Does this suite come with a bar?"

She shook her head. "I can call room service."

I shook my own head. "I thought maybe I'd been drinking and forgot. Let me back up a panel. The job's to ask your blackmailer to go on blackmailing you."

"Yes and no. Is there much construction on the street where you live?"

"I live in Detroit. No one's constructed anything since Henry Ford was a junior."

"Bad example, then. Okay, maybe you've been stuck someplace where you had to put up with a constant noise. After a few minutes you think you'll go crazy if it doesn't stop. An hour goes by, then another. It goes on for a week, day and night. Suddenly it stops, and the silence is so loud you think you'll go crazy if the noise doesn't start up again."

I grunted. The murk continued to clear.

"The details are simple. On the thirteenth of each month, I arrange to place the cash in small bills at Jillian Rubio's feet. She goes away and I don't have to think about her for another month. If I miss a payment, everything I've told you goes to the police. If anything happens to her, same thing. Remember, she thinks I'm a murderer, so she's fixed things so the information will be passed along in the event of her death or disappearance for three months."

"It doesn't take much fixing. All she needs is a safe-deposit box. In this country, a tax examiner has to be present when a box belonging to a deceased party is opened. Anything suspicious becomes public record."

"In my country, they pocket the loot. I'd prefer it in this case. Once it becomes known I lied on my visa application, I'll be deported home, where I'll stand trial, either for murder or treason or both. I might as well opt for both. They can only hang me once."

"The three-month bit could be a gag, or she could have left the stuff with a friend. Probably not, though. Any friend a blackmailer is inclined to make can be trusted as long as no one sneezes. Maybe her box rent comes due every quarter. The bank would have to have the examiner in to open it if she defaults. When did the noise stop?"

"On the thirteenth of November. The money was there; she wasn't. I thought she'd been detained and would be in touch to arrange another date. I have no way of contacting her. She always called me. She didn't, and she also missed December and January. Next week is three months." She made a hoarse little noise of amusement. "I ought to write a song about the situation; it's ironic enough to go platinum. As long as she went on bleeding me, I knew I was safe. Now she's stopped, and I can only wait for the other shoe to drop. That is the expression, isn't it? The other shoe."

"Uh-huh. She might be in jail or the hospital. Or she might be sacked out at home in front of *Days of Our Lives*, letting you work up a lather while she gets ready to raise her rates. Her kind is very good at psychology. It's their only weapon and they spend a lot of time polishing it."

"Or she might be dead."

"She might be dead," I agreed. "Even a blackmailer can get run over by an innocent bus."

"The flaw in the system. Except I don't suppose she cared about acts of God when she set it up. Can you find her? If she is dead and I know it, I can at least be prepared for what's about to happen. I can always run."

She hadn't convinced even herself of that. Her upper lip alone stood two stories high on billboards throughout the lower forty-eight, promoting her national tour, and you couldn't tune in MTV without seeing her stamp holes in Standards and Practices on one of her videos. She'd need more than Groucho glasses and a fright wig to go underground anywhere in the free world.

"Anyone can be found," I said. "The catch is the deadline. The FBI has been looking for a couple of mad bombers since the sixties, and I've got exactly one-tenth of one-thousandth of a percent of their manpower. The only promise I can make is it won't be next week. That would probably hold even if I knew where you've been meeting her to make the drop, but it would be a place to set up base camp. You haven't told me."

"It hasn't always been the same place. Anyway, I'm not the one who's been making the drop." She tasted the phrase "making the drop," not without pleasure. Everyone likes to talk like Joe Friday if he doesn't have to do it to eat. "You'll need to ask my business manager about the more current details. I put it in his hands."

"Nice to have a business manager you can trust with a toy like your life. They have such a good track record with life savings. Did you sic him on Caterina first?"

"I apologized for that."

She very specifically had not; but I let it flap. Unnecessary dead ends go with the work, like mad dogs and mailmen. Also I liked her. I liked the lift of her jaw and the way she looked at you closely when you talked, listening hard, and the snap of light in her eye when she heard something she didn't like, which in another latitude might have been followed by a stiletto from a garter belt.

Or a needle filled with Stelazine. Her Mata Hari defense had more holes in it than Mata Hari.

"So what's the name of this manager, and where do I find him? One missing person per case is my limit."

"Hector Matador."

This was a new voice, or rather an old voice in a new venue. I could have placed that guttural Hispanic accent, heavy on the *H* and dentilinguals, given the time and the circumstances, but as it was all I had to do was turn around. He'd let himself in the door from the sitting room, making no more noise than he'd made listening from the other side. Of course he'd have a key card to the suite.

He'd put on a little weight on the block, but you could still thread a needle with his narrow hips and shoulders and narrower head, if you had the right size needle and resisted the temptation to turn it around and shove it through his heart. He still wore his hair in little-boy bangs, although these days the black was probably aged in the bottle, and he hadn't lost his fondness for fawn-colored suits, pink silk neckties, and bench-made loafers. It would be the great-grandson of the outfit he'd had on the last time I saw him, when my testimony before a Wayne County jury had sentenced him to life imprisonment for first-degree murder.

FIVE

"Well, well," I opened; and no one ever sounded more like the second act of *The Chambermaid's Confession*. "Has it been life already? I still have a license plate with your mark on it."

Matador found a crumb on his shirt cuff and flicked it off with a shiny-nailed finger. "Still a shitter. The cops liked someone else more than they liked me. I gave them what they wanted, and they gave me a parole. What a country. You ought to treat me with more respect. I recommended you for this job."

"I recommended you for your last one. How'd you land this gig, references from Noriega?"

He pressed his lips tight and paled behind his pox scars. A sense of humor is one high they don't export from Bógota.

"Hector got me my first singing job," Gilia said. "He was the man to see in Los Angeles if you wanted to bypass the man at the door."

"He always did have connections in Hollywood."

Light snapped in her eyes. "I feel like I walked in in the middle. He told me he'd seen your work close up."

"He had it backwards. I saw him put three slugs into Frankie Acardo across the street from my building some years back. The Cosa Nostra didn't miss Frankie all that much, but we had a Renaissance going at the time. All those unclaimed bodies clogging the gutters don't help the convention trade."

"Nobody saw who shot Acardo," Matador said.

"That's true. You were just taking the February air in the shotgun seat of a stolen Camaro with the window down, five minutes before Frankie strolled out of my office into a lead storm."

"I did not know the car was stolen. You could not get good help even then."

Gilia said, "Hector told me all about his record. I could hardly hold it against him. Police are the same everywhere. A loose fit is tight enough to close their files."

"It took less than a week for the Colombians to sweep out the Sicilians after Frankie." I wasn't even listening to myself. I was tiring of the argument. Seeing Hector Matador ranging free was enough to tire out a tire. "You want another detective. I'm running a special this month on wardrobe mistresses. Write out a check for five hundred and I'll find my own way out."

Matador's smile was a paper cut in his narrow face. There wasn't life enough in his dark eyes to sustain it that high up.

"The lady has confided in you. Where would she be if every man she trusted with her secret just walked out? It is like apartment keys. The more of them that you allow to float about . . ." He shrugged a South American shrug.

I smiled back. "You vouched for my good character."

There was an absence of verbal exchange, full of rattles and gongs rung backward. All it needed was a gaunt yellow dog and three more men in ponchos. Gilia let out a lungful of air.

"Let him go, Hector. I'll get my checkbook."

Matador didn't look at her. "You can listen to me talk while she fills it out. In private. You have nothing to lose, gringo."

"Not in a hotel room," I agreed. "An alley's another country."

"I have a small suite across the hall. Just we two. Benito's responsibility is to stand in front of Miss Cristobal's door."

"I'm not worried about Benito. He comes at you from in front."

He opened his coat with a dreamy movement to show he had nothing beneath it but his shirt. There was no room for anything else beneath it but Matador. His tailor worked in subatomic particles. "The restrictions of parole," he said, almost apologetically.

"After you, Dreyfus."

He didn't know what that meant, but he resented it anyway. He rebuttoned his coat and turned his back on me.

Out in the hall, Benny asked him a question in Spanish and he spat a stream back, too fast for me to follow even if *Señora* Lipschitz and her compound subjunctives weren't as dead as ninth grade. The big man stiffened, graying a little, and nodded jerkily. Neither of them looked at me and so I decided I was the subject of the conversation. Matador fished out a key card and let us into a room cater-corner from Gilia's.

The suite was as small as a suite could be and still share a floor with the one across the hall. The sitting room came with a pocket-size refrigerator and microwave and an armchair upholstered in stiff fabric, unused since the showroom. The bedroom was just a room with a bed and related furniture in it and on the top sheet lay a Franchi Magnum shotgun, assorted semiautomatic pistols with chrome and composition finishes, a couple of tasers, and a Korean assault rifle with plastic stock and handgrips and a magazine the size of a toaster. Boxes of shells and police-issue speedloaders finished making a mess out of the housekeeper's hospital corners. Five men as large as Benny, one white, one black, the rest as brown as Mexican heroin, stood around the bed in shirtsleeves and clip-on neckties, monkeying with the cylinders and slides of additional handguns. They looked up when Matador entered.

He threw them out with his chin. They belted and shoulder-holstered their weapons, climbed into their Big-and-Tall suit coats, and left us, leaving deep footprints in the pile carpet.

"I didn't know singing was hazard work," I said. "Or was that the chorus?"

"Miss Cristobal averages three death threats per month. That is two more than John Lennon. She is permitted to carry a concealed weapon in every state, but where would she conceal it? All these men are licensed private investigators. Not that any of them has ever investigated anything. They serve but one client, and her full-time. The black fellow trained with the U.S. Marshals. He can punch a three-hundred-grain round through a two-inch oak board from six hundred yards."

"Handy, if she's ever attacked by a dining room suite. What about close up?"

"That's Benito. He's qualified in all the standard forms of Oriental dirty fighting. You caught him at a bad moment earlier. Yes, I am aware of everything that goes on within walking distance of Miss Cristobal. He has been reprimanded."

"And he's still manufacturing hormones? You've mellowed. Does the parole board know about all this ordnance?"

He leaned across the bed, grabbed the coverlet, and twitched it over the firearms. "This is between you, me, and the sheets. Strictly speaking, it is permitted as long as I don't actually handle the weapons, but my p.o. has a linear mind. He thinks guns lead to shooting. And so this is a secret you have on me as well."

"Close friendships have been built on less," I said. "But not today."

He sighed a Latin sigh. "You are an unforgiving soul, Anglo. The People of the State of Michigan have decided my debt is repaid. Is it not lonely to be the solitary holdout?" He perched himself at the end of a love seat covered in industrial-strength chintz, crossed his slim legs, and spent a minute adjusting the crease in his pants. All he needed now was a slim Cohiba, and he selected one from a calliope-shaped case made of glossy brown leather.

"Lonely as the grave. Which is where I almost was when you turned my police bodyguard after I talked to the grand jury. I'm holding the grudge. Call me petty."

"That was not personal. Nor is the assignment Miss Cristobal has offered. Would you have accepted if I were not in the picture?"

"What do you think?"

"I haven't that luxury. I do not know the Anglo mind. If I offered to remove myself from the situation, would you reconsider?"

"I might, if you used one of those removers on the bed."

He looked sad. "You may select one, if that is truly how you feel. It should not be difficult for an experienced man such as yourself to arrange the evidence consistent with a self-preservation defense. It's unlikely the Dearborn Police will lean very heavily upon the forensic anomalies. *El muerto es solo verdad.*"

"The boys from the chorus might be a little more difficult to arrange." I wondered where the conversation was headed. People like him played Russian roulette with no empty chambers, and they were just too polite to go first.

"They are paid to protect Miss Cristobal. If they took a bullet for anyone else they would be fired for moonlighting." He made an elegant gesture with the cigar, which he hadn't set fire to. "Since I cannot appeal to your emotions, perhaps your bank is the more direct route. Miss Cristobal promised you a bonus of ten percent of the seventy-five thousand dollars *Señora* Muñoz was alleged to have cost her. I offer you the entire seventy-five thousand in return for evidence that the woman who calls herself Jillian Rubio is alive or dead. This, too, is a bonus. You will receive your customary five hundred dollars per day and expenses meanwhile. But only until the thirteenth of this month. After that the point is *inconsecuencial*. Moot?" He lifted his eyebrows.

I left them up there. His English vocabulary was better than Lord Cecil Harrumph's and he knew it. "Does the lady of the house know what her money's doing when she's not around?"

"She spent that much on a dress. You may mention the transaction to her. I insist upon it."

"If I took the offer, and I'm not going to, I couldn't hope to collect without a place to start. I know five hundred a day is what she tips limo drivers, but they take her where she wants to go."

"I can provide what you need. Miss Cristobal is too famous to go skulking about with blood money in her purse; she cannot step out without trailing a string of paparazzi, which is a class I would eliminate if I were not such a reformed character. But I am speaking of paying extortion. It has never been my custom to entrust such an errand to anyone but myself. You may say that in my late profession we encouraged loyalty by slaying those who betrayed us. That is an expensive alternative, and hardly erases the original transgression. I am the one who made the drops."

"All except the last three."

His fast draw was one for Pecos Bill. If he'd been armed, I'd have had a hole in my chest before I gave any thought to the revolver I wore under my coat. He whisked the envelope from his inside breast pocket and tossed it at my feet. It made an expensive thump when it hit the carpet. I found my reflexes and stooped to pick it up. There was nothing greater than a fifty inside, but the packet was too thick for the flap to close properly.

"That is fifteen thousand. You may count it if you wish. I offered each time to return the unclaimed five thousand to Miss Cristobal, but she told me to hold on to it and add it to the next payment. Consider it your retainer, to be repaid after you have deducted your fee and expenses in the event you are unable to determine the Rubio woman's fate."

I flipped the envelope onto the bed. It landed with a smack. U. S. Grant's eyes glared at me above the notch.

"I'd be tempted, if I thought you weren't blowing Spanish smoke up my chimney about separating yourself from the action."

"I was not. Of course, I would prefer it be on my own two feet instead of the alternative we discussed. You will report directly to Miss Cristobal. If you call her first, using the private cellular number she will provide, you will not so much as smell my cigar." He seemed to remember he was holding it then. He snapped a flame out of a gold-and-enamel lighter and started it burning. It smelled like the inside of an exclusive club, the front door of which would always be closed to me.

"You hesitate still." He frowned at the ring he'd blown; as circles went it was a bubble off perfect. "I will raise the bonus. One hundred thousand dollars. The difference to come from my own pocket."

"That must be quite a work-release program they have there in Jackson," I said. "Most ex-cons have to settle for minimum wage."

"Let's just say I settled for smoking Dominicans and saved my pennies."

"What's your end? Gilia is gilt-edged now, but the market in futures isn't looking too good. A man with your connections can always clean up a replacement. They dump the raw material at the L.A. bus station every morning and afternoon."

"You are mistaken. There is but one Gilia to a century, and the century is no older than this cigar. More important, there is but one Gilia in my life."

I laughed in his face. He looked at the ceiling and forgot to squirt smoke. It found its way out of his nostrils in twin blue threads.

I picked up the envelope and thumbed through the bills. There was fifteen thousand there all right. I tapped a corner against my lower lip. "She could be guilty, you know."

"Of revolutionary activity? But of course. She has said as much."

"No, the other."

He appeared to consider it for the first time. "It is as good. Better, maybe. A woman who would kill for love is a precious thing."

"It spices up the Friday night fights." I put the envelope in my inside breast pocket. "Keep your hundred grand. Gangster dollars never stay with me long. I can't walk past a church poor box with them in my wallet, and I have to burn the wallet after. It's a new wallet."

He lifted his eyebrows again. Then he placed his cigar in a glass ashtray as big around as a bicycle wheel and let it smoke. "I will tell you what you need to know to start. Then we will return to Miss Cristobal's suite and she will tell you what you need to know to finish." He lowered his eyebrows, and with them the lids of his eyes. "I sold you very hard to her, gringo. I hope you will not make me out a liar."

I shrugged him a North American shrug. It wasn't as fluid as his, but my ancestors came from a colder climate. Maybe he was in love with her after all. Weasels fell for chinchilla wraps every day.

SIX

He was standing alone on hell's hilltop, swinging a saber at a half-naked warrior while another warrior took aim at him with a captured revolver. All of his companions were dead or in the process of being butchered, and what this all had to do with selling beer was somebody else's mystery. I'd had the Anheuser-Busch advertisement framed and hung on the wall of my office so long I couldn't remember what sort of stain it was hiding. In all that time, Custer hadn't made any headway toward subjugating the Sioux and Cheyenne, and I was no closer to retirement than I had been the day I bought him in a junk shop in Redford.

I was waiting for a callback on a message I'd left with a number in Milwaukee, and the cheap print was the only thing worth looking at in the meantime. The two olive green file cabinets—retro chic now, no longer just a pair of stove-in saurians inherited from the back room of a mortuary—were full of dust and dead cases, the rug had given up its pattern to the sun, and the desk was just a desk and the man behind it just taking up space in obedience to the first law of nature.

Hector Matador had made the October blackmail payment to Jillian Rubio in a restaurant in Milwaukee, a dark wood erzatz German place with decorative steins on shelves all around the main dining room. The personnel who answered the telephone there didn't remember either customer, but then four months had elapsed and at the time they were up to their *Lederhosen* in Oktoberfest. That meant a hotel search, and I remembered a detective there I'd tagged for help in the past. A recording had kicked in on his end, referring me to an 800 number, never a good sign. There I'd gotten a recorded directory, pressed the nearest option to what I needed, and left my name and number.

The telephone rang, taking me away from the Little Big Horn. A deep masculine voice with some evidence of radio training asked me if I was with A. Walker Investigations.

"I am A. Walker Investigations. Is this a party calling itself Millennium Confidential Services in Milwaukee?"

"This is the Milwaukee office. We also have offices in Madison and Green Bay. I'm Lester Ziegler, special agent in charge. What can I do for you?"

"I'm looking for Dan DiNapolitano. I didn't think I'd need to do detective work to find a detective."

"Don't know the name, sorry. He might be one of the independents who sold their practices to us last year. We offer a very comfortable buyout package whenever we open a new office."

"I wouldn't think there was enough work in Wisconsin to support three branches of an investigation firm. Dan barely made his rent shooing home lost cows."

The deep voice grew an edge. "We're a little busy around here to discuss mutual friends you and I don't have. If this is a business call, tell me what you need and I'll tell you if we can deliver."

I said I needed someone to run through registrations, airline manifests, and railroad passenger lists for a certain week in October. I said I had a name and a description but no picture; that was bad. We discussed the difficulty of flying under an alias during the current situation; that was good. He quoted me a rate that made me feel like a discount dentist at a convention of microsurgeons. I asked him about his professional rate. He said that was his professional rate. I gave him the name and description and then he asked me about my credit history and I told him the name of my bonding company. All this took as long as

Dan DiNapolitano would have needed to do the first two hotels.

When we were through with each other, I thought a bit about Dan. I didn't know him that well, just a monotone over the wire and the noise of an electric typewriter munching in the background. But he'd found more to say to me than Lester Ziegler of Millennium Confidential Services. I wondered how comfortable their buyout package was. Maybe Dan had had his fill of clerks, jerks, and boulevard Turks, not to mention the twice-breathed air in the county hall basement and the monoxide haze in the break rooms where taxi drivers drank their brimstone coffee and griped about their lousy marriages and their bratty kids and their rotten fares. Maybe one more fifteen-minute tail job that lasted a week had been one too many. Maybe he was out shooting badgers.

I had another call to make, but that line was busy. The buzz-buzz woke up my stomach and it began to grumble. I remembered I was supposed to feed it every twelve hours. When I told the girl at the answering service I was going out for a while, she tried to keep me on the line with some original remarks about Michigan in February. For all I knew I was her only customer. As I hung up it occurred to me that one of these years I'd dial the service and a tinny voice would direct me to another number that would be answered by Millennium Voice Mail.

My bank was on the way to the soup-and-sandwich place where I was eating my lunch this century. The teller—a stranger; they changed them with the ballpoint pens—looked at me with mild interest when I laid fourteen thousand in cash on the ledge in front of him, but in the absence of an eye patch or a parrot on my shoulder he returned to his computer and handed me a slip indicating I would have whiskey and Velveeta for a few more weeks. The remaining thousand was snug in my wallet, waiting to bribe the surly border guard, buy the last vacant compartment on the Shanghai Express, snag the seedy little hotel room overlooking the Bay of Dirty Deeds, or procure a can of beanie-wienies at the 7-Eleven around the corner from home. Preparation is everything in grizzly-tracking and detection.

The restaurant wasn't much, even by downtown standards. It

averaged five critical violations per inspection and the counter help smelled of reefers. But it was handy to the office and I liked the old-fashioned flatware with its perforated pink plastic handles that looked like Band-Aids. I had a bowl of tomato soup, which couldn't have too much happen to it between the can and the pot, and watched the cook grill my cheese sandwich. The place was Arab-owned and had a new American flag tacked inside the window that faced the street. I smoked a cigarette for dessert and read the review of Gilia's concert in the *Free Press*. The reviewer wasn't impressed by the butterfly finale but allowed as how the star seemed to perform as if she was aware there was an audience present. He was a Sinatra man and only referred to the Chairman's final appearance in Detroit five times in four columns. A sidebar feature mentioned the video Gilia was shooting all week in Mexicantown and what was left of the warehouse district.

Barry Stackpole swung his counterfeit leg into the opposite side of the booth and followed it in. As usual he wasn't wearing a coat, just a pink cashmere sweater over an Oxford shirt, prewashed jeans, and Keds high-tops. As not so usual, he had a deep tan and his normally sandy hair looked bleached. He was carving it close to the skull these days, which made him look even more like he'd cut algebra to sneak a smoke in the boys' room. We were both looking at fifty from the same slim distance, but middle-age morbidity had hit him like a haulaway. He was fighting it with everything but fission.

"Man," he said, "you've got to start eating in better places. You're starting to look like a cop."

I folded the newspaper. "I tried to call you a little while ago. Richard Simmons wants his sweater back."

"This is the hot color in Miami this season. Once a girl thinks you're a man who is comfortable with his masculinity, you're as good as in the stirrups."

"Maybe she just wants you to offer her a good price on a rinse and set."

He had on that toothpaste smirk that made women wonder why they were angry at him and made men want to push it through the back of his head. The week his father had died and left him his motorcycle collection, he'd joined a Harley club, discovered Viagra, and given up tennis for sex. He was going out with women who weren't born yet the day a car bomb took off his leg, two fingers, and part of his cranium. The scars from his steel implant showed through the extreme haircut. The incident hadn't prevented him from making celebrities out of a couple of hundred public enemies who would rather they'd stayed below the radar. Call him an underappreciated press agent.

"Sam Lucy's kid, Peter, bought a place called the Lagoon," he said, apropos nothing. " 'The Nugget of the Gold Coast,' he calls it. Or he did. The Miami Hotel Owners Association is looking into the purchase."

"Were they looking into it before you went down there?"

"I wrote a guest column for the *Sun-Sentinel.* Could be coincidence. I sent you a postcard. Drew an arrow pointing to my room."

"Didn't get it. Maybe Lucy has friends in the post office. I'm guessing when you drew that arrow it wasn't your room anymore."

"My new hard-on didn't drain all the blood from my brain." He helped himself to a pickle chip off my plate. "I was on my way to your dump when I saw you through the window. Thought I'd show off the tan."

"It's like the first robin of spring." I asked him how his contacts were in Gilia Cristobal's country. I didn't mention Gilia.

"Mostly dead. Revolution's dead, too, but the government keeps on executing rebels. A rebel being anyone who slaughters one of his own chickens because he can't afford the tax on meat."

"I'm checking a client's story. It has to do with a love triangle and murder."

"I need specifics. That's how all the love triangles end down there. The national flag is a broken heart on a field of daggers."

"This one has a political twist. A rebel leader slept with two women and one of them wound up with a skinful of poison."

"Rings a bell. What kind of poison?"

"Something called Stelazine."

"Yeah, I know it. I went undercover in a booby hatch once. It can look like a heart attack or a stroke if no autopsy is performed. That's the advantage. The disadvantage is it's a hard drug to get hold of down there, unlike heroin or coke. The authorities keep a tight cap on all the legal narcotics. You'd have to have access to a locked hospital cabinet. The hospitals are all owned by the government, so that means there's an armed *soldado* standing in front of it."

"I only need what was in the newspapers. Also anything you can get me on any political prisoners who might have vanished about the same time as the murder. Vanished as in escaped."

He nodded. He never made notes on anything of a criminal nature. All the photographs in his memory were front-and-profile. "Anything in it for me?"

"Not now. Probably not ever. It's a personal favor. Quid pro quo to be named later."

"Shit. Sex, murder, and politics. Put them all together, they spell Pulitzer. But it seems to me I already have one of those in the attic. How about lunch?"

"I just ate."

"I mean me. All you can get in Miami is fish and clams. They couldn't do a steak if you sent them to school in Omaha for a year. I skipped the delectable turkey loaf aboard the plane; saved my empty gut for the beef medallions at the Blue Heron."

"They don't serve lunch there."

"They'll serve me. INS was all set to deport the head chef until I made a couple of calls to DC. Been on their VIP list ever since."

"B.F.D. That stands for big freaking deal. What am I supposed to do, drink fizzy water and watch?"

"My friend the chef will have to hot up the grill and prepare the meat. By the time it gets to the table you'll be hungry again. We'll stop and pick up my laptop and I'll have what you need before the appetizer. You'll have to pay for yours, though. All you ever did for the Heron was bleed in their parking lot."

"If you don't have to pay for your meal, what do you need me for?"

He slapped his smirk back on. "Company. I don't like to eat alone."

"Since when?"

"Since Pauly Cicero stuck a knife through the back of my booth in Allen Park last Easter. I wouldn't be here, except he hit a stud. Not this stud. A stud inside the seat. Think you can keep an eye out for Paulies?"

"Only all my adult life." I slid out of the booth.

SEVEN

Her name was Mariposa.

On formal occasions, when filling out documents or when her parents lost patience with her and addressed her by her complete designation, it was Mariposa Niceta Ignacia y Villanueva Flores, and there was evidence the family had owned El Salvador and a fair chunk of Guatemala through the generosity of Philip II of Spain, but their personal fortune had gone the way of the Armada. A great-to-the-fourth-power grandfather, the Conde de Villanueva, had fled the homeland to avoid his creditors and run out of ocean on the island where Mariposa would be born four hundred years later.

Many generations of hardscrabble existence followed, but by the 1950s the Flores family had done very well in coffee and invested some of its profits in the presidential palace to maintain its piece of the monopoly on foreign exports. Mariposa's great-aunt nailed the deal by betrothing herself to the minister of the treasury. Then the military laid siege to the capital and the president committed suicide by shooting himself with eighteen rounds from a two-hundred-pound Krupp fifty-caliber machine gun. That threw a damp sheet over the wedding ceremony, and the reception was called off when the generalissimo who had taken charge nationalized the coffee industry and the Floreses found themselves once again without property or cash. (The great-aunt changed out of her white gown into a black sheath after her groom was herded along with the rest of the former cabinet into a soccer stadium and shot in front of a Dr Pepper sign.) When Mariposa was born, thirty years later, you couldn't tell the descendants of the Conde de Villanueva from the rest of the islanders who supported their families by picking the bugs off leaves on the government-owned plantations.

There was a brief dusty ray of hope in the overcast: A representative of the government-controlled radio station heard sixteen-year-old Mariposa singing in the choir at Our Lady of Perpetual Pain and booked her on the air to interpret the sentimental country ballads that were decreed suitable to keep the peasantry contented with the cards as dealt. At first she sang with two other black-haired girls, introduced as *Las Palomas Negritas*, the Little Black Doves, but within a few weeks her rich contralto moved her out from between them into solo spots. Then in a little harbor town where nothing ever happened her brother Fernando jerked the pin out of a grenade in a cafe frequented by soldiers, and the revolution was on.

Actually, it had been going on for a year in villages and provinces throughout the country, but when prison laborers shoveled up what was left of Fernando and the half dozen men in uniform he'd taken with him, it threw its tentacles around Mariposa. Her father had died some years before between rows of coffee plants, so the arrest order named the remaining Floreses for conspiracy to overthrow the government. Her mother was removed to an undisclosed detention area and was not seen again. Mariposa eluded the soldiers who came for her at the radio station. For a time after, she was reported to be traveling with ragtag squads of revolutionaries, including a charismatic and well-educated young commander who was believed to have been the man who brought her the news of Fernando's death and her mother's arrest and bundled her out a back door while the government troops were coming in the front.

Apart from unconfirmed sightings, however, she did not reappear in the news until the rebel leader's longtime female companion, a former cabaret dancer and part-time prostitute named Angela Suerto, died in a mountain camp, the victim of a lethal dose of Stelazine. A new warrant was sworn out in Mariposa Flores's name for suspicion of murder, but it was never served. Her name quietly evaporated from press accounts after six months, when all the leads had been beaten flat.

By then the revolution was past tense. The rebel leader was in prison waiting to hear whether he was to hang himself in his cell or be shot down in the approved manner while scaling a wall, and most of his confederates were drawing flies at the base of riddled billboards or dangling from makeshift gallows in the villages where they surrendered.

That was the sum total of what Barry managed to bring up on his portable computer screen from AP and UPI features that had drifted onto American soil. They wouldn't have gotten that far without the songbird revolutionary–turned–passion killer hook, and there was something musty and brittle about even that, like a John Gilbert movie based on a novel by Gertrude Atherton. Without photographs, sound bites, or tape footage to sustain it, the entire episode withered away in back numbers of *U.S. News & World Report*. Aristotle's dentist never got any deader.

I had most of the worthwhile details in my notebook by the time two platters of beef medallions came sizzling to our table in the Blue Heron in West Bloomfield, but Barry was still working on the angle involving the escaped political prisoner—Mariposa/Gilia's alibi—over the after-dinner wine, a fortified Madeira he'd chosen to go with the afternoon's theme of castanets and cordite. It tasted like old Valencia and kicked like a shotgun.

"Most of the wire accounts would be based on local reporting," he said, rattling keys between sips. "They take their gag orders literally down there. The government newspapers wouldn't be eager to report breaches in the penal system, and the rebel sheets couldn't without laying open their sources to arrest or annihilation. Redundant terms in this case."

"If there was an escape," I said.

He looked up. "This is pretty Spy vs. Spy for a domestic gumshoe who prefers his steak smothered in onions." He'd noticed I hadn't cleaned my plate.

"The medallions were okay. That grilled cheese I had two hours ago could hold up an overpass." I poured down the rest of my wine to break it up. "Try entering 'The Lincoln Question.' "

"What's that?"

"Maybe the Net knows."

The Lincoln Question was the trick with the red-hot penny Gilia had told me about, the one that had blinded the prisoner she said she'd helped smuggle out of the country the night the Suerto woman was killed.

He typed it in, waited. "No matches. Could be the equipment. I'll try it again on the desktop later."

"There might not be anything. It sounded pretty gaudy to me when I heard it."

"What happens to the case if there isn't?"

"The case stays the same. It may go pretty hard on the detective."

I spotted my brown shadow eight blocks from the restaurant.

He was driving a three-year-old Chevy Corsica in dusty gold, the nearest thing to a plain paper sack on wheels, and I could tell it was breaking his heart because he was hunched behind the wheel like a teenage kid hoping his friends wouldn't see him out with his mother.

I might not have noticed him at all except he was following all the rules of maintaining a close tail in the city: hanging back a block, observing the limit without becoming a fanatic about it, laying off the horn even when a woman carrying a Jacobson's bag stepped off the curb right in front of him on Northwestern. He was being so unobtrusive he stank.

I wanted a better look. I found a residential street, swung into it without signaling, and stopped in the middle of the lane. I counted two beats, then he turned in behind me. His brake lights winked on when he saw the Cutlass, but by that time it was too late. He accelerated and went around me. Neither he nor his partner on the passenger's side looked right or left as they passed within arm's reach. They were cruiser class, columnar necks sloping into football shoulders, wearing dark suits as invisible as the car. The driver was Hispanic, thick black hair cut short, Anglo fashion, conspicuously without a moustache. His companion was black, but tipped out of the same double-wide mold. They continued at the same pace to the end of the block, then a volume of thick exhaust spilled out of the tailpipe and they scooted around the corner with a bubble of rising tachs.

I wondered how long it would take them to circle the block.

The license number didn't mean anything and I only committed it to memory out of habit. It would just trace back to whatever rental company they'd used, and I knew whose name would be on the order. The pair in the car had been among the men I'd seen in Hector Matador's suite at the Hyatt in Dearborn. The black one, the former U.S. Marshal, would have the legs for the job in case I found a parking space and they didn't and I took off on foot. It was a professional arrangement.

I gave them a moment to get back into position, then turned around in a driveway and went back the way I'd come.

I picked them up again when I passed a picture-framing shop with a turnaround in front. This time they didn't bother to try to blend with the scenery. They'd be with me until a cellular call to Fearless Leader could alert the relief team.

EIGHT

In my travels I've managed to assemble an impressive collection of road maps, no two folded the same way and all of them taking up space in the glove compartment that would otherwise go to waste on registration and proof of insurance. Some of them go back to when they gave them out free in service stations, back when there were service stations; and those are strictly of historical interest. Others are more up-to-date, and each one tells the story of a routine local tail job that had taken me twice around Circe's island and past the cave of the cyclops.

The one I selected, after I parked in the Tonka-size lot a block over from my building, was a cute pop-up affair that featured the Rust Belt in all its El Niño-battered glory. It was as easy to fold as a conventional accordion map, with the added advantage of not being as detailed. But I wasn't using it to attack Bastogne.

None of the customers in my waiting room could distract me from my higher purpose, even if there were any; the trade off the street in that neighborhood would drive a pusher into real estate, and anyway you can't expect to just walk up two flights and hire an investigator on a whim. You need to bring your wallet.

I found out from the service no one had called, and grunted at the girl when she asked me if it was snowing yet. I guessed the switchboard room didn't have windows. Mine was sealed with a nail from one of Alexander's horseshoes and the panes had cataracts. I spread open the map on the desk, sat down, and found the red pen I employed to keep the accounts.

Matador had met Jillian Rubio for the first time last February in Chicago. Five thousand dollars had changed hands in return for letting the woman who called herself Gilia go on being Gilia. I drew a scarlet *X* on the little circle that marked Chicago on the map. In March it was Indianapolis, in April Des Moines. I marked them. Des Moines again in May, then clear up to Duluth. Another *X*. Omaha, Omaha, Chicago again. Scratch scratch. Milwaukee for the first time in October. The upper Midwest was beginning to look as if it were stitched together with crimson thread.

Milwaukee again in November. That was the first time the blackmailer had failed to show. Matador had decided, in view of the Rubio woman's propensity for returning to the scenes of earlier crimes, to go back to the same place in December and January, adding five thousand to the envelope each time to bring his client's account out of arrears. It was a sensible plan, only Jillian wasn't having any of it. We were coming up on the first anniversary of the arrangement next Saturday, also three months since anyone had seen the extortionist vertical and breathing, and that was as long as she was supposed to stay missing before the whole thing came spewing out into the living room of Mr. and Mrs. America.

As itineraries went it wasn't Magellan's. All the locations were within twelve hours' driving distance of one another. Whoever had drawn it up either lived somewhere within that twelve hours or wanted whoever looked at it to think that. The last was an unlikely hypothesis; blackmailers made life inconvenient for other people, not themselves. A related theory was that if the person did live in that area, the one place she would *not* set up a drop would be the city where she lived. It would be bad form to be recognized by an old acquaintance while committing a felony.

I excavated the big Sherlock Holmes magnifying glass someone had given me in the spirit of jest, and which I used far more often than the someone had intended, although hardly ever to magnify anything. Its heft made it a good tool for rehanging pictures, and in this case it functioned equally well as a compass. I laid the glass on top of the map, lining it up so that all the marked cities showed, with Milwaukee and Indianapolis on the extreme right edge at top and bottom, Duluth and Des Moines framing the center, and Omaha at the left. I used the red pen to trace a circle around the glass, then pushed aside the magnifier and with one eye closed and my tongue between my teeth marked a bold red *X* in the circle's exact center. Then I leaned back to admire my artwork.

The cross of the *X* fell squarely on the Mississippi River where it divided Minneapolis and St. Paul. Which were the only bold-faced cities on the map where Jillian Rubio had never arranged to meet Hector Matador.

I enjoyed the moment, then tossed the map into the wastebasket. It wasn't even good enough to drive around with anymore. Life doesn't work out like a crossword puzzle. If it did, it wouldn't have any place in it for angle-bangers like me. But it so happened I knew someone I could call in St. Paul, if Millennium Confidential Services hadn't gotten to him first.

Sometimes life does work out like a crossword puzzle. My hand was on the telephone when it rang, and it was Lester Ziegler at Millennium. He'd oiled the rollers in his deep voice, and now he sounded like the man who describes toaster ovens on game shows.

"Nothing yet," he said, "but my people have a few more places to call. If this Rubio woman drove and paid cash, she could use whatever name she liked. Only these days people notice when you pay cash."

"You called to report nothing?"

"Not exactly. I ran your name through TRW after we spoke. They never heard of you. I've never come across that before. If I didn't think it was a computer glitch, I'd swear you had no credit rating at all."

"Go ahead and swear. I haven't."

"That's impossible. Everyone has a rating, even deadbeats. It's like you don't exist."

"I've been told that."

He got tired of waiting for me to tack something onto the end. "I checked with your bonding company. You're covered for up to a million, but that's strictly boilerplate and it only protects your clients in case you take their retainer to Brazil. This isn't a cash-and-carry business. We need a secured method of payment."

"We aren't in the same business, Mr. Ziegler. You're Big Oil and I'm a pump jockey. I don't owe anybody and nobody owes me. That makes me a nonperson where the credit companies are concerned, but from where I sit it means I haven't made any enemies. Not the kind they'd recognize as such, anyway."

"You could send us a check."

"Will you keep your people on the case while they're waiting for it?"

"I can't do that. Our plate is full of paying customers. I only got this started because you sounded professional over the telephone and I was sure you would have some kind of credit history and we could decide whether to proceed depending upon what it was. This agency belongs to a corporation. The board wouldn't enjoy explaining to the stockholders why it accepted a phantom for a client." Something tapped a beat on his end—a pencil or more likely a keyboard. "I'll waive the standard ten-day waiting period while the check clears. Get it in the mail today and we'll be back on the case day after tomorrow."

I glanced at the bank calendar on the wall. I knew what the date was day after tomorrow. I just liked to look at the picture of Tahquamenon Falls. The attraction hadn't changed in more than a century. No new owners had acquired it and anyone who wanted to could go up and look at it for free. He didn't need a credit rating. "The case blows up in five days, Mr. Ziegler. I'm not going to sit on my hands for two of them waiting for your people to make half a dozen calls I could make myself if I knew the names of their contacts."

"Well, the contacts are what you buy." He'd lost interest. "I hope for your sake your luck holds, Walker. It's the only thing keeping you afloat."

"Does that mean I shouldn't expect a comfortable buyout package?" But I was barking down a dead line.

I replaced the receiver carefully, then rechecked the number on my desk directory and dialed. A voice that sounded like a dump truck downshifting through gravel answered on the third ring.

"Twin Cities Detective Agency, Corcoran."

"Corky, this is Amos Walker in Detroit. How's every little thing in St. Paul?"

"St. Paul-Minneapolis," he corrected automatically. "We're up to our tits in snow and there's more coming from Alberta. I had to get a jump this morning to start my electric razor. Hope you're the same." His tone had changed to one of cordial malice.

"Not a flake so far. I'm cooking out Valentine's Day." It was good to hear his voice, even if it did mean running a Chapstick around inside my ear afterward. Sid Corcoran employed five full-time investigators and a secretary and held a degree in criminal law. In addition he did security work for some of the local flour mills and advised law enforcement agencies on the state of the art in electronic listening devices. His operation was just big enough to attract the attention of a cruising shark like Millennium and just small enough to be swallowed whole. "I've got a missing-person case that just pointed your direction, maybe, but I can't remember who owes who at this point."

"Whom." Other telephones purred on his end, a regular chorus of them, with a different tone for each agent. "Last time was that runaway from Mendota Heights you found hustling line workers in the parking lot at Chrysler," he said. "So you're in the black. What's the ruckus?"

I gave him Jillian Rubio's name—just that one, the one she used stateside—date and country of birth, height, weight, eyes and hair, citizenship status unknown, some other bits of slag from the notebook. "Minneapolis-St. Paul's a hunch," I added. "If it pans out, she has a car, or at least a driver's license, so she ought to be on file at the secretary of state's office. No picture, sorry. Try the morgues and hospitals. She missed three important appointments in a row beginning the middle of November."

"Department of Motor Vehicles issues licenses here, not the secretary of state." It was the absent tone he used whenever he lectured someone on regional terminology or the rules of grammar; he was the first detective in a family of university professors. "There might be something in that bout with infantile paralysis. I don't guess she gets around on crutches, or you'd have mentioned it. Maybe not, though. One time a police inspector described a missing witness for me, tattoos included, very detailed. Left out the fact the guy was a Siamese twin."

"No help there. She was always sitting down when the contact arrived. It's a lead if you can make a lead out of it. She might need a regular prescription. Any doctors or pharmacists on your snitch list?"

"Don't need 'em. I'll see what Bill Gates has to say. Not plugged in yet, are you?"

"Computers make me nervous. 'Select any key to proceed.' Too many choices."

"The technology keeps changing. If you don't hop on soon, it'll leave you behind."

"My first reaction to that is to say good-bye."

He switched gears without pausing. "Want us to hang on to her?"

"No contact. Just let me know where she can be reached." I breathed in and out, dreading what came next. "This one has a deadline. She has to be alive on the thirteenth."

"Shit. Of February? Shit." More telephones purred. Someone on the other side of a thin partition was arguing on a separate line. The sound got muffled—Corky's big paw cupping the mouthpiece—the head of the firm yelled. When he came back on, his was the only voice I heard. "I'll put Spitzer on it. He can make the Dalai Lama take a swing at him, but he goes through dead bolts and doormen like shit through a pigeon. This might tip you over into the red. His bailbondsman's into me for twenty grand already."

"How's my credit history?"

"What the fuck's that?" We swatted some more insults back and forth, and he said I'd hear from him. He didn't say good-bye. His superstitions went back to the Inchon invasion.

I hung up with the snuggly feeling that Minneapolis-St. Paul was covered, for whatever it was worth, lit a cigarette, took two puffs, put it out, and got up to peer out through the film that covered the window on both sides. The dusty gold Corsica was parked across the street with both men inside. It reminded me of the day Frank Acardo took three in the belly, but that wasn't what was bothering me.

Matador hadn't changed the guard after all. That meant he intended for me to see them, which meant either he was trying to throw some kind of scare into me or he had a stealth crew staked out somewhere else, to pick me up in case I ducked the first team. I couldn't figure out why he'd want me scared, and in any case I'm easier and less expensive to scare than the situation seemed to demand. So the bottom line was if the surveillance broke off for any reason, someone in the ranks was going to be reminded that *matador* is Spanish for more than just a killer of bulls.

A lot of Gilia's money was being spent to find out what became of Jillian Rubio. A lot more was being spent to find out what the detective found out at the very moment he found it out.

It seemed like one more angle than the case should have; especially a case that had started out with an employee accused of simple disloyalty and snaked its way into a jungle filled with mosquitoes and guerrillas and red-hot pennies and poison. It was time to go back to the well.

NINE

If there are any conservationists out there interested in preserving the physical evidence of what made Detroit Detroit, they'd better rope off a piece of the warehouse district today, because tomorrow there will be condominiums or a casino standing on top of it.

It's shrinking faster than the Brazilian rain forest, this homely stretch of riverfront with its acres of crumbling warehouses, tangled miles of narrow-gauge track, and columns of cold smokestacks. Bricktown bulldozers are snorting in from the west and Rivertown backhoes are scooping out basements from the east, busy making the neighborhood safe for knickknack collectors, penthouse playboys, and blackjack dealers. The landscape is as bleak and hostile as they get, full of gaunt shells with empty windowpanes like missing teeth, and inside them rats and termites, but while they stand it's still possible for anyone who cares to go down and see the exposed living organs of an American industrial city. I don't imagine there are many who do.

A pair of large black Detroit police officers in leathers and earflaps lowered their hands to their belts as I approached the barricade, leaving their cigarettes to smolder between their lips. I guessed the sergeant was the one with the words, so I showed him my ID, folding back the part with the badge, which wouldn't have impressed him, and said I was working for Gilia. He had a thick black moustache that looked as if it had been poured while molten and hardened in the Arctic air off the river.

"You with the band?" This came from his partner, a slightly younger version of his superior, with humorous eyes and only his lower teeth open to view. I'd been wrong again.

"Just a jobber," I said. "I'm checking in."

Somewhere down the decaying length of dead-end street an electrocuted cat sang out its anguish. It stood my scalp on end. The sergeant with the poured moustache rubbed his nose with a leather-sheathed finger. The officer with the humorous eyes went on watching me through the smoke rising from the end of his cigarette. I figured either they were wearing earplugs under their flaps or they'd gotten used to the noise.

I pointed with my chin. "Spanish invention, the guitar. Took two hundred years to become the most important folk instrument in the world."

The cop with the words spat a flake of tobacco from between his lips without dislodging his cigarette. "How about that."

"Then they had to go and add electricity."

"My kid plays guitar," he said. "But then whose kid don't? They're doing what you call a sound check, for a video. No Gilia today. You ought to know stars don't stand around freezing off their famous asses till showtime."

"They told me at the Hyatt she's here."

"I guess that's why you had to fight your way through the crowd." We were the only things breathing within a block of the barricade.

"Could be she's incognito. You know, dark glasses and the Monday mink. One of us could go back and check. You're on duty, so why don't I volunteer."

Someone took another whack at the guitar. A flock of seagulls took off from one of the loading docks, creaking like hinges.

The sergeant stirred, drew three yards of blue bandanna handkerchief from a slash pocket, and blew his nose with enthusiasm. The honk would have sounded loud if it hadn't followed the guitar lick. It might have been some kind of signal. His partner tossed his cigarette, turned his back on me, and walked down toward the river. He had that swagger you just can't help with the Sharper Image for Cops winter catalogue swinging from your belt.

The wind buzzed around a brick cornice. Otherwise the sergeant and I stood up to our hips in silence.

"Getting ready to snow," I said.

He smoked and said nothing. His eyes followed a white panel truck clattering a loose lifter up Jefferson.

I tried again. "I know, because my rib's giving me hell. I broke it on a bullet a lot of years ago."

"My right knee," he said after a moment. "Throbs like a bitch. Thirteen-year-old puke with a zip gun cracked the cap. Department offered me a disability, but what's that. So I roll an Ace bandage around it when it rains or snows."

"I thought zip guns went out with mumblety-peg."

"He was the last of his breed. The very last."

"Yeah?"

"That's why I'm not a lieutenant."

The conversation ended there. A minute later the other cop came back into view. He stopped to light a cigarette, turning his back to the wind and cupping the match with both hands, then resumed; taking his time while I felt the cold.

"Okay," he said.

He didn't move the barricade. There was a steep curb on either side, and I was making up my mind to climb one when the sergeant with the kneecap lifted the sawhorse and pivoted it to make a space twelve inches wide. I sidled through.

"Who're you, Sir Radar O'Reilly?" asked his partner.

"You ever been shot?"

"Shit. No." The partner rapped a gloved knuckle against the wooden crosspiece.

"Then shut the hell up."

Cops. They start out all different shapes and sizes and personality types, and at the end of five years' erosion you can't tell them apart.

The street led between a row of brick piles with concrete loading docks and a long frame hangarlike affair that had sheltered everything from kitchen stoves to bootleg hooch to Cabbage Patch Kids in crates, going back to when Cadillac was a pup; in a couple of years some sheep-faced woman in a green suede vest would be raking up plastic chips on the site. Over on the Canadian side of the slate-colored river the electric sign of the Hiram Walker distillery blazed against a bank of dirty-looking clouds. I'm told I'm related, away on the wrong side of the sheet.

There were lights on the American side as well, hot ones bouncing off silver reflectors on the same dock where the rum-runners used to tie up while the grandfathers of the two officers on the barricade did pretty much what their grandsons were doing now. A couple of dozen people dressed adrogynously in navy peacoats and Thinsulate milled around, adjusting lights, hoisting shouldercams, swinging microphones on aluminum poles, tormenting Stratocasters, and drinking from steaming Styrofoam cups. There was a pulsing rumble going on underneath it all; I felt it first in the soles of my feet and as I got closer I heard it, growling inside the insulated shell of a generator the size of a refrigerator truck, parked on the broken pavement near the dock, with tentacles of cable leading from it out to where the action was.

"Who the hell picked this spot?" someone said. "We could've gone to Moscow, seen the Kremlin."

The speaker was the man with the guitar, a Popsicle stick in Goth black with a crysanthemum head of bright yellow hair. I'd seen him backing up Gilia at Cobo. The hand he strummed the strings with, out on the end of the dock, was swollen and as red as Lizzie Borden's. He blew on it and tortured another cat.

"I did. You want to make something of it, or would you rather go back to the Hyatt and practice 'Stairway to Heaven'?"

This came from a slender technician in Orange County Correctional Facility coveralls and a Dodgers cap with a curled bill. A pair of mirrored sunglasses called attention to her Castilian cheekbones. Someone ought to tell them that eyeglasses only worked for Clark Kent.

The Popsicle stick folded in on himself. "I'm just cold, okay?

The whole reason I left Bismark was to get away from this shit."

"We're all cold, Kit. That was the plan. If we shoot one more video in Southern California, the palm trees are going to have to join Equity. Why don't you get a cup of coffee?"

"I can't hack the caffeine."

"Not to drink, *hombre*. To warm your hands. They're what I bought. The rest of you just came for the sights."

I slid up beside the Dodgers cap. "You need a set of false whiskers. You look just like someone who's trying not to look just like Gilia."

She peered at me over the tops of her glasses. The sun broke through then, and here was someone in show business who hadn't bought her orthodontist a beach house. One of her front teeth had crossed a little in front of the other. "I should've known a smart detective like you would track me down."

"I have special equipment. Fifty-two weeks of the *Free Press* for ten bucks off what I'd pay at the stand. When the factories let out, you're going to be combing rubberneckers out of your hair."

"I'm not on the schedule till tomorrow. I like to drop by, see how my money's being spent. Speaking of which." She'd lowered her voice.

I shook my head. "Picking up, not delivering. Where's Scarface? Matador," I added, when her forehead dimpled.

"*¿Quien sabe?* We are not as the saying goes joined at the lip."

"Hip; as if you didn't know. Lupe Velez wore out that act when your grandmother was in jumpers. Are you sure he isn't somewhere close, disguised as a caterer? Parole boards take a dim view of ex-cons wandering too far from their tethers."

"I'm paying you to find a blackmailer, not my business manager."

"I'm on it. So, apparently, is your business manager. I've been trailing a couple of carloads of your personal security all around town. I hope they found a parking space in the neighborhood. The downtown situation's pretty tight."

She took off the shades. Behind them in the gray light her

pupils had spread and the irises were nearly all black. "Why would he do that, do you think?"

"That's what I came here to ask. I've got a fair idea, but he might be able to talk me out of it. He's got a lot more experience hunting than protecting. I want to ask if being back in Detroit confused him about his current job description."

"This means what, in *inglés*?"

"This means I didn't hire on as a spotter for the Colombian branch of Murder, Incorporated. The deal was to bring Jillian Rubio back alive, if that's what she is. With her back on the payroll, the profits dip. Less money all around."

"That's loco. If she's dead, there is no profit. I'm a gallows bird."

Her voice rose a little on the last part. A woman built like a Teamster—she might have been a Teamster—standing nearby in a shapeless jogging suit and knitted cap looked our way with her eyebrows in her hairline. We moved off into the lee of the generator. The motor thumped and putted behind two sheets of aluminum separated by six inches of rock wool.

I grinned. "You're getting the vernacular down. Look, I don't know what goes on in Matador's head. I don't spend a lot of time trying because it's even harder getting back out. I look at a killer and a killer's what I see. Life's much simpler that way, and you know what? Life is simple. People don't change. Maybe they get a little more refined, hire someone else to do their drive-bys so they don't get nitrate all over their French cuffs. A mug's a mug in Thom McAns or Italian loafers. Especially in Italian loafers."

"And what do you see when you look at me? A killer also?"

"Now that you mention it, I'm having a little trouble locating that political prisoner you were helping escape while Angela Suerto was getting herself poisoned. May I call you Mariposa, when we're alone? I actually prefer it to Gilia. It's less like the name of a venomous iguana."

If I expected her to curse or spit, shout *caramba* and dance a flamenco on my chest, I was disappointed. Not a muscle moved in her face. "You've been tracking me as well. When do you find time to look for Jillian Rubio?"

"It makes sense to look back before you pull out into traffic. In my business we don't ask for references, but it can save time later if we test a client's story for leaks. It would speed things up if the prisoner had a name."

"We did not use names in the resistance. The less each of us knew, the less we had to tell under persuasion. I would say 'torture,' but the word doesn't do justice to the cleverness of the soldiers of the government. Pencil sharpeners and old-fashioned crank telephones have many uses beyond what their inventors intended." She put her glasses back on, erasing the last bit of expression from her face. "We went where we were told and did there as we were asked. I never saw the man before that night, and I haven't had so much as a Christmas card from him since. I don't know what offense he was in prison for, or whether he was guilty or innocent. The distinction isn't all that great when you consider how few activities there are that do not violate some law there."

"Okay," I said.

"Okay?" She didn't put an *h* in front of it, a surprise. Her English had a way of becoming slow and thoughtful when she spoke of home, with fewer contractions and an occasional misplaced accent.

"Okay as in that's as far as I can go for now. I'll be back when I can think of some more questions. I may even have a couple of answers. Meanwhile you can tell Matador to blow his whistle."

"His whistle?"

"Whatever he uses. His dogs are distracting me and I'm too busy to find out why."

"So now I'm your messenger."

"I'd tell him myself, but he knows more places to hide around here than I do."

"And if he says he doesn't know what you're talking about, which is probable?"

"He might want to find out. I have some favors outstanding in Lansing, never mind what or who. He's got the longest leash of any Jackson parolee I ever met. Somewhere he has to have bent the terms of his release. Up at the capital they hate like hell to shorten a life sentence. They don't need much of an excuse to reinstate it."

Her glasses reflected the city skyline, stepped black against gray. "You're stupid, *hombre*. Not brave. Stupid."

"I get that a lot," I said. "But this is the first time I've been stupid in two languages."

"I've got a video to set up." She walked away from me, raising her voice and clapping her hands for attention.

The cops were still smoking at the barricade when I climbed around them. I looked at the one with the humorous eyes. "You were right. She wasn't there."

He thought about that hard. His lower lip worked at the end of his cigarette. "We never get the really good celebrities. If we did, they'd pull us off and put two other cops in our place."

I left them and cranked my car out of a patch of gravel and broken glass. Back by the river, the electric guitar screeched again, then played a snatch of honest music: "Stairway to Heaven." Kit's fingers had thawed out, along with his sense of humor.

TEN

It's eight hundred square feet on the border of Hamtramck and the United States, too small for a house and not quaint enough for a cottage. I acquired it from a foreman at Dodge Main who'd bought it for a starter home in 1940 and moved out thirty years later into his daughter's house after she caught him trying to replace a spent fuse with a shotgun shell. After twenty-five years I don't guess it's a starter for me either. It's a place to smoke a cigarette without alerting Detroit Vice, and maybe the only place in the solar system where a man can tell a visitor to go screw himself and make it stick. It needs a new roof, a coat of paint, and while we're at it a cellar stocked with vintage Amontillado, excellent before dinner and when entombing enemies. I'd settle for the paint.

The open tail I'd been touring with most of the day had evaporated sometime while I was parked in the warehouse district, replaced by a pale blue Bonneville with tinted windows; it had taken forty-five minutes of aimless driving to pick the car out of rush-hour traffic. After that I'd torn the wrapper off some tricks I'd learned in my varied and ultimately pointless career, but this one didn't shake. Unlimited drug money and then the Gilia Fund for Unemployed Parasites had taught Hector Matador the value of hiring quality. I returned to conventional driving. I'd only been amusing myself. If the threat I'd passed through

Gilia was worth the breath it took, the second team would go away on its own. There was no sign of the Bonneville when I'd pulled into my garage; which whether it meant something or nothing I was too tired to decide. Nothing is more draining than a day of asking questions without answers.

I heated a bowl of chili for supper, cooled it down with two beers, and took stock of my panoramic view of the neighborhood. In the dying light I saw no vehicles I couldn't assign to a regular, but that was similarly inconclusive, so I stopped thinking about it. I read part of a mystery that had more holes in it than Augusta. I watched two figure skaters stumble out of Olympic gold on TV and went to bed. I had as much on my mind as Big Top Pee-Wee and I dreamed I was asleep in bed dreaming of nothing at all.

When the telephone rang I switched on the light to read the alarm clock.

"It's three-fifteen," I answered. "Do your kids know where you are?"

"I don't even know if I have any. I always give a phony name."

It was Barry Stackpole, sounding as bright as the moon. "It's chipper," I said. "Its news must be good."

"There is no bad news, only bad reporters. Where can we meet?"

"I'd offer my office, but since you didn't say after breakfast I'd say give it to me over the telephone, but since you won't do that I'll say the Atheneum. They're open all night and you need a baseball bat to stir the coffee." Barry wouldn't order a pizza over a land line and he never touched cordless. He'd been tapped, bugged, and black-bagged under Nixon and Clinton, and under the present conditions all the cops needed to listen in was a thumbs-up from an Eagle Scout or better.

"Thirty minutes." He clicked off.

It was snowing finally; bitter, streetwise flakes that rolled off the hood of the Cutlass like buckshot. I found a space near the six-story slot machine that used to be Trappers Alley and hung up my coat inside the Atheneum: a counter, six booths, and a scatter of tables on gray linoleum as old as the wine-dark sea. The restaurant was one of the few left in Greektown that hadn't gone to ferns and stainless steel.

There were only three customers on-site. A couple with overcoats still on over their party clothes dined in chilly silence in the far booth. Barry was nursing a mug of coffee at the end of the counter. He wore no coat as before and the same clothes he'd had on earlier that day.

I slid onto the stool next to his. "What happened to guarding your back?"

He pointed to a convex mirror mounted above the blackboard menu. The Today Only Special on baklava had entered its third consecutive year. "Sir and Lady Laughalot took my first choice."

"What's their story?"

"What do you think? They lost two bucks on the slots and spent a thousand trying to get it back at blackjack."

"Talk to them?"

He shook his head. "I ask questions for a living. You never ask one you already know the answer to."

The counterman, thickset and hatchet-faced, with a long scar on his left forearm where a tattoo had been routed out, poured thick black coffee into a mug and set it in front of me. I hadn't ordered it. I figured he was a disciple of Barry's.

I drank. The barely saturated grounds crawled down my throat and threw open a couple of hundred thousand brain cells. "What couldn't wait eight hours?"

"Northwest Flight 166 to Islamabad," he said. "It leaves at seven, and I need to be there by five to make sure my underwear clears security. An arms dealer I've been in close contact with longer than my first marriage is over there peddling a missile guidance system to a fellow whose most recent address was Kabul."

"I didn't know you were married."

"If I had a nickel for every fact you didn't know about me I wouldn't have to fly to Pakistan." He took a fold of paper from his shirt pocket and stood it tent fashion on the counter next to my coffee.

I opened it up. It was one of the sheets of newsprint he used for making notes when he bothered to make notes. It contained a 212 area code and telephone number scribbled in pencil in his left-hand slope, nothing else.

"New York," I said.

"Columbia University. It belongs to a professor of Romance languages."

"Does he have a name?"

"You'll have to get it from him. I spent an hour and a half on the phone just getting permission to give you that number."

"He sounds like you."

"He's got a good reason. He only has one eye, and he didn't start out in life that way."

We were speaking in murmurs. I waited until the counterman pushed through a swinging door into the fragrant kitchen. Even then I didn't raise my voice. "The Lincoln Question?"

Barry said, "Yeah. I installed a four-barrel carb in the home computer a week ago—the works, including air scoop. It gets into corners the laptop doesn't know existed. I got a recipe for heating pennies and a list of names. This one kept coming up. He's the only one not still in prison down there, not counting the ones they buried in the yard and the ones unaccounted for, who are probably buried next to them. Emigrated two years ago. State Department looked down his throat, looked up his birth certificate, and granted him asylum. Notwithstanding all that, he still pisses his pants whenever someone addresses him in Spanish with an island accent. Down there they don't put erasers on pencils. They hate to make mistakes."

"The two years is good. What else?"

"The name Mariposa rang a very big bell. I guess someone slipped up and called her by it on the way down to the boat."

"Thanks, Barry." I started to refold the sheet. He snapped his fingers and stuck out his palm.

"Memorize it. I only wrote it down because you're the visual type."

I unfolded the paper again, mouthed the number a couple of times, closed my eyes. I dropped it on his palm. He plucked a matchbook with THE ATHENEUM printed in red on the cover from a glass bowl full of them, set fire to the sheet, and dropped it into his empty mug to burn out. The couple in the booth didn't look up, but the counterman pushed in from the kitchen sniffing the air, spotted the flame, and said, "Hey, hey!"

Barry said, "Opaa!" and put his hand over the mug to snuff it out.

ELEVEN

New York and Michigan share the same time zone, a fact that seems to be lost on everyone but people who live in Michigan. It was too early to call the number I'd memorized and too late to go back to bed, but I tried bed anyway and gave up after an hour and a half locked in combat with three slugs of Greektown coffee. I had a cup of my own and tomato juice for breakfast and drove to the office unsatisfied. Drinking Juan Valdez after the Atheneum was like chasing single-malt Scotch with Kool-Aid.

The temperature had risen, turning the snow that was still falling into a gluey mixture of rain and loose ice crystals. But the temperature of the pavement was still below freezing and I had an interesting moment with a patch of black ice and a city salt truck I'd just as soon not remember in my next life. For what it's worth, I appeared to have lost all tails, open and closed. The salt truck and my Cutlass were the only vehicles abroad at that hour.

I had my choice of spaces in the little lot near my building. The attendant, usually an inexhaustible source of unsolicited gossip, stayed inside his plywood booth out of the drizzle, nursing a Thermos and watching *Mr. Rogers* on his portable TV. I surprised Rosecranz, the building superintendent, mopping the foyer and passed a member of the cleaning crew lugging a bag of trash downstairs. The grand panoply of early morning had opened itself up to me in all its variety.

A visitor was snoozing in my outer office. He was a long loose number in a cable sweater and unpressed Dockers, slouched on the upholstered bench with a seasoned mackinaw bunched up behind his head to protect it from the maple rail and his feet spread in clunky sneakers with waffle soles. He was too tall to stretch out full length. His mouth hung open, but he was breathing quietly; those lanky types aren't snorers, as a rule. He had a nice head of chestnut curls and he needed a shave. I didn't know anything about him, except that he was good with locks. I had a dead bolt on the door and I always used it when I went home for the night.

A black duffel slumped on the floor at the foot of the bench. I unzipped it and poked among the clothes inside, opened the cheap vinyl toilet kit, and found nothing more interesting than an electric razor and an unhealthy obsession with L.L. Bean. I put everything back, moved a stack of *National Geographic*s to one end of the coffee table, and sat on the edge, facing the sleeper. I didn't want a cigarette, but I lit one and blew the smoke his direction. After a little while his face twitched. He rubbed his nose, shifted positions, and slept some more. I leaned forward and blew a cloud into his face. He snorted, coughed, and opened a pale blue eye.

"You're Walker?" He didn't even sound hoarse. He would be one of those individuals who dropped off when they wanted to, slept the programmed length of time, and woke up with all the circuits intact. My father was one, by vocational necessity, but that was in the days before truck stops and sleeper cabs. Nowdays it seems like showing off.

"What did you use on the door?" I asked.

He stirred, reached into a pocket of the Dockers, and brought out a flat worn gray suede case that closed with a snap. "Most people think it's a nail kit," he said. "I used to be able to get it through airport security without questions. Now I have to check it. I'm not a B-and-E man, I just needed to crash for a little. Been up twenty-four hours."

"No Continental breakfast, sorry. You can't expect that for the rates."

After a second he showed his teeth in what someone had told him was a grin. The other eye opened. He had heavy lids and he liked to look out from under them. That and the sneer made him a bully of the classic schoolyard type. I studied him the way you stare at a loose shingle—something that would have to be dealt with, and sooner was less expensive than later.

"That makes you Walker," he said. "Corky said you were quicker on the draw than what's good for you."

"Corky as in Sid Corcoran of St. Paul?"

"Minneapolis-St. Paul; but fuck that. They don't correct you in Minneapolis." He returned the burglar kit to his pocket, groped in the one on the other side, and showed me a Minnesota private investigator's license. Alvin Spitzer was the name.

"They call you Alvin or Spitz?"

"Neither, if they admire their bridgework. Al's okay. What about you?"

"You seem comfortable with Walker. Tell me why we're introducing ourselves."

He put away the ID, sat up, and cracked his neck, my favorite habit after chewing tinfoil. "You gave Jillian Rubio to Corky. He gave her to me and I tracked her through the DMV to a duplex in Coon Rapids. Neighbor on the other side hasn't seen her lately: months or weeks, he couldn't say. She keeps to herself. Why are they always the ones that go missing?"

"Because the ones that don't turn up quicker. People notice when they're not around. What did you get out of the duplex?"

He showed his teeth, thought about running a bluff, then remembered where he was and how he got in and moved a shoulder. "She's a good Catholic, or wants people to think so. A cross in every room and spares on chains in all her drawers. All her books and magazines are in English. Only things in Spanish were some letters I found in a box on the bureau in her bedroom, all in the same handwriting and from the same address. Most recent was postmarked November third of last year. No mail in her box, so she probably stopped delivery, but you need a court order to find out for sure. I took the letters and gave them to Maria at the office, to translate. They were from Jillian's mother. Newsy as all hell. The telephone book should be so dull."

I hadn't told Corky about Gilia or blackmail, but if the mother were part of that, it seemed likely she'd make some mention of it in a letter. Or maybe not. She came from a country where mail was opened and read in transit. "Return address Detroit?"

"You guessed it. West Vernor Avenue?"

"Mexicantown. You don't have to be Mexican to live there, but life's easier if Spanish is your first language. You could have given me this over the telephone. I don't like charging clients for unnecessary travel. Somehow I don't think Corky does either."

"He's eating the expenses. There's a subpoena on its way to the office in St. Paul with my name on it. We thought it best for everyone if I wasn't there to take delivery."

"He said you don't make friends easily."

"The advantage being that when I do, they're worth keeping around. So you're getting my considerable services for free. Use them or don't. If not, give me the name of a good cheap hotel. I can take in a couple casinos and maybe the Ford Museum while I'm here."

I let that one swing. I knew he was good with locks, and Corky said he ran a good gag, but I didn't like him by a mile. I saw discipline problems in my future. "What name is the mother using?"

"Miranda Guzman. I guess she remarried. I gathered from the letters she owns dogs. Dogs don't like me any better than people. If I'm going along, don't count on me to scratch them behind the ears."

"We can pick up some biscuits on the way."

"That mean I'm going along?"

"Until you forget who's boss actor. I'm not as easy to get around as a doorman."

He uncased his incisors one more time. No wonder he didn't get along with dogs; they're territorial. "Corky told you about that, did he?"

"He also said you're into him for twenty thousand in bail. I have to work in this town. If you queer that, I won't go to Corky. You don't want to wrestle with me. I don't have any more friends than you."

He rose. He stopped rising at six-two and none of it was suet. His hands formed fists at his sides, as if that was the position they found most natural. I didn't feel like getting up. I took my cigarette out of my mouth, rested my hands on the edge of the coffee table, and kicked him in the nearest shin. He took in air through his teeth and bent to grasp it.

I stood up. A member of the cleaning crew was standing in the doorway, holding a broom and dustpan and a square bucket filled with spray cans and bottles. He was a deaf-mute in his fifties with thick pads of scar tissue around his eyes and his nose spread all over his face. He watched us without blinking.

"You can give me the rest in the brain box," I told Spitzer, shaking out my keys. "I've got a bottle of Old Smuggler in the desk, good for applying internally or externally."

"I'd bust it over your head if I didn't need it." He finished rubbing his shin and tested it with his weight. "Maybe sometime you'll get to St. Paul."

"Minneapolis-St. Paul." I opened the door and herded him inside.

It was my second visit to the neighborhood in as many days, and I was just as happy that none of the people who were beginning to brave the slush appeared to be related to Caterina Muñoz. I wasn't so sure I'd get the friendly end of a bottle of mescal without the presence of Gilia's wardrobe mistress to curb her nephews' protective instincts. The awnings were coming down and the steel cages were going up in front of the bakeries, paleta shops, tortilla factories, and corner markets with plucked fowl dangling upside down in the windows. A thin boy of about twelve, with black bangs and the face of an old man framed by the hood of his parka, pedaled a bicycle along the sidewalk carrying wrinkled brown chiles and cans of refried beans in the basket attached to the handlebars. West Vernor in February looked like Mexico City in a science fiction film about a new ice age.

Spitzer glowered out the window on his side. "You got an ugly winter. I thought you had the lake effect here, too—fluffy drifts, the works. Looks like the inside of a goat's stomach."

"Tourist Council wanted to put that on our license plates. Wouldn't fit." I looked for addresses. There ought to be a law requiring they be posted prominently on places of business.

"You got to wonder what the Mexicans think. What makes a man move his family from Chihuahua all the way to the fucking North Pole?"

"Automobiles. Minimum wage is higher than their maximum."

"Not high enough for me. I'd still be working in Florida if it wasn't for my ex-wives. It got so I couldn't follow one restraining order without violating two others."

"There are forty-nine other states," I said. "One's California."

"I thought about it. I could put up with the crowds and the traffic and the goddamn Democrats and the fat overcooked tourists and their fanny packs. I just didn't want to have to get used to a whole new set of natural disasters. God threw us out of paradise and He gets sore when we try to crawl back in. So He sends hurricanes and earthquakes and fires and floods and droughts and mudslides and paid lobbyists. I'll take my chances with snow and ice. It beats listening to a movie star sitting on her redwood deck blubbering over the fate of the spotted owl."

"I didn't know there were movie stars in Florida."

"There are movie stars in Miami and Phoenix and Santa Fe and wherever the sun shines warm. That's why I picked Minnesota."

I almost missed the address. It belonged to a narrow, butter-colored house with a high peaked roof wedged in between a cinder-block restaurant with a bullfighting mural painted across the front and a discount tire shop. I'd driven down Vernor at least twice a month since I learned to drive, and I'd never noticed it before. I U'd into a space across the street and looked at Spitzer. "How are you with women?"

He made the thing he thought was a grin. "I never had any complaints."

"That's what I thought you'd say. I'll do the talking."

Three painted wooden steps led to the front door. There was a wicker shade in the window next to the door and in one corner a square of white cardboard neatly lettered in black Magic Marker:

AUTHORIZED PRESA CANARIO BREEDER
CHD FREE GUARANTEED

"Presa canario." Spitzer mangled the words, however they were supposed to be pronounced. "Sounds like a pasta plate."

I pressed the button next to the door. I got a jingling buzz from deep in the house and then a deep, rooping bark I could feel in my testicles.

Spitzer said, "Shit," and backed down a step.

I reached behind under my coat and loosened the Smith & Wesson in its kidney holster. I'd had business with mean dogs before. A normal-size man in good health is more than a match for most if he keeps his head, but there was more than a hundred pounds behind that bark.

Inside, someone yelled. The barking stopped. A floorboard squeaked and the door came open wide enough for the woman inside to insert her face into the gap. It was a strong Hispanic face, framed between corkscrews of dark hair that had come loose from the pins. Very large, very dark eyes, good skin, and the beginnings of jowls. She'd gone light on the lipstick and eyeliner, a good choice. There had been great beauty there once, and she still had a claim on handsome if she didn't try too hard to hold on to it. I had her down for fifty.

"Mrs. Guzman?" I said.

Her eyes flicked from my face to Spitzer's and back to mine. "You're early. I haven't fed them yet."

"Feed them," Spitzer said. "We'll wait."

"You look like fighters," she said. "The skinny one especially. I don't sell to fighters. It's against the law, and even if it wasn't

I wouldn't. You said over the phone you were interested in show dogs." She had a little accent, most noticeable when her tone turned accusing.

The wicker shade buckled and a square head the size of a toaster oven pushed a black snout up against the glass. A rosy tongue spilled out of a wide, wrinkled grin filled with ivory teeth. The head was looking out the top pane. Something rustled behind me. Spitzer was standing on the bottom step now.

I said, "Is that dog standing on something?"

A sheet of steel slid down behind the woman's eyes. They hadn't been soft to begin with. "You're not the man I spoke to on the phone. He had a lilt."

"Maybe Fido ate his balls," Spitzer said.

I gave her one of my cards. "There's a misunderstanding. I didn't call you. Are you Mrs. Guzman?"

" 'Investigations,' " she read. "I have all my papers. My dogs are tested regularly for CHD. If you take one home and it develops problems, I'll replace it or I'll refund your investment. I'm a breeder, not a puppy mill."

"What's CHD?" I asked.

"Congenital hip displacement. If you don't know that, why are you investigating me?"

"Again, a misunderstanding. We're not with the kennel club. We're private detectives. Do you have a daughter named Jillian Rubio?"

She took that in. Then the door slammed shut. The dog, startled, began bellowing. The black snout dissolved into pink gums and flashing teeth. The glass fogged over. The window jumped against the frame and I joined Spitzer down on the ground.

"Fish make good pets," he said. "You don't have to shut them up and when you get tired of them, you give 'em a flush. What's the deal with the Rubio woman? She wanted?"

I said, "We'll come back after feeding time."

TWELVE

Blackmail, huh? Who's the mark?"

"Barbara Bush," I said. "She used to dance topless at Planet Hollywood."

"Fuck off. You don't trust me?"

"I don't trust Corky, and I trust Corky. I wouldn't have told you about the blackmail, except it's possible you have a right to know what you mixed into. The dogs put an edge on the situation."

We were sitting at a table in the restaurant next to Miranda Guzman's house. It was a square room lit with fluorescent troughs, with colorful bottles of hot sauce standing on a shelf that ran around the walls and a large Mexican in a clean undershirt stirring something lethal on the griddle behind the counter. The smell was making me rethink ordering just coffee. He'd just opened for lunch and he must have been a good chef because it takes an expert to keep all the spatters on the cooking surface.

"Presa canario," Spitzer said. "What kind of dog is that, do you think? She must've bred a Great Dane with a Clydesdale."

I looked at the photocopied flyer I'd torn off a crowded bulletin board inside the door of the restaurant. "Spanish breed, it says here. From *presa español.* Cortez used them to hunt Aztecs. This strain comes from the Canary Islands. They run a hundred to a hundred fifty pounds and they snack on pit bulls and Rottweilers."

"I bet she gets a lot of business here. They come for the fajitas and go home with a man-eater."

"It's a complication."

"No shit. We had an eighth of an inch of glass between us and a torn throat. What would you have called that, a serious miscalculation?"

"Every time I come here they sic something savage on me. Last time it was four big Hispanics. What this operation needs is a little less improvisation and a little more finesse."

"What it needs is a lot less me. I'm going back to St. Paul. Lawyers only tear you up on the witness stand."

"Suit yourself. We'll get your duffel out of the trunk."

When the cook came with Spitzer's burrito, he asked him to call a taxi.

"*¿Qué?*" He had kind sad eyes in a big round face like the map of Sonora.

"El cab-o, Pancho. Redtop. *El grande remo.* Today, if possible."

"*¿Qué?*"

I said, "I think you just ordered a big canoe paddle."

"You ask him, then. I bet you know all the words to 'La Cucaracha.' " He cut into the burrito with the edge of his fork and released a cloud of steam.

I held a fist up to my ear and dialed in the air. The cook said, "*Sí, pronto,*" and trundled back around the counter. He returned with a cordless telephone. I pecked out a number I knew by heart and the dispatcher said he'd have a cab in front of the address in fifteen minutes. I gave back the instrument, told the cook *gracias*, and between hand signs, a scatter of leftover Spanish nouns, and his own superior command of English, I managed to get in an order for a pound of raw hamburger to go. He looked puzzled, but he had too much self-possession to shake his head on the way back to the kitchen. I recalculated his tip at twenty percent.

"You better add this if you want to put the dogs out of commission." Spitzer pushed a bottle of Mad Apache hot sauce across the table. The cap was floating a half inch above the container.

"I want to make a friend, not kill an enemy."

"Good plan. That way you can be buried next to your wife *and* your parents." He ate two forkfuls, emptied his water glass on top of them, and belched propane. "Man, I wouldn't want to be the guy sitting next to me in coach."

A few minutes later, Alvin Spitzer gave his driver the duffel, got into the backseat, and rode out of my life without so much as a "hasta la Viagra." I heard Sid Corcoran fired him sometime after, while he was in jail awaiting arraignment on a charge of assault and battery. He'd found a doorman he couldn't con and a lock he couldn't pick, all in the same week.

I put my paper sack with the wrapped hamburger on the floor of my car, drove around the corner for the benefit of whatever dogs and mothers might be watching through Miranda Guzman's window, and parked next to a Dumpster piled high with take-out cartons and shredded rims. The street that ran behind the restaurant and the tire shop and the house between was wider than an alley but just as vacant, and no more in need of repaving than a street in any other neighborhood, which meant that the cracks in the asphalt qualified for wetlands preservation.

I was still improvising. I wanted a door with an easy lock, a look inside an unshaded window, a glimpse of something that might indicate there was someone living in the house besides Mrs. Guzman and her breeding stock. Even a Mr. Guzman would be a nice change, but I was counting on a set of luggage monogrammed J. R. or maybe Jillian Rubio herself, sipping a Tequila Sunrise and scratching the belly of an orgasmic hippo of a canine. The raw meat might work on Miranda, if the dogs weren't having any.

The block presented an encouraging lack of around-the-clock residents with time on their hands. Across the street was a lumberyard with stacks of boards protected from the weather by blue plastic tarping, with a circular saw zinging away inside the galvanized walls of the accompanying truss building. Vacant lots yawned on either side, where a couple of HUD houses had probably stood, never occupied and rotting, until the city knocked them down to discourage crack dealers from setting up shop inside. Detroit is a city of empty lots and lumberyards, churning out plywood to nail over the windows of unoccupied houses on their way to becoming empty lots. The odds of a concerned neighbor spotting a private agent snooping through windows in that vicinity were agreeably low.

Getting to the windows was a problem. A rectangular backyard of winter-killed grass extended from a kennel built behind the house to the street, enclosed in a chain-link fence eight feet high with razor wire on top and a padlocked gate. Inside was a scatter of rubber dog toys and a well-gnawed hunk of bone and gristle that looked disturbingly like part of a human pelvis. It was probably a hambone. There was scarcely room to squeeze between the house and the buildings on either side, and less opportunity to beat the street in the event of discovery. I couldn't get that chewed-up hambone out of my mind.

A knee-high door in back of the kennel slid up while I was contemplating the situation and the first of eight dogs ducked its huge square head to bound through into the yard. The rest came in all sizes, not including small, but the first was the biggest and the most impressively built: deep-chested, with a short bluish brindle coat, Chippendale legs, and a scooped-out belly like a greyhound's. It made a beeline for the hambone, and after two or three seconds of scraping the surface with its teeth, down on its elbows and bracing the bone with its great round paws, something cracked, a sound that turned my bowels to water. The dog was the same one that had been watching me through the front window earlier.

The cracking ended its obsession with the bone. It lowered its haunches, let its tongue hang, and amused itself watching the others with paternal interest. They romped, dug at the hard earth, licked themselves, wrestled, and pretended to worry at one another's throat. The growling sounded serious, but in the absence of bleeding I assumed it was play. The other loner, a female slightly over two-thirds the top dog's size, whined and yipped and clawed at the base of the fence facing the street, paused now and then just long enough to sniff the air, then went back to work with fresh enthusiasm. I figured she had caught the scent of a pheasant roosting in one of the empty lots.

"What are you doing? What have you got in that bag?"

I hadn't seen Miranda Guzman sidling between the house and the tire shop. She was standing near the fence gate, wearing a heavy, hip-length sweater over her stretch pants. Her feet were stuck in an old pair of industrial work shoes whose steel toes had begun to wear through the cracked leather; either that, or the dogs had started on them when they got bored with their chew toys. Her hands were knotted into fists in the sweater's pockets.

I looked down at the sack. I'd forgotten I was holding it. "Leftovers. I never could finish a plate of Mexican in one sitting."

"You're trespassing."

I was standing on a public sidewalk, but I didn't make an issue of it. "I'm looking for your daughter. No one's seen her in three months. Her friends are worried."

"She doesn't have any friends. Did *she* send you?"

"Who?"

"Don't be estupid. The one who calls herself Gilia Cristobal." The accent was thickening.

"What do you know about Gilia Cristobal?"

"I know she's a whore that gets her picture taken in her underwear and parades it around in front of God and everyone. Dragging my daughter's name through filth."

"When was the last time you saw your daughter?"

"She came here for Thanksgiving. Get off my property." She took her hands out of her pockets. She was holding a big ring in one with a key dangling from it.

"If you saw her then, you're the only one who has since the first part of November. Did she say where she was going when she left?"

"She didn't stay for the holiday. Happy?" She grasped the padlock on the gate and stuck the key in the slot. "If I were you,

I'd start running now. These dogs can take down a horse in full gallop."

The dogs had stopped playing and were gathered on the other side of the gate, eyes bright and their stubby tails wagging; all except two. The big bull stood apart from them, staring at me with thoughtful anticipation. The bitch near the street was still trying to get out her own way. She was too preoccupied to notice what was going on.

I reached back under my coat and pulled the revolver out of its holster.

"Have it your way." Miranda Guzman sprang open the lock and undid the latch. The bitch near the street heard the noise. Her big head swung that direction.

I brought the Smith & Wesson around, at the same time taking hold of the paper sack by its bottom and shaking out the contents. The ground meat struck the sidewalk with a splat and separated. The woman must have thought it was poisoned, because she said something sharp in Spanish and tried to slam the gate shut. She wasn't fast enough for the bitch. The dog was already running, and knocked two others sprawling and got her broad chest and shoulders through the space. For a moment she was pinned between the gate and the frame, but she twisted and got her hips free. The gate clanged to behind her, drawing yelps from one or two of the other dogs when the chain link struck their muzzles. The bitch slipped on the turn, scrabbled for traction, and came straight at me, ignoring the hamburger. I took aim on her chest.

"Isabella! *¡Aqui!*"

The half-hysterical command was lost on Isabella. My finger was tensing on the trigger when she abruptly changed course and loped past me. A string of slobber detached itself from a pair of blubbery lips and plastered my left pant leg. Tires cried in the street; the bumper of a delivery van that had just turned the corner stopped an inch short of collision with a hundred pounds of muscle and flesh. The bitch, taking no notice, bounded over the curb on the other side, crossed a sidewalk, and stopped briefly when she came to the board fence that surrounded the lumberyard. Whimpering and yipping, she ran back and forth along its base, then found a narrow gap where a board had come loose and wriggled through on her elbows, jostling the board off its nail. It fell with a clank.

I left Miranda fumbling with the padlock and trotted across the street. I was still holding the gun. Out of the corner of my eye I caught a glimpse of a pale face behind the windshield of the delivery van, which was still stopped in its lane. That wasn't something that had anything to do with me. I wanted to know what was more interesting to a dog than trespassers and fresh meat.

Ducking under the fence rail, I tore my coat on the bent nail, but I didn't spend any time on it. The presa canario had followed her nose to one of the stacks of lumber covered in blue tarp. She clawed at the plastic, got a strip between her teeth, and pulled, snarling and whistling through her snout. I was moving that way in long strides, but Miranda Guzman overtook me, bustled past, seized Isabella's thick nylon collar, and tugged with both hands. But the bitch set her feet. Her shoulders bunched as big as coconuts and the tendons in her neck stood out like guy wires. Her stubby ears lay flat and saliva cooked in her constricted throat. Nothing was going to move her from that spot this side of Gabriel's horn or a slow mailman.

I changed hands on the .38, got a grip on the tarp, and tore it free of the clothesline someone had tied around it. Something long and gray slid off the top of the stack of boards and flopped over the edge. Flakes of scarlet enamel still clung to the end, bright as cardinals in a winter landscape.

"*Madre de dios.*" Miranda's voice was a whisper. Only her hands on the bitch's collar prevented her from crossing herself.

I'd been wrong about a pheasant being the cause of the commotion. Pheasants don't have fingers.

THIRTEEN

I hadn't visited Inspector John Alderdyce's office on its rarefied upper floor at Detroit Police Headquarters in many months. He'd been promoted practically out of my orbit, got his picture taken with chiefs and mayors and white city council hopefuls who needed the black vote in order to nod when the mayor spoke, and probably hadn't visited a crime scene since Jeffrey Dahmer was in short pants. But the office hadn't changed: The same academy class picture hung at the same crooked angle on the wall, the same framed photos of his wife and two children, now out-of-date, stood on the corner of the same gray steel desk. A credenza I remembered groaned beneath stacks of what might have been the same fat case files and yellowing reports.

Alderdyce himself had changed, but in a straight predictable line. There were glints of silver in his close-cropped, tightly curled hair, he'd taken on baggage around the middle after the fashion of heavy-muscled former beat cops approaching their thirty, the eyes in the brutal face had gotten a little older and a whole lot less happy, if they'd ever been happy to begin with; I'd known him since childhood in the dear dead days of integration and couldn't recall ever having seen him cut loose with so much as a yippee. His tailoring was always flawless, the material of his gray winter-weight suit in keeping with his upper-story salary and his necktie woven from equal parts spun silver and moonbeam.

He sat in his chair without touching the padded leather back, listening to the receiver he held to his ear and looking straight through me as if I were a window to a view he didn't care much about. After two minutes of almost complete silence on his end he thanked the caller and hung up.

"Medical examiner." He'd given up using initials like *ME*, *APB*, and *GSW* about the time *Cops* worked them into America's everyday vocabulary. "Dead two months anyway, possibly three, intermittent bouts of cold weather considered. No visible wounds as yet. It's hard to tell when you can poke your finger right through the rotten skin."

I nodded understanding. I'd stood back and burned tobacco to distract my nostrils while the morgue crew had shoveled the body of what appeared to be a young woman in an advanced stage of decomposition from the top of a stack of lumber into a rubber bag on a stretcher. Miranda Guzman had retreated into her house to throw up and possibly cry. I'd helped her haul a determined Isabella across the street and into the kennel, and had used the telephone in her front room to call 911. There had followed a cloud of uniforms, a plainclothesman and -woman from the local precinct, and then the lab rats, who had directed the photographers, examined some loose pebbles in the yard, and taken away the blue tarp and clothesline to check for prints, DNA, and Malay sailor knots.

The cops had been polite enough, in their suspicious way; frowned a little when I said I'd have to check with my client before identifying said party and underlined the answer in their notepads, but made no mention of truncheons or hot irons or the Lincoln Question. The owner of the lumberyard, a knobby Dane in a Carhartt coat who looked like the man on the Brawny paper towels package, had stared at me throughout the operation as if I'd been smuggling out two-by-fours up my sleeves.

That particular stack of wood, he'd said, had been seasoning since last fall. No one connected with the yard had had any reason to look under the tarp and wouldn't until the construction season started up in March. He'd asked the detectives if the state disclosure laws required him to inform customers that their wood had been contaminated by a corpse. They'd referred him to the Attorney General's Office.

" 'Female, five-two, eyes and hair brown, aged twenty to thirty,' " Alderdyce read from the notes he'd made on his blotter pad. "She had on a light cotton dress, ordinary lingerie, flat pumps. The shoes don't often stay on; but whoever dumped her might have put them back on her feet, either out of respect for the dead or a compulsion for organization. How cold did it get in November?"

"As I recall it was mild," I said. "But a lot of people don't dress for cold weather until they can't stand it anymore." I thought of Barry Stackpole.

"She was wearing a small crucifix on a gold chain. The examiner had to cut it off. Bloating. That could make her a Catholic—the crucifix, not the bloating—but not necessarily. The Guzman woman didn't give us a positive, although she recognized the clothes as her daughter's. We'll ask her again when she's had some time, but by then we'll know for sure anyway. You know how they take prints in cases like these?"

"They cut them off the corpse and make finger puppets out of them."

He made a grumpy noise, as if I'd stepped on his punch line. "In Washington they use holographic photography. Here we're still using ducking stools. Who's paying your expenses?"

The abrupt change of subject was supposed to catch me off guard.

"I'm still trying to reach the client," I said. "It isn't a question I get to answer until I do."

He didn't get mad. He'd booted that habit on the advice of a physician. "The mother says Jillian Rubio came to visit November tenth, intending to stay through Thanksgiving. On the twelfth she packed an overnight bag, saying she had an important appointment and would be back on the fourteenth. She wasn't, but Mrs. Guzman wasn't too worried. Apparently the daughter was an unstable type, couldn't be counted on. Went months without telephoning or answering letters; then she'd show up in person, right out of the blue. Diagnosed manic-depressive, or whatever they're calling it this season."

"Bipolar. It's like a code. They change it whenever too many people understand it."

"That's checkable, although she thought of that, too. The mother doesn't know the name of the doctor."

"Who thought of it, the mother or the daughter?"

"Detectives weren't sure. Mrs. Guzman's a cool character, they say. Must come from living with animals that can eat you alive the first time they figure out they don't have to sit or stay just because you say so."

"If her daughter was taking medication for her condition, it ought to show up in the toxicology report."

"Which if so, in her depressive phase she walked across the street, ditching the overnight bag somewhere we haven't found it, climbed up under the tarp, and committed suicide. That'll fly."

"Dicier cases than that have." I thought about the former president of Gilia's country, shooting himself with a machine gun that required two men and a tripod to operate. "But in those cases the system had some incentive to make them fly. Jillian Rubio wasn't that important."

"She was to someone."

I saw it was coming again and threw something in front of it. "Did Miranda Guzman see her leave?"

"She went out to catch a city bus on the corner. We're checking that. Obviously she missed it. Maybe someone offered her a ride. Whoever it was didn't take her very far. Who's paying your expenses?"

Well, I hadn't really expected it to stall him for long. I had a cup of coffee sitting on the desk in a blue-and-gold DPD mug I'd forgotten about. I took a sip and said nothing. The coffee wasn't as bad as you hear. But it was cold.

Alderdyce leaned back, fished in a pants pocket, and slid two quarters and a dime across the blotter. "Try the client again. There's a pay phone in the hall."

I always obey the police when there's no reason not to.

Tapping a public telephone means a world of hurt for the locals who try it, but the Supreme Court is less specific about outside listening devices. In the hall I felt all around the box for a bug, unscrewed the mouthpiece and then the earpiece and looked inside, groped under the shelf. All I found was a petrified wad of gum. That left low-tech. A hangdog type with a fringe of ginger-colored hair was slumped on the wooden bench nearby, with nothing to do but check his necktie to see if the tomato stain was still there. He was probably a detective lieutenant. I turned my back on him and called the Hyatt.

I argued with someone I may or may not have argued with before, and just as Gilia came on a male operator broke in to tell me I was out of minutes. Gilia asked him to reverse the charges. I waited to make sure he'd gone away, then made my report quick, on the same theory that if you yank off a Band-Aid all in one motion you spare the patient extra pain. It doesn't work with Band-Aids and it didn't work with Gilia. She rattled off some gutter Spanish that made a lot more sense to me than anything I'd heard from *Don Quixote*.

When she stopped for breath I said, "This goes back to before she missed her first appointment. A good investigator might have made a better start at it then, but homicides take time. The cops just broke a case that took place at the Airport Hilton a dozen years ago; they had to wait for genetic science to catch up. I need to move a hell of a lot faster, which means I need your consent."

"Consent on what?" She sounded like someone who'd bought the Brooklyn Bridge and was waiting for the bank to tell her the check had already cleared.

"I'm going to have to give the cops something. I've been in the jug before. It's every bit as bad as they say, but the food's decent—thank Amnesty International for that—and they let you alone with your thoughts. Only I wouldn't be any use to you in a cage."

"Tell them everything. What's the difference? The axe is going to fall either way. She was pretty clear about that."

"I wouldn't be so sure. Most blackmailers are lazy or they'd find a less risky living. The information could be parked under a rock somewhere. If I can get the cops to cut me some slack I may be able to find the rock. Information's the only card they accept. The honest ones, anyway."

"I guess it's too much to hope that this inspector isn't one of the honest ones."

"Yeah. There's never one of the others around when you need one."

I heard canned music on her end, conga drums and vibes. She had the radio tuned to an Afro-Cuban station. "If he's your friend and you tell him, will he keep the confidence?"

"Police inspectors aren't anybody's friend, least of all mine. They have people to answer to, the people they have to answer to have people to answer to, and sooner or later one of them is a politician. It will get out. So our priority is not to give them anything we don't want to get out."

"The blackmail—"

"Is one of those things. Even if we don't say what it was about. Especially then. That kind of thing just makes the darlings in the press want to run out and dig up whatever it is you've been paying to keep buried. Which they will, eventually. It's all public record, remember."

"But if they haven't found it out on their own by now . . ." She saw where that was going before she finished, but I kicked it home.

"So far no one's had a reason to match up all the files," I said. "The minute they find out you've been paying extortion, they'll have a reason. It's called circulation and ratings. They call it truth."

"Give the police my name. I can stall them with lawyers, and bad publicity won't hurt me as long as no one knows the details of how I came to be mixed up in a murder. I'm a pretty notorious character already. It might even get me a European tour." She was starting to sound like the public Gilia now; shoot first and flash your breasts on the recoil.

"No good. They're bound to find out Jillian Rubio's real

name, and then they'll guess the rest. Giving them a head start would be a bad idea."

"But what *can* you give the police to satisfy them?"

I let two seconds trickle into Ma Bell's purse. I was pretty sure the putative cop had gotten up from the bench and left, and when I looked around I was right. Mostly I wanted to enjoy the moment. "Hector Matador," I said.

FOURTEEN

Bullshit. Hector Matador? Bullshit."

When John Alderdyce employed his favorite compound word, it was usually the last in the argument. But this time there was a light in his eye. He was too much cop to dismiss a fresh opportunity to tie the Colombian drug lord to a murder. His telephone had begun ringing the instant I gave him the name, and he'd reached for it out of habit. Now he withdrew his hand and let it ring itself out.

"I was as surprised as you," I said. "He says he's a reformed character. The parole board seemed to agree with him, and there wasn't any red bank dye on his money, so I took the job."

Gilia's reaction had been similar, but after I'd explained my reasons—different reasons from the one I'd given the inspector—she'd agreed it made sense, in a P.I. kind of way. The police held no fear for Matador. Once prepared for the encounter by his client, he could stonewall a little thing like a big-city homicide until whales beached themselves on the shore of Lake St. Clair. The fact that once he got clear he'd come after me with his private army was immaterial. He'd been waiting to light candles at my head so long I was already dead on general principle. It was a small enough price to pay for sleuthing time.

Alderyce said, "I didn't realize you'd been Born Again. The last time you two were in the same room, he tried to kill you."

"No, the last time was when I testified against him in Recorder's Court. One might say the two things canceled each other out."

"If you needed the money that badly, why didn't you rob a church?"

"If I only worked for people I liked, I'd be sleeping in a refrigerator box instead of the palace I live in now."

"Ah. The solvency defense. Somehow I never expected to hear it from you. But then I blacked a kid's eye in third grade when he told me the Easter Bunny died."

"The Easter Bunny died?"

He wasn't listening. He was looking at the pictures of his boys in their duofold frame, thinking I didn't know what. They were school shots: hair combed, shirts bright and chosen by a maternal hand. One of them had started college. His brother was on a carrier in the Persian Gulf. If I'd known that at the time, I might have played things differently. Probably not, though. The game is tricky enough when the human card doesn't turn up.

I opened a palm. "The job looked okay. Matador had a standing appointment with Jillian Rubio the thirteenth of each month. After she missed three of them he got worried."

"Appointment for what?"

"He didn't say."

"Bullshit."

"Jillian didn't either, at least to her mother. If it was the same appointment. Maybe they had a pact."

"It got broken this afternoon."

"Good luck with that," I said. "Matador wouldn't tell a cop his blood type if he blew an artery."

The telephone went off again. This time he answered it. He said "yeah" three times, wrote a name and a time on his blotter, and cradled the receiver. I glanced at his scribble. The name meant nothing to me and probably had to do with another case. He always used military time, not that he'd ever served. About the time I was scaling walls at Fort Campbell, he was riding around in the back of a police car, memorizing the names of streets.

He said, "So that's your story."

"Matador's staying at the Dearborn Hyatt. You can confirm it with him."

"I never thought I'd see the day you used him as a reference."

"Times change. We're chummy with China now."

He played with his gold pencil, standing it up on its eraser, sliding his fingers down from the top, reversing ends, sliding his fingers down from the top. Finally he blew out a lungful of coffee-flavored air and threw the pencil hard into a corner. It rattled off two walls and rolled to a stop at the base of a particleboard bookcase stuffed with Michigan Manuals. He'd inherited them from a predecessor who thought they had something to do with the law.

"Feed it to me plain," he said. "No understanding by implication, no conclusions based on omission, no bullshit about what the definition of 'is' is. You accepted a blind assignment from Hector Matador. No other parties involved."

I met his glare. "Yeah."

"You're a goddamn liar."

"I've got a thousand dollars of his money in my wallet. I put the other fourteen grand in the bank. Want me to empty out my pockets?"

"I want you to take a lie detector test."

"Can you do that? I'm just asking. A lot's changed since last fall. They used to post the Bill of Rights in the room where you conduct strip searches. It was kind of quaint, like the 'God Bless Our Home' sampler in the warden's office at Jackson."

"So you're refusing."

"It's not the machine, it's the guy who operates it. He smells like old magazines."

"I could book you as a material witness. No habeas corpus need apply."

"I wish you would. I can use the free advertising. The *Free Press* charges too much and all I can get from Channel Two is thirty seconds between nine-hundred numbers. The last time I did that a guy proposed marriage."

He smoothed his necktie. It already clung to his shirt like a seal's skin. "I guess I should've seen this coming when we started letting presidents lie under oath. Then we lost the Boy Scouts. The Boy Scouts! I guess Mickey Mouse is next. He's been selling secrets to Woody Woodpecker. It's like a fucking virus. Call me Huck Finn. I never thought it'd worm its way around to you."

"Still don't believe me?"

"I do. That's what's depressing me." He drew an ordinary pencil out of his leather cup. "You know where the elevator is. The way my day's going you probably won't fall down the shaft."

"Isn't this supposed to be the part where you tell me not to leave town?"

"You can leave the fucking planet. Hubbell can use another snooper."

I got up. I was home free, but I just had to stop and ask to be thrown out at the plate.

"How long do you figure on that toxicology report?"

When he scowled, he looked like one of those tiki gods carved for the purpose of sacrificing virgins and porterhouse steaks.

"Lansing's been backed up since the coed murders in sixty-nine," he said. "Ten days just to eliminate the nonprobables. Minimum."

"You might ask them to test for Stelazine. That's a poison."

"I know what it is. I used to work hospital detail. Why might I?"

"I like the word. Rhymes with 'nectarine.' "

"In Branson, maybe. Are you withholding evidence in a homicide?" He laughed, explosively and without enjoying himself. "Look who I'm asking."

"A hunch isn't evidence. Anyway, I didn't withhold anything. You can write down the exact time I brought it up." I looked up at his quartz clock. "Oh six hundred."

"That's six A.M. I thought you were a veteran."

"Just a dogface. The brass kept the time."

The scowl went away. He still looked like a pagan barbecue grill.

"I hope I get to lock you away for obstruction of justice," he said. "It might save our relationship."

"I wasn't aware we had one."

"That's what makes it work."

I let myself out. It was the nicest thing anyone had said to me in days.

FIFTEEN

Eastern Standard Nighttime lay on the cophouse steps as stiff as a dead cat, dragging down the thermometer and turning the afternoon thaw into a sheet of glaze. Blue salt crystals scattered by a city employee were eating holes in the ice and eventually the marble underneath, but I hung on to the railing and tested each step before committing my weight to it. I hadn't dodged a bullet inside just to break my neck out front.

A ticket was frozen to my windshield where I'd parked in a slot reserved for police vehicles. That angered me; the phony MEDICAL EMERGENCY sign I'd clipped to the visor was plainly visible. I chipped the ticket loose and stuck it in the glove compartment with its near relations. I'd pay them when the lid would no longer close.

Just for a driving exercise I remembered the telephone number Barry Stackpole had given me, a number without a name that belonged to a professor at Columbia with the power to corroborate or destroy Gilia's alibi for the night Angelina Suerto danced her last tango. He wouldn't be there at this hour, and anyway I had another more urgent hole to plug. It was named Miranda Guzman.

The Matador gambit had an expiration date. His connection with Gilia wasn't public and he would know how to keep it that way, but I had a few days at most before the cops gave up on him and dug back far enough in Jillian Rubio's history to find out she shared a name with the hottest Latina entertainer since Charo cooched her last cooch. But I didn't have even that much time if Jillian's mother decided to spill what she knew. So I had to persuade a grieving mother to lay off on the woman who by now she may have convinced herself had something to do with her daughter's murder. I should have brought more raw meat.

I rang the buzzer, got some barking from the direction of the kennel behind the house, but no Miranda. The boss dog didn't come to the window and I missed its deep bass among the others. I thumbed the button a second time just for laughs. I stepped down to the sidewalk and put my hands in my pockets.

I pictured Miranda's living room, where I'd used her telephone to report the body in the lumberyard. It ran pretty much to type: sofa and love seat, a little worn but a matched set, clean and with those arm-condoms in place to slow down wear and tear, a wicker coffee table with picture magazines on top, not too much of a chore to read for a resident who spoke English but thought in Spanish, a Spanish Bible on a side table with a rattan mat, an elaborate crucifix on one wall, carved in meticulous detail from what looked like ancient ash. That would have come over with her and Jillian. A votive candle guttering on a decorative shelf underneath. A religious person, Mrs. Guzman. I bet she and Mr. Guzman, whoever and wherever he might be, had discussed long into many a night the merits of Jesus' claim to messiahhood. Maybe I'd lose my bet. There are probably a lot of Roman Catholics named Guzman, just as there are plenty of Jews named O'Reilly, Presbyterians named Washington, and Muslims born in Salt Lake City.

Three Catholic churches serve the growing Hispanic community, and all three are a hike from the heart of Mexicantown; but a bus ride to Mass is nothing compared to an old-time pilgrimage, even when it's in a city bus. I logged up a bunch of blocks on the Cutlass' odometer, committed more parking violations outside Most Holy Redeemer and Most Blessed Sacrament, got no Guzman in either place, took my leave. Nearing Most Holy Trinity, I hit the brakes and almost lost control in the slush. Someone had tied up a dog the size of a library lion in front of the stark Norman facade.

I found a space on Porter with a sign saying it was reserved for expectant mothers. I didn't know if that was enforceable, and I toyed with the VISITING PRIEST sign I keep for variety, but with a steeple so close I figured God already had the range, so I put it away.

Most Holy Trinity was the second Catholic parish founded in Detroit, a palm for the Irish when they came by the boatload from the potato famine of the 1830s. The present building has been standing nearly 150 years. The presa canario bull, unimpressed, lifted a leg against the bottom step as I passed. The dog looked miserable and was probably thinking of the hambone it had left at home. It seemed a pretty valuable property to leave out on the street, but the rippling growl that had come from its throat as I'd approached the church reminded me it came with its own security.

Inside the entrance, a bronze plaque depicting an angel and a departing soul in a gondola in relief contains the names of the twelve altar boys and five adults who died when their excursion boat collided with a steamer on the Detroit River in 1880. The pastor, a survivor, called it the Massacre of the Innocents. I took off my hat.

No service was taking place. Miranda Guzman and I had the cavernous interior to ourselves. She was in the third pew from the back, kneeling on the padded rail with her head down and her hands clasped in front of her. She had on a cloth coat with a monkey collar and a lacy black scarf covered her hair. I slid into the pew behind her and waited.

I'm not a Catholic. I'm not anything, although I spent two years of Sundays reading Bible stories at St. Paul's Episcopal on Woodward and waiting for something to take. Still, it's tough to remain an agnostic in the presence of so much ancient iconography. There are no atheists in foxholes, and very few in Most Holy Trinity. I thought holy thoughts and wondered if Miranda intended to break for supper.

After a little while she crossed herself, rose from her knees, and sat back. She never turned her head, and gave no indication she knew I was there until she spoke.

"Why are you here? Can a woman not pray for her child's soul in peace?"

She was looking straight ahead, toward the life-size crucifix behind the altar. Her voice was barely more than a whisper.

I said, "I'll go if you ask me to, Mrs. Guzman. I need to speak to you tonight. You choose where."

She was silent for a long time. I didn't know if she was thinking or praying.

"You can do your speaking before the Lord," she said finally. "If you have the courage."

"Did your daughter tell you about her arrangement with Gilia?"

"No one of that name exists. Not now."

Her tone had a steel rod through it.

"Fair enough. We'll call her something else. How does Mariposa sound?"

Not being able to see her face I was at a disadvantage. The back of her neck seemed to redden a little, but the red might have been there a while and I'd just noticed it. A church that size has drafts no matter how hard you try to heat it in winter.

"My daughter told me very little about her life in Minnesota. That was her stepfather's fault. Noah Guzman was a cruel man. I suppose I am to blame also. I did not interfere with his cruelty. It drove her away from us when she was seventeen."

"Are you divorced?"

"It is not permitted. He died. Strong drink was the cause."

"Did Jillian's father die? You and she came to this country without him."

"He had our marriage annulled so he could wed another. Such things are possible in the country of my birth, if you are willing to meet the bishop's price. He made me *una puta* and his daughter *una bastarda*. It is why we had to leave, and why I changed her name."

"If she was staying with you near the end, you and she must have reconciled."

She seemed to shrug. She might have been adjusting her coat.

"I think she told you what she was up to," I said. "Or you guessed. You knew there was an entertainer running around using your daughter's birth name. It would be a topic of conversation between a mother and her estranged offspring; safer than something closer to home. Even if she didn't tell you everything, you would've been able to supply the rest. You're nobody's idea of a dumb wetback."

"I'm not a wetback!" It made an echo. An altar boy or something who had come in through a door near the front looked our way briefly, then genuflected before the altar and set to work with a scraper removing bits of wax from the rail. Tiny orange lights flickered in the soles of the running shoes under the hem of his robe. Miranda lowered her voice to its former level. "I'm not a wetback. My great-great-grandfather was a marquise. Your ancestors would have been flogged for failing to lower their heads when a member of *La Casa del Rubio* rode past."

"Yeah. Scratch a rolled *r* and doubloons spill out like gumballs. Your land grant's shrunk to a kennel in Mexicantown and you swapped your sceptre for a pooper-scooper. Let's confine the conversation to something since Galileo. Are you planning to put the bite on Gilia, or are you going to the cops?"

She hesitated. "I don't know this bite."

"The tariff. The tithe. The bee. You know: El Grande Suckarino. It's all in the breeding. Blue blood, blackmail."

"*¡Puerco!*" It rang clear up in the clerestory. The altar boy dropped his scraper. He looked at us again, crossed himself, picked it up, and resumed scraping. It sounded like a jazzman brushing a snare drum.

Miranda had swung around, resting an elbow on the back of her pew. Bright patches glowed on her cheeks. She had a fire-stoked beauty that would be with her on her deathbed. Beside it, Gilia's was all youth and cosmetics. *Señor* Cristobal had been a donkey to throw it away. "I would kill you if we were not in the house of the Lord." It came out in a hissing whisper.

I nodded. "Okay. I apologize, Mrs. Guzman. I was just playing picador. What we call needling. I was tired of looking at the back of your neck."

"Speak of me as you will. You did not know my daughter, what she went through just to cross a room or climb a flight of stairs. When she was six months old they said she would never celebrate her first birthday. When she was a year old they said she would never walk. Until she was two, she did not know a day without hot and cold compresses on her poor withered legs."

"You nursed her?"

"She had nurses. We had money. The Rubio women were raised to marry well, nothing else. When she was twenty, she still used a cane. She was using it when she came to visit me in November. This woman who calls herself Gilia was born with the gift of health, and what does she do with it? She dances half-naked on the stages of the world. It is right that she paid."

The boy hummed in time with his scraping, clearly and with unpracticed accuracy. His vibrato resonated in the nave. In New York or L.A. or Branson or Nashville, some producer with a confession to make—there were plenty of those—might have heard him and talked to his parents and signed him up for lessons and a recording contract. But it was Detroit, and the boy would sing in the choir and scrape wax until his testicles dropped.

"So you knew," I said.

She closed her eyes, then opened them. It was a kind of nod. "I knew. I did not judge, and I did not take any of the money when she offered it, even though all I have is my house and the dogs Mr. Guzman left. I do not blackmail. I go to the—cops—instead." She tasted the colloquialism, didn't like it. It was as alien to her as the thought of nursing her own daughter.

"What would that do?"

"Avenge Jillian. Gilia. My Gilia. Who would kill her if not that whore of an imposter? She has killed before."

"The whore of an imposter is in town this week. Your daughter died three months ago."

"Then so was she. Or an assassin in her employ."

There was no reason, when she said "assassin," that Hector Matador came into my mind, except that his picture should appear in Webster's next to the definition. "Your daughter made arrangements to expose the secret in the event of her death. Killing her wasn't an option."

Her eyes flickered slightly. Then she raised her chin. It hadn't been low to begin with. "I ask again: Who if not her?"

"I don't know."

"Ha!"

"It will take some time to find out," I said. "You're the only one who can give me that time. It runs out when you tell what you know."

"Who are you that I can trust you?"

"Not the police."

It was just something I'd said to plug a silence that scared me more than her dogs, but it worked on a level I hadn't thought out. "Police" didn't mean the same thing to her that it meant to me. To me it was an annoyance at worst. Cops; a joke term for an occupational liability. But twenty years away from home hadn't been enough to wipe out pictures of dignity squads in Gestapo caps and jackboots wading through peaceful assemblies with clubs and hauling motorists out of their cars and slamming the doors on paddy wagons that only carried their cargo one way and never came back except to take on a fresh load. And if she did manage to forget, we had more than enough of that kind of thing on video here in the U.S. of A. to remind her.

"You will find the monster who did this thing to my Jillian?" It was hardly louder than a prayer.

"I don't know. I can try to prove that Gilia—the other Gilia—didn't. The one might flush out the other, but I can't swear to it either way. If the police decide to pin it to her, that's as far as they'll look. If she's innocent, he'll still be out there."

She crossed herself and turned back around. I was staring at the back of her neck again. "Unless I am asked if the woman who calls herself Gilia is responsible for my daughter's death, I will say nothing. For now."

"How long is for now?"

I was pretty sure this time it was a shrug.

"*La Casa del Rubio* was never celebrated for its patience."

I knew a curtain line when I heard it. The big church door drifted shut on the boy's humming, sealing it off from the world I lived in. Out there all I got was the dog's growling as I passed within two yards of where it was tethered.

SIXTEEN

A famous calendar shot of the Detroit skyline shows the daytime scape reflected on the surface of the river at night, gray granite and blue sky above, black onyx and lighted windows below. As I drove away from Most Holy Trinity, the picture rotated on its axis, nightside up. Half of the city was going home from work and the other half was going to work from home, signing out squad cars with engines still warm from the eight-to-four and grasping the handles of drill presses still slick from the sweaty palms that had operated them by daylight. Every day the two half worlds pass each other on the Walter P. Chrysler and the John Lodge and the Edsel Ford freeways with only a narrow median separating them. I was the only one who belonged to both.

I didn't feel like going home. I didn't feel like going anywhere especially, and when I feel that way I go to the office.

It's an old building even by local standards. John Brown might have ridden past it in a four-in-hand on the northern spur of the Underground Railroad. In any other city it would be an archaeological treasure, and a slot for it on the National Register would be someone's cause of the month, but in our town it's just another empty lot in waiting. The corporation that owns it budgets just enough to prevent that, paying an old Russian Jew to bang on the radiators and a crew to sweep out the butts and unclog the waterspouts shaped like griffins. I like it because they let you smoke in the offices. You can probably sacrifice a goat if you want to badly enough.

Old buildings, like old musicians, are never silent. The chords they strike after dark belong to a nocturne. I wasn't the only one still working, but the typewriter chatter and booming file drawers had shifted to a minor key and the whir of a vacuum cleaner and bass note of a floor buffer came out front. When a telephone rang, it was no longer part of a chorus: more of a soprano solo. Probably it was just a telephone. Your head fills with fuzzy poetry when you work at night. It's like drinking alone.

I got organized. I moved the dignified old Underwood from its lonely aerie to the desk and typed up a report on the Jillian Rubio case. The dignified old Underwood's keys had begun to drift loose and it typed a wacky line that looked like sheet music from the score of a Looney Tune. It lent some pizzazz to the bald facts. I didn't write that I had committed to solve a murder. That would have looked even wackier. It played silly enough inside my head.

I tore out the last sheet, drummed the pages even, read them through, snapped on a paper clip, and filed the report under *D* for delirium tremens. That was getting to be a thick file.

Just to keep the pink snakes at bay I broke the downtown bottle out of the desk and poured an inch into a glass. Good Old Smuggler. You can't get it in Michigan, despite the fact it's imported by my cousin-six-hundred-times-removed Hiram and bottled in Southfield, thirty minutes from where I sat warming my hands around its inner light. You have to follow a bigamist all the way to St. Louis and buy a couple of jugs from the liquor store across the street from the apartment where his second family sits around waiting for Dad to come home from his business trip to Detroit. It has a pirate on the label and you know it's cheap because of the way your lips go numb when you sip it. In Edinburgh they use it to prep patients for root canals.

I decided to hold off sipping until I tried the telephone number I'd been carrying around in my head since I'd talked to Barry Stackpole in Greektown. I didn't expect to get anything but an empty ring or a recording telling me the offices at Columbia University were closed and please call back during normal business hours, in free verse if possible. It rang three times and someone picked up.

"Hello?" A mellow rounded voice, perhaps male, perhaps with an accent. You can't get much more than that from hello.

"My name is Walker," I said. "I got this number from Barry Stackpole. I didn't know if anyone would answer this late."

"Yes, Mr. Walker. I remember the name. I'm leaving on a business trip soon. The dinner hour is the best for clearing one's desk." He didn't introduce himself.

"I'm calling about Mariposa Flores."

I didn't know if the name would mean anything; Gilia had said no names were used in the resistance. There must have been a leak, though, because I could almost hear the coin dropping into the pan. Some of the mellow went out of his voice.

"I cannot discuss this over the telephone, Mr. Walker. I would prefer not to discuss it at all, but Mr. Stackpole was very persuasive. Perhaps you could tell me why it's important."

"She's under hack for murder. You may be the only person who can get her out from under."

"I do not know this hack."

I blew air. My next client and all his contacts were going to be one hundred percent American. Nothing less than the name of an ancestor on the *Mayflower* manifest would persuade me to take the case.

"Professor—" I said, and paused when someone gulped oxygen on his end. "It is Professor, isn't it? Mr. Stackpole didn't seem to think that was a secret."

"It is possible I was not specific upon the point. Yes, I am a professor. Of Romance languages. A pretty term. Consolation, I suppose, for the loss of the Americas. Please go on."

"There's murder in the business, and a little matter of a visa obtained under a false identity. The State Department is more concerned with the visa. If they pull it, she goes back to stand trial for murder. You may be able to prevent that, if you'll agree to answer one simple question."

"I have been asked questions before, Mr. Walker. They are seldom confined to just one and they are almost never simple."

I asked him to hold on one second. I hung the receiver on my shoulder, picked up my glass, and threw the Old Smuggler off the end of the plank. It pickled my throat tissue and brought a flush all the way to my ears. Conversation with the learned gentleman was enough to wean Henry Ford off weak tea. I plunked down the glass and got back on the line.

"Sorry, Professor. I had to answer another call. The question I'm proposing has nothing to do with Abraham Lincoln."

He was silent so long I thought he'd hung up while I was fortifying my defenses.

"Just who are you, Mr. Walker?"

I got a psychic flash from six hundred miles away; a picture of a man touching a dead eye socket.

"I'm a private investigator, engaged at the moment in trying to prevent my client from being deported. There's a hell of a lot more than a red-hot penny waiting for her at home."

The silence this time was filled with someone's memories of home. They didn't come with harmonica music and the old swimming hole. I heard paper slithering.

"I'm flying out to California day after tomorrow," he said. "One of those useless seminars that are just an excuse for grown academics to behave like college freshmen on spring break. Apparently it is my turn. I am changing planes in Chicago. How far is that from Detroit?"

"Four hours driving. Not much less flying, under current conditions. I don't know if I can spare the time. When this thing blows it'll blow all at once. What airline?"

"Northwest."

"Detroit Metropolitan is Northwest's hub in the Midwest. Their planes go in and out like buses. You could change there and we could meet in the airport."

He took my number, said he'd see what he could do, and he'd call back. He sounded eager. I didn't know what to make of that. I hoped it would do me some good. I wasn't sure if I'd recognize it if it did. Once again I'd taken a straightforward missing-person investigation and turned it into an abstract equation, a voyage of discovery, a *Bildungsroman*; as if there weren't enough languages involved already, with no more romance to any of them than Punch and Judy. They ought to put me to work designing aptitude tests to be given out by companies that aren't hiring.

What the job needed was a CPA. He'd sort all the facts into tidy piles, sweep them into envelopes, hang tags on them, and mail them out with a bill for services rendered. Thank you and please call again. I can help the next person in line.

I'd found Jillian Rubio. That was the job. Now I'd volunteered myself to wrap up two murders, or at least separate them from Gilia Cristobal *née* Mariposa Flores. That was not. My Pimpernel Complex was showing. I'd grown a tail that made me curious. A young woman to whom everything in life had come as hard as iron, even blood money, was dead, her body left out to season with the white pine. It all had something to do with the client, and before I handed it over to the CPA I needed to know if the job I'd finished had nailed a killer or framed an innocent. Maybe I was just bored. When it's February in Michigan it's been winter forever, and when something interesting comes bumping along in the sluggish current of the longest short month on the calendar, you snatch at it and hang on to see where it leads. Even if it's a murder. Especially if it's a murder. I collected them like driftwood. No two were ever alike and displayed together they made intricate tortured patterns, like the work of an alcoholic Swedish sculptor.

While I was waiting I tore open the mail I'd dumped on the desk earlier, kept some of it, and threw the rest away. Nobody wanted to give me something for nothing, there was no invitation to sail to an uninhabited island and raise a race of beautiful naked savages. There wasn't even a second notice to indicate that a smooth efficient capitalist system had snagged itself on my empty checking account. If a letter drops through a slot and no one cares if it's answered, is the stamp still good?

I figured the telephone call that interrupted this exercise in poetical philosophy had been placed by someone on business from Porlock.

"Samuel Taylor Coleridge," I answered.

The professor was up on his English literature. He hesitated only a second. "Did I break in on *Kubla Khan*? A thousand pardons."

"One would be too much. And thank you for not asking what gives."

He chuckled; a dry academic sound, like a dusty thumb riffling through Newton's *Principles*. "When you've sat in on a few Ivy League conversations, you learn to tune in quickly. What jackasses we must sound like to the janitor. Perhaps not, though. At Columbia the odds are better than even he has a Ph.D. in pre-Christian theology." Stiff paper rattled. "My flight gets into Detroit at nine-ten A.M. Friday. The layover is two hours. Which, given the present security situation means we will have fifteen minutes. Satisfactory?"

"Tickles me pink." I gave him the name of a bar and grill in the Davey Terminal. "Should I scribble PROFESSOR X on a sign and hold it up?"

This time he hesitated two beats longer. Making up his mind.

"Zubarán is the name." He spelled it. "Miguel. I doubt identification will be necessary, at least in my case. I have an idea you'll know what to look for."

I wrote the name on my telephone pad. Then I scratched it out thoroughly. I'd had to memorize even his telephone number. "Zubarán like the painter?"

"I'm told there is no relation. You know a good deal about arcane matters for an American. How old are you?"

"Too old for your classes, Professor. My generation talks back."

"It would be a refreshing change. All those sheep's faces and their ubiquitous Walkmans sometimes make me want to vomit. I shudder to think what will happen to the world in hands such as theirs."

"Yeah, and after we took such good care of it."

He let that one drain down the line. "Good-bye, Mr. Walker. I cannot say I look forward to our discussion, but taking part in it will be my privilege. One so seldom gets the chance to give something back." There was a plop and then the little silence before the dial tone, like the space between novenas. Or was that twenty-four hours? I'd been too much in church of late and too little of faith.

I wrote 9:10 A.M. on the Friday square of my calendar. My eyes jumped to the next row. Ash Wednesday was coming up next week. It was also February 13th: the date of the fourth consecutive appointment that Jillian Rubio would fail to keep with Hector Matador. No date since Lenin's birthday had lost its significance so fast.

SEVENTEEN

Breakfast is the most destructive meal of the day. It diverts blood from the brain, where it's most needed at that hour, and it soaks up too much caffeine. But not counting the cardboardy supermarket sub I'd slammed down the night before on my way home from the office I couldn't remember the last time I'd eaten. The work is like that sometimes, all fuel consumption and empty miles. I stuck a hard-fried egg between two slices of toast and admired Hector Matador's picture on the front page of the *Free Press*.

It was a police mug shot from an eight-year-old arrest. His hair was shorter now and he was a little less gaunt, but sullen arrogance is a quality untouched by time. Take away the nifty numbered placard, sling a hundred-dollar necktie around the bare throat, and it might have been taken last week.

Inspector John Alderdyce was quoted, saying that Mr. Matador was not a suspect, and that foul play had not yet been established in the case of the young woman whose body had been found in an advanced stage of decomposition in an unnamed lumberyard on the southwest side. The woman had been identified, but police weren't releasing the name pending notification of next of kin. That was so much eyewash, next of kin having discovered the body, but in a nonelection year the cops never miss an opportunity to keep the press uninformed. Mr. Matador's history with the authorities filled up much of the article, whose byline belonged to the reporter who had covered his trial for first-degree murder in the matter of Frank Acardo, deceased. I wasn't mentioned, but then I hadn't been interviewed. That was some more poker-playing on the part of the thin blue line; otherwise the reporter would have made the connection with my trial testimony, and the lead story on the fighting in Kandahar would have been bumped below the fold. That would have meant more officers assigned to media liaison and fewer on the street.

I didn't mind, except that the free advertising might have come in handy later. I had some sleuthing of my own to do, and it's tough enough climbing through windows without trailing the guardians of the First Amendment from my heel like so much toilet paper.

There was another, much smaller item of interest in the World section: six inches tucked in an inside corner about the prison suicide of a former rebel leader in a country no one read much about these days. He'd begun six years before by organizing a walkout by government hospital workers and ended up hanging from a bedsheet in his cell. In between there had been some rough mountain fighting and one successful engagement against superior numbers of government troops that for a moment had distracted the attention of the world from the rest of its squabbles. Then came the reversals, a lieutenant's betrayal, arrest, and two years of trial postponements while a case for treason was being built. Now the only question was who had tied the knot in the sheets. It wasn't raised in the article, and it certainly wouldn't be in the capital, although it might have come as a surprise that prisoners were even provided sheets. In the end it didn't really matter whether they did it to you or helped you reach the decision on your own. You were just as dead. As dead as the revolution.

No mention was made of the murder of the rebel leader's girlfriend. There wasn't room for it, even if it had come in over the wire. They would have had to drop a comic strip to make room, or reduce the size of the crossword so you'd need a magnifying glass to read the clues. Someone would have written an angry letter to the editor, someone else would have dropped his subscription, and the dominoes would start to fall. It was a wonder they'd found space for the rebel leader to begin with.

I finished breakfast, called Sid Corcoran at the Twin Cities Detective Agency in St. Paul, and got him on the first ring. He was always the first man in the office and the last to leave. He said he'd been about to call me. The local cops had been all over Jillian Rubio's duplex in suburban Coon Rapids. The neighbor on the other side of the common wall had told them a detective had been around asking questions about Ms. Rubio a day or two earlier; he still had the man's business card. That had brought them to Twin Cities. Corky had told them his role in the agency was strictly administrative, and if they wanted to know what one of his operatives was working on they would have to ask him. That had sent them back to headquarters for more ammunition, but he knew they'd come back and he wanted to talk to me before he ratted me out for the sake of his license.

"Go ahead," I said. "The cops here know all about it. I just called to find out how fast they were moving. How's Spitzer going to take it?"

"Who gives a shit? I suspended him without pay. A summons server was waiting for him last night when he got off the plane from Detroit. The whole reason I packed him off was to buy time until we could work out a deal with the court. What the hell happened to him back there?"

"A dog barked at him."

"He ain't been barked at till he's been barked at by me. One more bonehead play like that and I'll can his ass."

"I don't know why you held on to him this long."

"Got under your skin, did he?"

"Nothing a kick in the shin couldn't cure. I meant the dog thing."

"It takes all kinds to run a carnival. Anytime you get tired of the one-man band, come see me. Climate's the same here, but you won't have to scrounge for your supper."

"I'd miss the scrounging. Thanks, Corky. Don't forget to send me a bill."

"That's the day I leave my balls on the bus." He sounded cheerful. A little out-of-town murder made a nice break from credit checks and deadbeat dads. We called each other a couple of names and stopped talking.

Someone knocked at the front door while I was knotting my tie. I started that way, then spotted the *Free Press* front page on the corner of the kitchen table and went back for the Smith & Wesson. I was holding it behind my hip when I opened the door on a mahogany-colored suit with gold buttons. Big Bad Benny had to stoop to look at me under the top of the frame. The studs glittered in his broad Basque face.

"He wants a word," he said.

I showed him the .38. "Tell Mr. Matador my office door is always open, even to him."

He looked at the gun as if it were a quarter tip. "He wants a word."

"You deserted your post," I said. "Who's throwing groupies off the boss lady's balcony?"

"Don't make him say it again. Benito's a stuck record. He missed the CD revolution."

This came from behind me. I relaxed my spine and turned my head to look at the black man I'd seen in Matador's hotel suite and again in the Chevy Corsica that had followed me from the Blue Heron in West Bloomfield. Matador had said he'd trained with the U.S. Marshals, and he had the build for it, as wide as Benny across the shoulders but narrower through the middle; a big, hard, athletic-looking thirty-five in a navy suit cut by someone who knew how to make room for muscles and firepower. His weapon was a European-style semiautomatic with a brushed steel finish and a bore as big around as a marble. He held the gun tight against his hip and didn't wave it around. His voice was a warm rumble and his face was friendly enough, if you didn't look at the eyes.

I said, "I'm having combination locks installed. Someone's been selling my keys on eBay."

"Locks are for rich people," he said. "You don't have a thing worth stealing. You heard Benito. The man wants a word."

Benny stuck out his paw. I laid the revolver in it. "Okay if I close up? I don't want the neighbors to find out how poor I am."

"Let me. I picked the back, I can unpick the front."

The Corsica was parked on the street. I looked back at the black man. He'd put the pistol in the side pocket of his coat. We both knew he still had it. He gave me a pained smile.

"I didn't pick the wheels. When they told me I'd be working with Colombians, I thought I'd at least get a good ride."

Benny said, "I ain't Colombian."

"He's Chicano this week," I told his partner. "He thinks no Anglo can tell the difference."

Benny opened the rear passenger's side door and held it. When I started to get inside he put a palm against my back and shoved hard. I twisted around so my shoulder took the impact when I hit the opposite door. I almost dislocated it, but I saved my skull for later.

"Take it easy," the other said. "Matador wants him talking."

"*Señor* Matador."

"Don't get your jalapeños in a wad, *muchacho.* I taught Irish accents to better than him when I was with WitPro."

Benny drove. His partner squeezed in next to me. We turned the corner and headed west. I wondered if we were going to Mexicantown or the Hyatt.

I said, "You were with the Witness Protection program?"

"Not long. I quit when they wouldn't transfer me to the Air Marshals. I didn't train to be a baby-sitter. You ever watch a snitch try to read his new ID papers? Their lips wear out before they get to the end."

"So now you sit with celebrities."

"They're not so bad. They're not so good, either. Most of them think you're a cheap analyst. You'd think they'd know how much the tabloids pay for tips. They're not the brightest buttons in the box. Benito could beat the whole gang in a spelling contest." He shifted positions, grunted, removed the pistol from his pocket, and laid it on the seat between his hip and the door. There wasn't that much seat. "I should've stuck with the service. Who knew the demand for air marshals would go up overnight?"

"You talk too much." Benny's eyes were hot in the rearview mirror.

"Maybe you don't talk enough. It might just put our friend in the mood."

"Gilia tell you the story of her childhood?" I asked.

"Ask Benito. I never got closer to her than the outside of the crowd."

We turned south. If we were going to Dearborn or Mexicantown, we were blazing a new route.

I took another shot. "I didn't check my service today. Yesterday we were all working for the same party."

The black man grunted again, picked up the pistol, and slid it back inside his pocket. He couldn't seem to get comfortable. "Seen the papers today? You ought to throw over this line of work, friend. You'd make a dandy press agent. Except Matador's the reclusive type."

"It was either give them him or give them Gilia. I'd expect him to understand that."

"Say it in Latin, it makes as much sense to me. I'm just the guy on the edge of the crowd, like I said. Maybe he's pissed at you for some other reason. Maybe he's pissed at the world. Most spicks are, for some reason. At least we had slavery. Maybe they never got over the Frito Bandito."

"You've been sniffing around behind me from the start. Or you were. Gilia seemed surprised to find out she'd been paying your bunch to duplicate my movements. You I can understand. These other guys aren't used to government work."

"You ought not to say that, friend. Not this year. This year the government's got Christ in a bucket."

I gave up then. Big Bad Benny was right. The guy talked too much.

We parked finally on Adelaide, in a block that looked like Bomber Row in a wartime photograph taken in London. Weedy desert lots peppered the neighborhood like shell craters, with paintless saltbox houses standing among them looking hardly less desolate; their owners had abandoned them for the suburbs under LBJ, then given up collecting rent on them under Nixon.

Shortly after the Spanish Mafia pushed out the original franchise, they'd been converted to heroin dealerships, but there had gotten to be such a choice of available houses the entrepreneurs had moved to better locations with more closet space. There is a hierarchy even among hovels.

We made a P.I. sandwich going in, Benny in front and the former marshal riding drag with me in the middle. The pistol was back out in the open, a sight that if there were any neighbors to see it in that neighborhood would excite about as much interest as a robin on the bum. You knew warm weather was around the corner when you spotted the first abduction of spring.

We entered without knocking. Inside was the sour odor of mildew and the ghost of boiled kidneys. The carpet, a thin pile job, once blue, was curling away from a plywood floor, and here and there a broken crack phial caught the light, twinkling like an extracted tooth. It was dank cold in the entryway, colder than the air outside because it lay there without circulating, but still not as cold as it should have been if the house had stood empty for years. I followed Benny down a narrow hallway lined with bulging Sheetrock and into a warm kitchen.

It was a smallish room, just big enough for the sink and major appliances and a couple of kitchen chairs but no table, and with the two men who were already inside and the three who joined them it was as crowded as a morning bus. The counters, the linoleum floor, and the stove and refrigerator were the same shade of avocado, a color scheme that had come and gone with H. Rap Brown, *I Dream of Jeannie*, and an evening of sitar music and magic brownies around the lava lamp. The stove was on. Someone had done meatball surgery on the gaspipe, rerouting it from the wall to a squat propane tank on the floor. A griddle lay across the burners, and one of the big Hispanics I'd seen taking inventory of the arsenal in Matador's hotel suite was standing in front of it in his shirtsleeves, turning something over on the surface with a wooden-handled spatula. It didn't smell like food cooking.

Matador sat on one of the chairs, cutting and rearranging the two halves of a deck of cards one-handed. Like many Latinos he had nervous fingers, and his stretch in Jackson hadn't settled them down. The suit today was charcoal gray, with a narrow lilac stripe and a tie and display handkerchief to match. Black slip-ons with tiny gold buckles glistened on his narrow feet.

"Lots of memories in this place," he said. He might have been speaking to the deck of cards for all the eye contact I got. "I held my war councils here when the dagoes started to push back. When they put fifty thousand on my head I stayed here a month. That's when I taught myself to cook. I planted a little herb garden out back. Cops dug it up after Jimmy Socks Mondadori went missing. They didn't find him."

I said, "Of course they didn't. That was a Sicilian hit. Everybody knows the Colombians leave 'em where they fell. You'd bend over to pick up a greasy nickel, but not a shovel."

Benny had withdrawn behind me. Clothing rustled and the edge of a steel girder struck a glancing blow off my left shoulder near the base of my neck. I felt a flash of agonizing pain. Then my left side went dead. The black man spun the other chair with one hand and got it behind me just as my legs folded. I sat down hard.

"You should appreciate Benito's gentle touch," Matador said. "He can split a two-by-four with that hand. Emmett?"

The former marshal had put away his pistol. He found something in a pocket, jerked my right hand behind the back of the chair, and yanked something tight around the wrist that didn't feel like wire or rope or duct tape, but that held it just as snugly. I assumed my other wrist was also involved; I had no feeling in it yet. The bond would be one of those plastic zip ties electricians use to secure cables. They've just about replaced steel handcuffs for space and portability.

Matador cut the jack of diamonds. "Those were good days. I had a new car every six months, quicker if I got bored with the one I was driving. Paid for them with suitcases full of cash. That was before the town went to shit. They tell me this was a meth lab last year. A meth lab." He leaned forward, curled back his upper lip, and spat through his teeth. The spittle splattered on the linoleum. He wiped his lips with the back of his hand. "I am still *un hijo del trabajador*, you see. The son of a working man."

"I heard a pimp," I said. "But I guess they put in their hours just like the rest of us."

"Benito."

Something pricked the back of my neck. Before martial arts training, Benny had been one of the best men with a knife this side of Bógota; excuse me, Mexico City. He could filet a fish in three seconds and a man in five minutes. Half an hour if he didn't like him.

Matador put the deck of cards in his side pocket, rested his hands on his thighs, and looked at me for the first time. "Thank you for telling Gilia you were tipping the cops. I had just enough time to prepare some answers."

I said nothing.

"You think I'm angry with you. You don't give me credit. Do you think I did not play the shell game when I worked in this town? Fortunately we all look alike to Anglos."

"Not all of you. The honest ones don't look like buttered eels."

I was trying to make him mad enough to work fast and unmethodically. It had begun to dawn on me what the silent man was cooking on the stove.

Matador smiled. He had good teeth, blue-white against his brown skin, but he was easier to look at when he was solemn. "The Rubio woman said she had documents," he said. "Newspaper articles in Spanish—detailed, not the watered-down accounts that appeared over here—her birth certificate, proving she was the original Gilia Cristobal. Some other things, probably. Nothing incriminating, unless it was all together. Then one could make a connection with the other Gilia. I had hoped to get them from her. For that it was necessary to play the meek little business manager; the lucky spick who lived upon Gilia the entertainer and could not bear the loss of his meal ticket should the truth come out and she was deported. That was not possible in the beginning. The woman was nervous, afraid to meet me in any but the most public place. However, I was patient. She came from a good family, and it was only a matter of time until the class system asserted itself. I am, as I said, a man of simple origins. We peons have known for centuries the power that is ours if we but hold our hats, lower our eyes, and employ the formal address when speaking to our betters. Your language does not even have such a thing, because of course you are all born equal under God." He almost spat again on the last part. I began to think he had emotions after all. I hoped it wasn't an act. Something clinked on the stove; the big silent man turning over the main course to heat the other side.

"It was working," Matador went on. "The last few times we met she had begun to become insolent. She called me *jíbaro*, which is a name that has no adequate translation in English. Formally it means a peasant, a man of no sophistication, unlettered, but it has come to mean so much more, as such terms will. Or rather so much less. The time was near when I would succeed in luring her into very much the same position in which you find yourself at this moment. Then a thing happened which frustrated me deeply."

"She stood you up," I said.

"*Sí.* I was disconsolate. The more so the second and then the third time. It was only when I remembered that Gilia was scheduled to appear in Detroit that I began to have hope. You see, I knew of a competent investigator in this place."

"Thanks for the recommendation. I'd wondered about that. So that's why I had company."

"That is why. When you observed that you were being followed, I knew that I had chosen the right man for the job. Now the time has come to ask you where are the documents. Felipe."

Something made a scraping noise and the man at the stove turned around. He had a pair of ordinary serving tongs in his hand with something that glowed between the pinched ends. I smelled red-hot copper.

EIGHTEEN

We can learn much from third world countries," Matador said. "Any American child can operate a computer, and our scientists have unlocked the secret of life itself. But who would have thought one could obtain so much useful information from the humble penny? It was generous of them to pay tribute to the United States by calling it the Lincoln Question. I assume the local coin carries the likeness of their current president or generalissimo."

I was barely listening to his droning. A thread of smoke curled off the penny in Felipe's tongs. Honest Abe's sad face glowed with rude health.

"Benito?"

Reaching from behind my chair, Benny folded my throat in the crook of his arm. I struggled, but he tightened his grip and cut off my windpipe. All I got from wriggling my hands was a raw burn on my wrists from the plastic tie.

"Let him have some air," Matador said. "I want him awake for this."

Benny made the adjustment. I sucked in sweet oxygen, coughed.

"The left eye, I think, Benito. That is usually the weaker of the two. I am not a vindictive man."

A thick thumb and forefinger prised at my eye socket. I

couldn't have closed the eye without a pry bar. The hot penny moved in close. I could feel the heat on my cheekbone.

Matador said, "The documents, *Señor* Walker. I would search your house and office, but if I enjoyed physical labor I would have stayed home and picked coffee beans."

"I don't have them." My voice was as squeaky as a cricket's.

"Brave, but unimaginative. Felipe?"

The penny was the size of a manhole cover. I couldn't see around it.

"We're on the same side," I croaked. "Don't you think I'd give them to you if I had them?"

"It's a hazard of my former calling. I think everyone is a criminal. There is a great deal of money to be made from that material, and you are a poor man in a line of work that in five years will cease to exist. Unfortunately, you will spend most of the money on devices for the blind."

I felt the heat on my cornea now. It was like staring into the sun. Felipe wouldn't have to move the penny any closer if he didn't want to; it would cook the retina in moments just where it was. Water ran out of the duct, drenching my cheek. In a couple of seconds it would be steam. My hands worked independent of the rest of me. They were becoming slick with sweat or blood.

"You're not thinking, Matador. By next week the cops will know Gilia's a fake. The documents won't be worth anything." I almost said, "won't be worth a penny." My eyeball felt poached. Smoke seemed to be rolling off it.

Silence sizzled. I thought it was something else.

"*Cristo.*" Matador's tone was a whisper. "Take it away, Felipe. Now."

The sun went behind a cloud. Green spots swam in the fluid that remained. They separated painfully, like old men climbing out of a pool. Light came between them and I saw Matador's face. Not the sight I would have chosen, but much better than none at all.

"Thank you, Benito. You may rest your arms now."

Benny let go. My eyes blinked with no help from me. I snuffled. Something bitter and viscous crawled down the back of my throat. I turned my head from side to side, testing my neck for breaks. Emmett, the big black former U.S. Marshal, was gripping the back of the chair Matador had been sitting in. His fingers were white.

Matador uncovered his blue-white teeth. He gave my cheek three smart pats.

"You make good sense, Anglo. I am not a savage, merely curious. If you knew where the papers were, you would have given me that answer instead of the one you chose. The trouble with the people who are used to asking this question is they want only one answer, and it is not always the right one. Often enough it is sufficient merely that the question is asked. No harm done. We are friends, yes?"

I kicked him in the crotch.

I didn't give it any thought beforehand, or to what would come after. I was sitting down and I couldn't get the leverage I wanted, but he was crouched in front of me with his feet spread and I had a clear shot. I found out he'd had onions for breakfast. He jackknifed and started making little mewing noises. That was no reflection on his masculinity; Manolete would have made the same sounds, and probably had when the horn went in.

"We are friends, no," I said. "Sorry to disappoint you, *jíbaro*. Jillian Rubio didn't call you that because your old man worked in a field. She guessed what you were. Maybe that's why you killed her."

Behind me, Benny coughed deep in his chest, the way a lion coughs, with a thud you can feel at the base of your spine. I heard a metallic *shink*, and remembered he had a knife.

"Not till you hear the order, *muchacho*." Emmett had dug his fingers out of the back of the chair and showed his foreign pistol. "Just now the *jefe*'s too busy to give it. Why don't you cut our friend loose meanwhile. He's had one shitty day, and it's not even noon."

"You don't tell me what to do," Benny's voice said.

"This little piece of Italian machinery says I do. Don't look to Felipe for help. He's just the cook."

The big silent man was standing next to the stove, still holding the tongs with the penny cooling between the ends. He tossed them clanging onto the griddle and lowered his hands to his sides.

After a moment I felt a vibration in my wrists; Benny sawing through the plastic tie. It came loose and I brought them around in front of me and rubbed the raw spots. The skin wasn't even broken. I thought I'd severed an artery at least. I stood up. I was a little unsteady on my feet. Matador remained in a deep crouch. He had his hands on his knees and all his attention focused on breathing in and out. Benny stepped in front of me and stooped to rest a hand on his shoulder.

"He's kind of a shrimp," Emmett said. "You don't notice unless he's standing next to one of us or bent over waiting for his balls to drop back down."

I said, "You wouldn't look any bigger. Nobody's unbreakable. Not even you."

"That's the trouble with you liberal types. Once they're broken you bleed all over them. Think he'll give me a reference?"

"Yeah, but you'll never know to who. You won't even hear the bullet." I snuffled again. He put up his pistol in an underarm clip, brought out a white handkerchief, and stuck it at me. I shook my head and took out one of my own. The tears had dried to a crust on my cheek. I rubbed at them, blew my nose. I always cry at tortures.

He watched me. "When you make your case, leave out conspiracy, okay? I just came along for the heavy lifting. Nobody told me the plan."

"Where was that snazzy gun when they were getting ready to fry my pretty brown eyes?"

"I was pretty sure it was a bluff. Turned out I was right."

"You always gamble with other people's money?" I put away the handkerchief. "I'm not making any kind of case. I've got two on my hands as it is."

Matador took in his first deep breath in several minutes, let it out with a shuddering whoosh. We glanced down at him, then back at each other. Emmett said, "So you figure he killed the Rubio woman?"

"How much do you know about that?"

"Not a damn thing before today, and I don't even know what I guessed based on what I heard."

I decided I was still too shaken up to try to untie that knot. "I don't figure it was Matador. I only said that to get a rise out of him. I was sore or I'd have waited until he wasn't so distracted."

"Yeah. These spicks put a lot of store in their *cojones*."

"So do Swedes and Albanians. The last time Matador paid off Jillian Rubio was October in Milwaukee. If he killed her because of something she said, he wouldn't have waited a month and commuted all the way to Detroit to do it. If he planned it that long, he'd have found out where the documents were before he killed her. He was a big noise in this town for a long time before the cops quieted him down. You don't get that big and last that long by going off your coconut every time someone calls you a nasty name."

"Too deep for me. I don't have any training in murder, committing or investigating."

"Me neither. It's all been on-the-job since I hung out my shingle in this town."

"You can have it." Emmett buttoned his coat. "Time to fly, boys. These two kids are past due for a play date."

Benny looked up from his boss. "We ain't leaving him here."

"You're forgetting the job description, Ferdinand. I'm a free agent now, but Gilia bought you that suit, not Matador. You don't walk in front of him, check his car for wires. Who's doing that for her while you're down here?"

Benny straightened, facing him. What he was thinking crawled across his face like the weather report. It was the old test case: martial arts vs. a loaded pistol in a holster.

It wasn't settled that time either. Felipe tipped the balance by reaching out and shutting off the stove. The fourth burner fluttered and went out with a pop. He twisted shut the valve on the tank, then got his coat off the back of the kitchen door and shoved both fists into the sleeves.

Some of the tension went out of Benny's shoulders. "Mr. Matador?"

The Colombian was breathing almost evenly now, coming up out of his crouch. He nodded. "Give him back his gun. I don't want you getting pinched." His voice lacked resonance.

Benny found the Smith & Wesson in his hip pocket. He swung out the cylinder, shook the cartridges into his hand, and dropped them into the side pocket of his coat. He smacked the revolver onto my palm hard enough to sting if I didn't already hurt in a few other places. I stuck the gun under my waistband in back.

"*Hasta mañana*, friend," Emmett said. "Don't say it's been real, 'cause it ain't."

"Is that all you got?"

He smiled and went out with the others. The Corsica started up and crackled away through frozen slush. With the load it was carrying, the frame must have been sitting square on the springs. I didn't see Emmett again after that, *mañana* or any other day. I never found out if Matador gave him a reference or if he went back to the U.S. Marshals. My life is a row of revolving doors and the only ones who ever seem to keep coming back in are the cops and the crooks.

In the awkward little silence that followed, I noticed the difference in room temperature with the stove turned off. It must have been getting colder outside, a lot colder. I swung a chair around. Matador looked at it, then lowered himself onto it, concentrating hard on not reacting. I reversed the other chair, straddled it, and folded my hands on the back. I watched him a while.

"Try an ice pack if it doesn't feel better later," I said. "You shouldn't need a doctor. In college I forgot to wear a cup the one time the other guy decided to give me an uppercut to the chin by way of the inseam. He had both feet on the floor and he got his weight behind it. Ice did the trick that time. I didn't hit you as hard as he hit me."

"Did you win?"

"On my back, by default. Boxing has rules."

He pulled out his pocket square and used it on his forehead. He spent some time folding it with the sweat inside. "I heard what you told Emmett. You were right. I didn't kill her."

"Of course you didn't. If you had, you'd have left her where she fell, like I said. Either that or you'd have made sure no one ever found her. Stashing her under a tarp was half-ass. You've been guilty of plenty, but never of not finishing a job once you'd started."

"I didn't finish the job on you. I've had several years to think about that."

"You made an honest try."

"I'd try again. If it mattered." He met my gaze. His eyes had no more expression than a couple of pencil erasers.

"I know it. I'd have finished the job on you, only I didn't think Emmett would let me."

"No, you wouldn't. That is the difference between us, Anglo."

"Don't count on it. I need both eyes in my work. That was plain bad theater, Hector. You knew going in I didn't have those papers. If you didn't, you knew the cops would make the connection themselves eventually. There isn't anything in them that isn't public record."

"I do not think as clearly as I once did. I lost my edge in Jackson." He tried folding the square into three points, didn't like that and smoothed it out and started over.

"That didn't keep you from building a whole new career in Southern California. How'd you swing that with the parole board, by the way? They like you to stay in the same state where you were incarcerated."

"I didn't lose all my connections when I went inside. At that I am not a free man. Whenever I cross a state line I must register with the local police within twenty-four hours. On a tour like this I have had to place as many as three such calls in one day." He made a Latin shrug; no one but a Latino can do it without looking rehearsed. "My judgment was clouded. I put my heart before my head."

I grinned. "You don't have a heart, amigo. They open you up every three thousand miles and change the filter."

"I love her."

I waited. I wanted to sneer. I wanted to smoke, but I'd left the pack at home as well.

He put the square in his pocket the way it had been all along. He started to cross his legs, thought better of that, and returned his foot to the floor. When he couldn't think of anything else he sighed, and damned if he would have looked out of place in the rosebushes strumming a guitar.

"Even so," he said, just as if I'd said something, "I love her. This is a difficult confession. I am twice her age and I have already a wife in Bógota, if she has not died or divorced me. Why else do you think I did not abandon Gilia when she came to me with her trouble?"

"Payday comes to mind. You stand to make a million off her this year alone."

"She is an ordinary talent. Much as it pains me to say this about the only woman I have ever known for whom I would kill, it is the truth. I hired voice coaches to rid her of the things she had learned from her teachers back home, failures who passed on their inadequacies to all their charges in equal measure, so that when one closed one's eyes one could not tell which of them was singing. Dancing, fashion, cosmetics, surgery to remove a distracting mole from her upper lip. I made her a blonde. Booking offices were filled with beautiful Hispanic girls with glossy black hair. These things are universal. The rest was marketing. I sold Gilia with the same tactics I had used to sell drugs, including bribery and intimidation. These things were more personal, but by no means uncommon. I had been training for show business all the time I was in Detroit, and I never would have known it if I hadn't gone to prison. Probably I would be dead. It is possible I should thank you. I find the impulse resistible.

"What I did for her I could do for anyone with a spark of talent," he went on. "The bus stations crawl with possibilities, any one of them with the potential to be as big as or bigger than Gilia. But they would not be Gilia. I am telling you more than I would tell a priest, Anglo. A priest is of no use to me."

I got up and spun my chair back into its original corner. I still felt like sneering, but I didn't know at whom. If I believed his story it would mean going back and looking hard at a number of things I felt sure about, beginning with whether I was right- or left-handed. So I decided not to think about it.

"Happen to read the World section in today's Freep?"

"Freep?" He lifted his brows. "Oh, the *Free Press*. I did not get that far."

"That's right, you stopped at the front page. Gilia's rebel boyfriend hanged himself. Whose idea it was doesn't matter. He's dead."

"He is the one for whom she killed the *puta*."

"So you think she's guilty."

"I do not care."

"You should. If her alibi holds, it could buy her time with Immigration. They might manage to lose a freedom fighter's shaky visa application, but we got all the passion killers we need. They'd send her back. She might even hang herself in the same cell."

Matador smiled sadly. It was no improvement on when he was happy. "Then we must prove her innocent, no?"

NINETEEN

"There may be a hitch," I said.

"And what would that be, Anglo?" He was all positive energy, courtesy of a growing conviction that he would remain potent after all. The therapy is not recommended, because the results tend to vary.

"She might be guilty."

"I do not see this as a serious setback."

"You wouldn't."

He rooted inside his suit coat, produced a flat gold-and-enamel case with his monogram engraved on the lid. He offered it to me. I frowned, selected one of the brown cigarettes, and let him set fire to it with a lighter attached to the case. It tasted like burning mattresses. "I think the documents are in the mother's house," he said.

I blew the smoke as far away from me as I could. "You're welcome to look for them. Have you met Mrs. Guzman's dogs?"

"I have not had the pleasure. I find dogs to be overrated, except in the case of children and caninophobes. Did you know there are but seven varieties of bacteria in a dog's mouth, as opposed to seven thousand in a human's?"

"This particular dog swallows you whole. The smallest one is about the size of a calf."

He appeared to consider that. "We will put Mrs. Guzman upon

the back burner for now. I used to know someone, upon a purely casual basis, who specialized in breaking into bank safe-deposit boxes."

"Just for now we'll entertain alternatives to federal crime," I said. "Not to mention the fact that we don't know which bank, or even if a bank was involved. Forget the documents. They'll be irrelevant in less than a week. Who killed Angela Suerto if not Gilia?"

"A whore's life has the valuation she places upon it. Who would not?"

"Whoever killed Jillian Rubio."

He held his own cigarette between thumb and forefinger, like Peter Lorre. "I do not understand this reasoning."

"The only person who would have a motive to kill Suerto *and* Rubio is the one person we want to prove didn't."

"*No es verdad.* Rubio's death means exposure of the Suerto matter."

"Unless Rubio was bluffing."

"How can one know?"

I was pretty sure the brown cigarette was gumming up my gray matter. I threw it into a corner, where with luck it would catch something on fire and save the city the expense of demolition. "If she was bluffing, we'll know in a few days. Next Wednesday's the official deadline—three months since anyone's had contact with her—but when the cops release her name in connection with the stiff in the lumberyard, the jig's up. Or not. In the meantime I'm not waiting for miracles."

"You have the lead?"

"I have the lead." I watched him apparently enjoying his smoke. "You've got Gilia to look after. If there's anything to what we've been talking about, I wouldn't leave her in Benny's hands."

"People underestimate Benito. He is not a man of initiative, but he will follow an order into hell. He would have made an ideal soldier."

"For what army, Mexico's or Colombia's?"

"His mother was born in Tenochtitlán. He is part Aztec. One

makes allowances. I think I shall accompany you upon this search for truth."

"I think you won't."

He inhaled carefully, blew smoke out his nostrils. "We are still enemies."

"Always and forever. Not because you iced Frank Acardo, who was born to be iced, and not even because you tried to put me on the same block. I'm not exactly accustomed to people trying to kill me, but now and then it happens and I just have to put it down to the nature of the work. But I don't team up with gangsters."

"As far as the police are concerned, we are already a team. You are the one who convinced them of that."

"That was easy. They think I'm a crook on general principle. It bought me leg room. I plan to use it to find out who killed Angela Suerto, or prove Gilia didn't. They might turn out to be the same thing."

"And what shall I do?"

"Whatever you'd be doing anyway. Buy a senator. Hijack a truckload of Acapulco Gold. Call up a pharmacy and ask if they have Prince Albert in a can. Whatever draws flies to you and keeps them off me."

"And the Rubio murder?"

"One for the cops. Maybe she was blackmailing someone else and tripped up."

"I do not believe you. I think you wish to tie up both cases as they say with the pink bow. To this I have no objection, provided that the box does not contain Gilia."

"No guarantees, amigo. She could turn out to be Lady Macbeth."

"That is neither here nor there, unless the police are persuaded to do something about it. In which situation I will ice you."

"You can try. Until then I won't climb into your yard and you don't climb into mine. Next time I look over my shoulder and see a brown face, I'll push in yours."

"You can try."

I watched him stand up. A spasm took him, but he covered it

with a last drag on his cigarette. He dropped it and ground it into the linoleum.

"What if the lady says no?" I asked. "She probably gets a thousand proposals a week, some of them from men without a rap sheet."

"She will not say no, because I will not ask. I said I was in love. I did not say I intend to take any action beyond that which I am doing. I am not so foolish as I appear."

"You and Cyrano. I don't see it."

"It is not necessary that you do." He smoothed back his polished hair with both palms, straightened his tie, fiddled with his cuffs. By the time he was finished I wanted to kick him again just to see if he could put himself back together as completely every time. "You may wish to consult with your client," he said. "She did not hire you to solve any murders."

"Now and then I have to solve one so I can concentrate on the job I was hired to do. I'll drop around this afternoon. Where's she shooting?"

"She is not. There is some trouble with her permission to use Mexicantown. She does not have it. That was the second item on my list for today. You will find her in her suite."

He said he was parked around the corner—the blue Bonneville that had followed me after the Corsica broke off—and offered me a ride. I said I'd catch a bus. I'd had enough of his careful English and tailoring for one day. "What happened to those testosterone jobs you used to zip around in?"

"In Detroit I prefer to maintain the low profile. You are not the only enemy I have in this town. Fortunately, I still have friends who owe me favors. Not Camaro favors, alas. There has been a devaluation in the local currency since high-grade cocaine passed out of fashion. Also in my stature. The name Matador is largely unknown to the methadone-and-Ecstasy generation."

"Sorry to hear it. Are you going to kill all of them?"

"If I were, I would wait until the economy recovers. There is more satisfaction in allowing a man to climb to the top of the ladder before pulling it from under him. He has so much farther to fall. I am joking, of course," he said. "I am a monument to the success of the prison rehabilitation system."

"Uh-huh. If I were you I wouldn't clear-cut. Show business is riskier than peddling drugs. You never know when you might need to borrow another Pontiac."

"You are more out of fashion than I, Anglo. There is more to the world than good and bad."

I said I'd heard that. It always seemed to be the bad guys who said it.

TWENTY

I walked the last five blocks from the bus stop with my lapels standing and my fists jammed deep in my pockets. I felt like Dustin Hoffman. Matador's Armada hadn't given me time to grab an overcoat on the way out. The air was stiff enough to fold and the streets had that naked granite look of nuclear winter. I wanted to start the car warming and soak my feet in hot coffee and bourbon. What I got was Inspector John Alderdyce standing on my doorstep.

"I called your office," he said. "Your service told me you hadn't checked in yet. What'd you do, get lucky last night?"

He looked as big as the county jail in a fur hat with flaps all around and a tan double-breasted camel's-hair that hung below his knees. His breath clouded around his head like smoke from the burning bush.

"Yeah, I found a penny." I tried putting my key in the lock. My fingers had all the feeling of balloon animals. He took away the ring and unlocked it for me. He held the door open and trailed in behind.

In the living room he glanced around at the little bookcase, the rack of vinyl, the TV and VCR, the one good easy chair, a dust bunny or two threatening to turn feral. "Still keeping the decorators off the welfare line, I see. What you need is a wife."

"I had one. What I need now is a drink."

"It must be past noon in Borneo."

"Lent starts next week. I need something to give up."

I went into the kitchen, filled the coffee filter, poured water into the reservoir, and checked the cupboard above the sink. The bourbon bottle was empty and I wasn't desperate enough to try Scotch in coffee. So I added another scoop to the filter and turned on the machine. Alderdyce had followed me in. He got out of his coat and hat and gloves and dumped them on the table in the breakfast nook, on top of the *Free Press*. He looked even bigger in his midnight blue suit with an American flag pin in the lapel. He wasn't as large as any of Matador's men. He could fill a ballroom with just his character.

"Why Stelazine?" he asked.

I finished rinsing out the cup I'd used that morning and stood it upside down on the drainboard. My hand felt hot. The circulation to it had been cut off twice that day and this time it had come back with an attitude.

"Get the toxicology report?" I asked.

"No, I guessed. Just like you."

"Any good cop knows about hunches. Even a bad cop gets a good one now and then."

"They made some kind of record up in Lansing. It helped that they knew exactly what to look for. If you say the word 'hunch' one more time I'll shove it up your ass and break it off."

The machine started gurgling. "Let's go in the living room. This is one of those days when I can't seem to get out of the kitchen."

I gave him the easy chair. Being a cop he would've taken it anyway. I found the one good spring on the couch and parked on top of it. I still felt some cold on my spine. I decided to blame the weather.

He took out a leather-bound notebook the size of a card case. The higher you got in the department the less things you had to put in one. "Toxicity five. The scale only goes to six, a short list that includes cyanide and cobra venom. I guess snakes are too awkward to carry around."

"How'd it get in her?"

"Did I forget to say I didn't come here to answer questions?"

"Okay, ask one."

"I did. You gave me the eleventh-week lecture on hunches. That was a good guess you made. You aren't that smart and you aren't that lucky."

I got up, opened a drawer in the table next to his chair, found a pack and a book of matches and went back to my seat. I got one going and made a contribution to the nicotine stain on the ceiling. I wondered what the toxicity level was on that.

"I had a case once involving Stelazine poisoning," I said. "I remembered it works pretty fast, especially when injected. If someone picked up Jillian Rubio in a car and didn't have to drive any farther than the lumberyard behind her mother's house to have a body to dispose of, that was one possibility that occurred."

"He could have cut her throat, or shot her in the heart or head. That's even faster."

"You didn't say there were visible wounds on the body. I didn't think that was the kind of thing you'd forget to mention. You said her mother told you she was diagnosed bipolar. Stelazine's one of the narcotics doctors use for treatment of severe depression. That's what got me thinking that direction. So's Thorazine. If I'd said Thorazine, would we be having this conversation?"

"You didn't, and so we are. Know what I think? I think you did have a case involving Stelazine poisoning. I think you're having it now. Ever hear of Coon Rapids, Minnesota? I didn't make it up; actually it's a suburb of Minneapolis, folks there probably wear shoes and hardly ever spit watermelon seeds over the back fence. Rubio lived there. The police checked with one of her neighbors. He said a P.I. was there a few days ago, pumping him for information." He glanced at the notebook. "Alvin Spitzer was the name on the card he gave the neighbor. With the Twin Cities Detective Agency in St. Paul. I'm waiting to hear what Mr. Spitzer has to say. Ever have any business in St. Paul?"

"As a matter of fact I have. As a matter of fact it was with the Twin Cities Detective Agency, and as a matter of fact the man they assigned to the case was named Spitzer. He probably still is. I told you yesterday I was looking for Rubio. What did Matador say? He's the client."

"*Señor* Matador was polite. *Señor* Matador was eager to cooperate. *Señor* Matador gave us *nada*. I considered tanking him as a material witness. His lawyer called from L.A. while I was considering it and gave me a Latin lesson. So instead I notified his local parole officer. Parole cops are mean as bloody turds. I'm thinking after they're through discussing the rest of *Señor* Matador's life in Jackson he'll come looking for us begging to hear what he has to say."

"Can I be there when he does? I want to see what you do to him after he spits in your eye."

His face got brutal, which was as brutal as any face ever got anywhere. Then he found the screw on the turnbuckle and smoothed it out. I wondered if that was easier on the nervous system than just hitting someone.

"Any idea where he is, by the way?" he asked. "He slipped out of his hotel suite early this morning, right out from under our surveillance team."

"You ought to pay them better."

"They're on suspension. I asked a question."

I answered it truthfully. "I don't have the slightest idea where he is."

"Where were you this morning? I froze my ass off outside for twenty minutes."

"My apologies to your ass. I took a walk."

"It's sixteen degrees. You didn't have a coat."

"I came back to get it."

"You're still a goddamn liar." He sounded calm.

I decided to get mad. "What if I am? Book me, if you can find a charge that covers it. You cops think crooks are dumb for asking an undercover cop if he's an undercover cop because they think if he says no and arrests them anyway they've got a case for entrapment. Then you turn around and threaten to arrest a citizen for obstructing justice when he tells a cop whatever comes into his head when the cop thinks it's any of his goddamn business where the citizen went when he went and what he did when he got there. It's probable cause in an interview room with a steno or a tape recorder present and there's a signature on the bottom of a formal statement. Anywhere else it's conversation."

I got tired of talking and took a drag. Alderdyce riffled the little notebook's pages with a broad thumb. They made a purring noise against the quiet of the neighborhood.

"You ought to take that to Congress," he said. "They might draw up a constitution or something. So where were you this morning?"

I laughed. He laughed. I shrugged. My shrug wasn't a patch on Matador's. "I went to a crack house downtown, where some people handcuffed me to a chair and tortured me for a while. When I got tired of it I had a smoke and came home."

He scratched one ear with a corner of the notebook. Then he put the notebook away. "Town's full of clams today. Even the mother's got a case of lockjaw. She's been taking a lot of walks lately too."

"She probably brought that over from the old country."

I was sorry I'd said it. I didn't want him to fixate on which old country that was. I didn't want him thinking about Miranda Guzman's fellow emigré in town. Now that what had happened in the house on Adelaide was over I was having a delayed reaction, taking stupid chances. But he didn't seem to be listening. After the torture story he probably thought I was still smarting off.

"What is she telling?" I asked.

"The sad story of Jillian's childhood. Seems she had polio or something related, still walked with a cane. Could have been the source of her emotional problems. The cane was confirmed by the neighbor in Minnesota: an aluminum job with a black composition handle. I'm wondering about that cane. It wasn't found with her body."

"Neither was the overnight bag."

"Yeah. An old tapestry case her mother lent her. The luggage she brought was too big and clumsy for a short trip. We've been through it. Nothing there. Clothes and cosmetics. Killer probably threw the cane and the overnight in a Dumpster. Now that I think about it, going through all the trash in the neighborhood would have been a good detail for that surveillance crew I suspended. Wish I'd thought of it; right now some poor bastards in uniform are out there rooting around in frozen dirty diapers and no doubt taking my name in vain." He gripped and ungripped his knees, spoiling the creases on his trousers. You knew he was preoccupied when he started messing with his haberdashery. He got up. "Your coffee's ready."

I put out my cigarette and stood. I'd forgotten about the coffee. "Don't forget your coat. It's sixteen degrees outside."

In the kitchen, he left the coat unbuttoned and stuck his gloves in the pockets. He pushed out a dent in the fur hat from the inside.

"I got more information out of that California lawyer than anyone I've been talking to in Detroit," he said, watching me fill my cup. "He's an entertainment attorney, with a firm that specializes in everything from contracts to criminal law. That's a big item out there these days, all those celebrities carving up their ex-wives and shooting horse and running over pedestrians. He says Matador's made his pile all over again as a business manager to the stars. He wouldn't say which stars; they're close about that kind of thing unless you catch them at a cocktail party."

I spooned sugar into my coffee and stirred it carefully. I usually drink it black, but I wanted to be doing something that didn't involve looking at him.

He said, "Our Colombian friend has a nice suite there at the Hyatt. Not as nice as the ones across the hall, according to the clerk downstairs. Guess who's staying in one of those."

"Gilia."

He was still. I blew across the top of the cup and watched the ripples. "I heard she's shooting a video here. Did I guess right?"

"Yeah. Twice in two days. I think I'll see if I can get an autograph. My kid on the *Ronald Reagan*'s a fan. Make him a big shot with his shipmates. What do you think?"

"Ask her to sign a CD. You can only listen to 'Anchors Aweigh' so many times."

He nodded, put on his hat. "A thing like that can get old. Don't burn your tongue on that coffee."

It was his exit line. I thought someone ought to introduce him to Emmett. They could punch up each other's dialogue.

TWENTY-ONE

I almost missed her call. I would have if I hadn't flooded the carburetor.

You can invest several hundred dollars in an old motor and merely give it an elevated opinion of itself. The Cutlass had decided it wasn't starting that cold day, and all I got for my pumping was the smell of raw gasoline, a fresh set of frozen fingers, and heat under the collar. The telephone was ringing when I went back in to finish the pot of coffee.

"Thank God," she said, with the true accent that came through when she was worked up. "Your secretary said you hadn't come in, and I tried you at this number a little while ago and you didn't answer. I was afraid you were in jail."

"Close," I said. "About jail, not the secretary. That was my service you spoke to. I've been in conference with your business manager and the police all morning. Not at the same time or in the same room, but if it had been any closer we might have had an embarrassment. I was just on my way out to see you."

"I've been going crazy not knowing what's happening. Every time the phone rings or someone knocks on the door I think it's the police and I look around wondering what I should grab to take with me, like when the house is on fire. In my country they don't give you even that much time."

"It's a little better here. They stand outside and wait while you get dressed. If you're going to need a toothbrush they'll tell you, and if it's a question of deportation or extradition they don't just whisk you out of the country in what you're standing up in. It can take months. You could pack six trunks. In the present case you could pack seven. They don't know about you yet." It didn't seem the time to tell her a police inspector was thinking of asking for her autograph, among other things. She sounded like a bird on a ledge. "I can be there in twenty minutes. Fifteen if I can get my heap cranked up."

"Not here. I'm sick of this suite. Is there someplace we can meet where I won't be mobbed by slender young men dressed up like Gilia?"

"Does that happen?"

"Yes. They're kind of sweet, and they look cute in their butterfly wings and backless gowns—cuter than me, some of them—but in a very short while you get tired of candy, and then they are just a bright blur with all the others, the gapemouths and fourteen-year-old girls in their training bras and those smelly little men with cameras. I wish to go somewhere there is no blur."

I said I could think of a place and gave her an address. I offered to pick her up.

She laughed. "If you did, your face would be on the front page of every tabloid for a week. After that you would be very forgotten, more forgotten than if you'd never existed. This celebrity thing is a virus. It runs its course quickly, but it leaves you worse off than you were before."

"So retire."

"I was talking about you, not me. I have a standard plan for sneaking out of hotels. It's expensive, but it never fails. I will meet you in one hour."

"If it doesn't work out, ask Matador."

"I have not seen him since yesterday, when I told him what you were telling the police. He said I would not for a while, that it would be the best thing for me. Do you think they will put him in jail?"

"He's getting to be one of those boys who hire people to go

to jail for them. You're supposed to be worrying about yourself. Be a celebrity. Narcissitate."

"This is a word?"

"It'll do until one comes along. I threw my dictionary at the houseboy last week. He took it with him and never came back."

She rang off laughing. It had been a silly sort of conversation, at least on my side, but it had gotten her off her nervous perch. It was a comfort to know that in five years, when according to Matador the last P.I. had hung up his Kevlar vest, I could put on a cap and bells and entertain the famous rich.

Well, they're no different from you and me, just more people know their names and they have more money than God. More than a third of them never went to college. Half of that third didn't finish high school, and in order to convince people they read books they spend as much on first editions as they spend on astrologers and personal trainers. More than half of them are as nice when you meet them as you hope they'll be; it's the louts who get drunk in first class and the sociopaths who fire off Magnums at parties who get most of the press and give the whole set a bad stench. Some, like Churchill and Errol Flynn, had whole other fascinating lives before they became icons. A tiny few climbed too high to approach and glowed brightly for decades. A good many more streaked across the sky with a cheesy green flash and piffled out. I could think of only one who had fought in a revolution. There may have been more. Truth is the first casualty of the studio biography.

You couldn't judge them until you peeled off all the foil. In a world in which Public Enemy Number One can fall in love with a nightclub act half his age, anyone is capable of anything.

The car started finally, with a racket like a washtub bouncing down the north face of Everest. I let it warm up for a minute, and when it settled into its bubbling purr I backed out and drove to the office. A snowflake the size of a corn plaster lighted on the windshield long enough for me to admire its open-weave pattern, then dissolved against the defrosted glass. The ones that followed were less intricate, or maybe I just didn't pay them as much attention. They say no two are ever alike, same as fingerprints. But that would mean having examined every flake and every finger that had ever been and comparing them to all those that ever would be. In an infinite universe, exact duplication is not only possible, but inevitable; and what does that do to meteorology and criminology? You can work up plenty of heresy driving through falling snow.

In the little waiting room where hardly anyone ever waited I dusted the fake plant and rearranged the magazines on the coffee table into a fan, then rearranged them again into stacks with the most recent issues on top. Inside the heart of the great machine the smell of stale cigarettes and desiccated spiders seemed stronger than usual, but I was inhaling it through Gilia's nose. I opened the window for a few minutes, stashed some unpaid bills under the blotter, blew the tobacco ash out of the corner between the desk lamp and the telephone, made my peace with the rest, leaned back in the swivel, and saw a smudge of dead insects inside the globe fixture above the desk. I couldn't remember when the last time I'd dumped it out was. I climbed onto the swivel and did that, disposing of the remains in the wastebasket.

I did office stuff: called the service and wrote down some messages, ignoring the ones that had been left by Alderdyce and one from a woman who had not left her name. That was my client. I'd spoken to both of them since. The others were follow-ups on other cases. I made three calls and closed those files. Just another day in the life of the gainlessly employed. Torture and bookkeeping.

After a while I felt a chill and remembered I'd left the window open. I got up to close it, and while I was doing that a Yellow cab smooshed to a stop against the fuzzy white curb three stories down. A woman in a long coat, red galoshes, and a white head scarf got out. When she looked up at my window I recognized the dark glasses.

I didn't move from the window after she found the front door and went inside. Two seconds after the cab pulled away, a stubby red Geo headed the same direction hove to on the other side of the street. A blur of pale face leaned over from the driver's side, hovered there, then withdrew. The exhaust pipe stopped smoking. I figured he had the number of the building; the rest would come later.

I didn't think he belonged to Matador. The car was too bright and there wasn't enough room in it to make a running shot.

She'd reached the landing by the time I got to the hallway door. Before she saw me in the dim light—she still had the cheaters on—she paused to remove the scarf and take the pins out of her hair. When she shook it loose, the fall of white gold gathered all the light there was in the narrow wainscoted passage and set it on cold fire. She almost cast a shadow in the reflected glow. The bleach job had been a good idea on her business manager's part. Leave it to a drug lord to know how to make a big impression.

She caught me looking and flushed.

"Go ahead and say it. I like to make an entrance."

"They pay you ten times the gross national product of Uruguay to do just that," I said. "Why be embarrassed?"

"I'm supposed to be incognito." It was a stage whisper.

"Then take off the damn glasses. You look like Dennis Rodman trying to look like Greta Garbo."

She took them off, using both hands the way they do. When she smiled, the hallway went negative. You can't get that from a dentist or cosmetician. You're born with it, same as dark brown eyes and a good singing voice. I'd been wrong before about her looks. You got away from her and you thought you'd fallen for the hype. Then you saw her again and found the faith you'd lost. She hadn't really needed the hair. I held the door for her and let it drift shut while I hurried across to hold the one to the inner office.

She took it in at a glance. "I could shoot a video in here. *Noir* effect. Do you own a trench coat?"

"No."

"Think about it. It could get you business."

"In Hollywood. Did you know you're being followed?"

Her face paled under the pigment. She went to the window and looked down. She said something abrupt in Spanish. "I gave the concierge a hundred dollars to keep him busy specifically."

"Who is he?"

"I was not aware they had names. Only cameras."

"Paparazzi?"

"*Sí*. A comic word for the lowest life-form on earth. I am afraid I have failed to keep you out of the tabloids."

"He probably gave the concierge a hundred to tell him when you gave him a hundred. I was afraid he was a cop."

"In that car?"

"All the unmarked units look like unmarked units. The agencies will rent a car to anyone, even cops and shutterbugs. Don't worry about him. I can use the free advertising."

"You do not know what you are saying, *hombre*. This filth will hound you to the grave and beyond. Ask Princess Di."

"She's the one who set the pace. You people kill me. You spend a hundred thousand dollars getting their attention and a million trying to avoid it."

"This one has been paying me attention for eight months. In Los Angeles it was a green Fiat. In Vegas, a yellow Neon. You never know what he'll be driving, except it's always small and bright, like a stinging bug. He snaps pictures and snaps pictures until he gets one of me glaring at him. Then a week later it shows up under a headline about my love affair with a cocker spaniel. I didn't come here to explain to you the contradictions in the life I lead. You will find that out yourself from the little fellow in the car."

"For only a week, you said. Then I'm confetti in someone else's parade. Let's have your coat."

She was still holding the scarf and glasses in one hand. She stuck them in a pocket, unbelted the coat, and took it off. It was one of those black all-weather jobs that glisten like a wet suit. Underneath it she was wearing rose-colored slacks and a matching blazer over a black bustier, above which was all her. It's funny how you can take a body you've seen naked, cover most of it, and wind up with something that makes you want to pound your fist against the wall just to have something else to think about. Before I could hang up the coat she rescued a pair of black slingbacks from the other pocket. She sat in the customer's chair to slip off her boots and slip on the pumps. The pale polish on her toes made me think about the chips of red Jillian Rubio had still had on her fingers. That was as good as pounding a wall.

I went around behind the desk, drew a sheaf of typewritten sheets out of a folder in the file cabinet, and pushed it across to her side. She asked what it was.

"The file on the Rubio case," I said. "Which isn't labeled the Rubio case. It would take a Navajo code talker to figure out my system, and then he'd have to know what all the initials stand for. My files were burgled a couple of years ago. Since then I don't take chances."

She removed the clip and sat back to read. I got into the swivel and drew a doodle on the telephone pad.

She glanced up. "Do you have to do that? You remind me of a booking agent I almost had. Who almost had me."

I speared the pencil back into its cup. I watched her read. Her eyes moved rapidly and her lips didn't move. The people who had taught her English could have chaired a department at Dartmouth, if they wouldn't mind the cut in pay. When she was finished she shuffled the pages back into order, put the clip back on, and laid them on the desk. "The poor woman. I was so busy thinking about myself I never realized her life was as hard as mine. Harder. My story came out all right. Or it has so far. Is the mother telling the truth, do you think?"

"About her daughter's health? Probably. You said you were told she'd died of infantile paralysis when you bought her birth certificate. The mother told me all this in church. People lie in church like they lie other places, even the devout ones. But I couldn't find a hole. One rough spot, but not a hole."

"What was it?"

"In a minute. Did you catch the news today?"

"I saw a black detective on television saying Hector isn't a suspect. *Muy fiero.* Ferocious."

"That one I could have figured out." It was as good a description of John Alderdyce as I'd heard in any language. "Not the local news. International."

I watched her get sad. Maybe it was sad enough. She was in show business, so I was just wasting my time. "Poor Nico," she said. "He was a bad general, I'm afraid. His one military victory was the work of his colonel, Fulgencio. Fulgencio died in the fighting. Had he not, the war might have ended differently."

"No tears for Nico? He died in his cell."

"He was the same as dead when they captured him. I did my crying then, when the news got here. It was Salazar, the Judas, who sold him to the government troops. Salazar was Fulgencio's replacement." You can spit a name like Salazar a long way. She got distance on it. "Nico was a healer. He walked out of medical school to organize a hospital strike. That was the beginning. He never went back. Even when he was living in the jungle he was a humanitarian first and a warrior second. That was why I loved him, not because he saved me from the troops at the radio station. People said it was because he was my hero, but I knew his weaknesses. I loved him for his strengths. He planned the prison escape, the one I cannot use to clear my name of his whore's murder. Beyond that, beyond the courage of his convictions, he was a weak man, easily fooled. The whore would have betrayed him had she lived that long."

She stopped talking. She'd seemed about to say more. She tossed her hair and looked at the window, as if she expected the little fellow in the red car to be peeping in from the ledge.

I said, "It's a good thing you're talking to me instead of the cops. You just gave them another motive for killing Angela Suerto."

"I did not kill her. I would prove it to you, if I could. You are not the United States government. You would protect me."

"Uncle Sam's more flexible than you think. Immigration fraud isn't murder. Does the name Miguel Zubarán mean anything to you?"

She looked at me. No recognition there. "Should it? It is old Spanish, that much I know."

"Very old. I looked up the surname in the encyclopedia. I'd heard it before, but didn't know the details. Francisco de Zubarán was a Spanish Baroque painter during the seventeenth century.

Religious subjects were his specialty. I thought you might have come across it sometime."

"You said Miguel."

"No relation, according to Miguel." I moved a shoulder. "It's not important. It was a long time ago—I'm talking about Miguel—and you said yourself you didn't use names in the resistance. But if you knew of the original Zubarán and happened to hear the name again you might have remembered it."

Her pupils got very large. They made her eyes true black. She leaned forward and her nostrils seemed to flare. They didn't, of course, but they wouldn't have looked out of place if they had. "You spoke to someone."

"Just briefly. We'll have a longer conversation tomorrow. Like I said, there's no reason you'd have heard the name if the revolution was so tight-lipped. But he seemed to know the name Mariposa Flores."

TWENTY-TWO

Who is Zubarán?"

"That's not my information to give away. I can tell you who he was. A university professor in your country."

She seemed to expect that. She was still leaning forward. "How did you find him? Where is he?"

"Same answer. Right now I'm trying to find out why he knew your name if you didn't know his."

"I don't know. I didn't tell him. Our training was specific about that. You never knew who was your friend, or how long he would remain a friend. Even those who did, once they were captured—"

"Yeah. What you didn't know you couldn't tell Abe Lincoln. Someone told Zubarán. It wasn't my go-between. His history makes yours and Jillian Rubio's play like the Olsen twins'."

"You mustn't meet with Zubarán."

"Uh-huh. Why not?"

"It's a trap."

I considered it. "Okay, say he's some kind of undercover spook sent here to pose as the man you helped escape from prison, find out what became of Mariposa Flores, kidnap her, and take her back to stand trial. What makes her worth the trouble? In this country, women of easy morals are killed every day in double digits. Your population is a lot smaller, but the percentage would be about the same. Why risk an international incident to bring back Suerto's killer?"

"Perhaps they know I'm not her killer. They want me for what I did that night."

"Same question. The revolution's as dead as Nico. You don't put down a rebellion and then turn around and antagonize a major world power just to scoop up the little fish that swam through the holes in the net."

"You don't know this government. It has a long memory and no concept of mercy."

"It also has to worry about mundane things like the budget and road repair and moustache wax for the minister of information. Even Hitler didn't spend all his time chasing Jews and crushing Poland. He had to make sure the Gestapo had enough rubber stamps. What makes you important enough to disrupt the daily bureaucratic routine? With apologies to university professors, that kind of government doesn't rate them much higher than the Suertos of the world. When they step out of line, they just throw them in the dungeon, and when they escape, where they went and who helped them takes on less significance with time. That leaves only one reason why you don't want me to meet with Zubarán. Your alibi won't hold up if I do."

Very slowly she straightened in her chair. Her face lost all expression. She rose.

"You were hired to find Jillian Rubio," she said. "You did that, and were well paid. There is no longer any business between us."

"Sit down."

She didn't move. Standing there with her chin raised she looked tall. She looked tall onstage as well. I didn't know how much of her was Mariposa and how much Gilia.

"Sit down, I said. I was ribbing you. I'm lied to a lot. Every now and then I've got to whack the piñata and see what comes out. If you'd gone on trying to convince me, I would've shown you the door."

"You believe me?"

"The part about being afraid Zubarán's a ringer. I guess when you've declared war on tyranny a little paranoia goes with the territory. The other part will have to wait until I've met with the professor."

She sat down, her spine straight. "If you'd accused my great-great-grandfather of lying, he'd have invited you to the field of honor. I suppose it's more civilized to take such insults without protest."

"Miranda Guzman gave me almost the same speech. What neither of you has said is both your great-great-grandfathers bathed every other Easter, peed at the dinner table, ate with their fingers, and wiped the grease off on the servants. We have manners now, noble and peasant. We use paper napkins and antibacterial soap and when we run someone through for calling us a dirty so-and-so we do it with the knowledge we'll answer for it later. I can't fence, but I'm a pretty good man in an interview. That's what you bought for fifteen thousand dollars. You probably spent that much greasing the help at the Hyatt to smuggle you out past the great unwashed, but it's ten times the minimum I charge for a missing-person investigation. I can either spend some more of it trying to untangle your little immigration problem or refund all but fifteen hundred and expenses and you can throw it at a lawyer. It should cover his telephone calls for a couple of days. Get one anyway is my advice. If you have one already—Matador does, so I'm sure you do—tell him what's going on. Otherwise he'll have to start cold when INS comes calling."

"If I do this, will you continue to investigate?"

"He might call me off. He probably has his own detectives, any one of whom keeps his fish in a tank bigger than this office."

"That isn't what I asked."

"I'm a nail biter. I get nervous when there are more questions floating around than answers. I'm also a community booster. Detroit had fewer homicides last year than it has had any year since before the riots in sixty-seven. I get more nervous still when a visitor is killed here. When there's reason to suspect the killer commuted here to do it, whether it was from Milwaukee or sunny California or the third world, I get downright peeved.

Another such incident and I might just lose my composure. Yeah. I'll continue to investigate, lawyer or no, until you call me off. Maybe even after that. My profit margin is so thin now I could operate for a year in the red before my creditors noticed anything unusual. I haven't a thing to lose."

"Except what Jillian Rubio lost."

"I wouldn't light any candles for her. She had some bad breaks. She would have anyway, whether you took her identity or not. She abandoned it, remember; you didn't take anything she needed or wanted. She only became angry because you made better use of it. Nobody else put that chisel in her hand. It was her decision, and she paid for it. The job now is to find out who collected."

"Even if it's me?"

"Especially if it's you. An attorney can afford to take on a guilty client. It's considered part of due process. A private eye just looks like a chump."

"It isn't me."

"I hope not. It's hard enough getting the innocent ones to pay once expenses eat up the retainer."

She shook her head, throwing off haloes. "You talk the good game, *hombre*. You don't convince me you're in it for money."

"I didn't try. The free exchange of currency for goods and services is what brought you to this country. I need some to keep the wolf from my door. If I needed more I'd be making my way through the classifieds. Hector Matador told me this morning my job will be extinct in five years. What do you think?"

"I think the same has been said of soldiers."

"I'd be okay with it if it were true, about P.I.s and soldiers. There isn't a good cop around who wouldn't welcome becoming unnecessary. That's the theory behind smart bombs and DNA fingerprinting and the Internet. But when all the indoor work is done somebody still has to wade in and clean up."

She sat back in the chair and rested her hands on the arms. When she did that her beauty hit you like a blow to the heart. "You mentioned a rough spot in Miranda Guzman's story."

I was back on the clock. I tapped the typewritten report. "She said her daughter came to spend Thanksgiving with her. Then she announced she had an urgent appointment, borrowed an overnight bag, and left. That was November 12, one day before she was to meet Matador in Milwaukee for her monthly bite. She only got half a block from the house, but that isn't the point. Why interrupt her stay for a date that had been prearranged for months? Why not wait until after she'd collected, then come for the holiday? It was still two weeks off. She could have shaken down everyone in the Top Forty and still been here in time for pumpkin pie."

"You said in your report she was mentally disturbed."

"Disturbed. Not challenged. Ted Kaczynski was as screwy as a waterspout, but he had a Ph.D. in mathematics and he kept the feds busy for seventeen years. And we only have Guzman's word she had emotional problems of any kind."

"Ask *Señora* Guzman."

"After I charge a side of beef to expenses. Her dogs won't even look at a pound of ground sirloin. Meanwhile I'm meeting Zubarán." That reminded me of something. "You wouldn't happen to have a photograph of Mariposa Flores."

"It wouldn't be safe. I left behind everything to do with my past when I came here. You have guessed that the professor would not recognize Mariposa if you showed him a picture of Gilia. That is the whole point. Ask him if he remembers the problem of the birds."

I drew a pencil and scribbled the words on the pad. They didn't mean anything more on paper than they had out loud. I waited, but she didn't add anything.

"Great. Another mystery." I socked the pencil back into the cup.

She laughed. "The professor will clear it up. Then he will know I am genuine and you will know he is not an imposter."

"Spy stuff."

"Another extinct profession the world cannot seem to do without. You said you spoke to the police this morning. Did you learn anything that is not in your report?"

"Only what killed Jillian Rubio."

Her face didn't change. It's all in the pupils if you know what to look for. Hers got small, as if I'd shone a bright light into them. "Not Stelazine."

"Yeah. Funny how you can go your whole life never hearing a word, and then suddenly you can't get away from it."

"I am cursed by God."

"Let's set our sights a little lower. The world's full of poisons and most of them are easier to get than this one. Anyone who would go to the trouble must have had a good reason. Tying you to the Rubio killing would be one; you already had a tag out on you back home involving the same poison. So the killer is someone who knew about Angela Suerto, and that you're not Gilia Cristobal."

"I cannot think who it would be."

"You told Matador."

"It is not him. I know what you think about him. It may all be true, and yet I know it is not him. I think he has a crush on me."

"Has he said anything?"

"No. The thing is impossible. He is an intelligent man and must see that."

"Beverly Hills is full of geezers and their baby brides."

"It is not age. When I marry, I will probably marry a man with skyscrapers named after him, who is on his third pacemaker. After he dies it will amuse me to fight with his grown children in court. But that is years away. Also Hector is too good a business manager to lose. Right now I am a property. Marriage would make me his property, and he would make mistakes."

"Love never stopped a killer, if he thought he couldn't have the victim. But I can't fit that to Matador. He hasn't the passion for it. His idea of murder is something you take care of between the dry cleaners and Wal-Mart. You might want to get ready for another round of blackmail."

She stiffened as if I'd slapped her. "Yes?"

"Maybe. Probably. If those papers don't turn up in a couple of weeks, someone has them. Rubio was killed for them, in a way that would destroy whatever chance you would have to strike a deal with the State Department. If that doesn't sweeten the pot, I don't know what would. And whoever did it isn't likely to be satisfied with five thousand a month."

"It gets better and better, doesn't it?"

"I'm not finished. Inspector Alderdyce found out you and Matador are neighbors. He wants an autograph."

She nodded. "I knew they would come sometime. Shall I lie?"

"Lie or tell the truth. Truth is better, but if you give it to them it won't be your truth anymore. Whatever you do, don't cage around. Cops love a tricky witness. They'll tie you up in your own evasions until you trip square into the truth. If they have to get it that way they won't cut you an inch of slack."

"I'll play the foreign card." She made her eyes round. " 'I am still learning the English, Officer, I do not know what you are asking.' "

"They'll get a cop who speaks Spanish."

"Then I'll be a celebrity." She smiled heartbreakingly. " 'Yes, Officer, Hector is my manager. No, I don't know why he would hire a private detective. I'd like to meet him. I play a private eye in the Bond film. Jillian Rubio? I don't know the name. I have all these lyrics to memorize, so many steps to learn. I haven't even time to balance my checkbook. Hector takes care of that.' "

"That'll work until they check Rubio's background and find out her real name is Gilia Cristobal. When they come back, they'll leave the charm at headquarters."

Her face flattened out. "In my country they are never charming. You and Hector are taking the same chances. I carried my weight in the revolution. Don't ever think I didn't."

"I never thought so. Go easy on the accent when you talk to Alderdyce. Lose the dumb blonde. You're not that good an actress."

She gave me a real smile this time. "*Hombre*, that's the best compliment I've gotten since I came to this country."

"One more question. Where was the mole on your upper lip?"

She hesitated, then placed a forefinger to the right of the dimple. There was no trace of a scar. "You've been talking to Hector. Is it important?"

"You never know. I once broke a case over a grain of sugar in a gas tank."

"Really?"

"No, but I'm sure someone did somewhere. What's the plan for sneaking back into the hotel?"

"I don't have one. In my set, you put more thought into sneaking out of places. Is he still there?"

I got up and looked out the window. The snow had picked up; the Geo was almost white. As I watched, a hole appeared in the frost on the passenger's side and irised out into a wide circle, cleared by a pale palm. "Did you expect him to go away?"

"I hoped a policeman had arrested him or something. He doesn't care which side of the street he parks on, or any other laws he breaks. Can we call and turn him in?" She sounded eager.

"A cop would just tell him to beat it. He'd drive around the block and come back." I sat back down, lifted the receiver off the telephone, and dialed. When a wheezy accent came on I asked the owner to come up. I put down the receiver and waited. Gilia lifted her eyebrows. I shook my head.

After five minutes someone knocked on the door and came in, a sad-faced balding party in the oldest pair of overalls this side of a textile museum. He looked like a refugee from the Crimean War.

I said, "This is Rosecranz. He was standing on this lot when they built the place, so they put him in charge." To him I said, "This is Gilia. She's an international superstar. She needs a way out of the building that doesn't involve Grand River, and transportation to the Hyatt Regency Hotel in Dearborn. What'll it cost?"

He looked at her without recognition or excitement. Nothing had excited him since the October Revolution, and the nine-inch Admiral that entertained him in his broom closet on the ground floor only got *Your Show of Shows*. "Fifty dollars, I think. More if I get a ticket for the broken taillight."

"It's a Dodge pickup," I told Gilia. "Truman rode in it. You'll have to walk the last couple of blocks. If Rosecranz ever saw his picture in the *National Enquirer* he'd fall and break his hip."

"Can he be trusted?" There is something about the old man that makes you refer to him in third person when he's in the room, and not at all when he isn't.

"He hasn't said anything about Jimmy Hoffa in twenty-seven years."

She rose. I got her coat and helped her into it. She spent some time pinning up her hair. When she'd tied the scarf and put on her dark glasses she looked like the second runner-up in a Gilia look-alike contest. "*Gracias*, Mr. Walker. You are *un caballero*."

"Yeah. Band leader, wasn't he?" I took out my wallet and gave Rosecranz two twenties and a ten.

He studied each bill, then got out his greasy handkerchief, folded them inside, and stuck the works in a hip pocket. "Who is Jimmy Hoffa?"

TWENTY-THREE

I'm not as patient as I used to be.

When I was just old enough to vote, I'd waited out a sniper about the size of my left leg for twelve hours, not moving a muscle, until he scratched his nose and I shot him through his right eye. But back then I'd had all the time in the world; time enough to read Kerouac and Gibran and Rod McKuen and realize they were gasbags top to bottom. The pisher in the Geo wasn't worth more than five minutes of a life half-lived. That was as much time as I gave Rosecranz and Gilia before I turned out the lights and closed the blinds over the window.

I spread two slats to watch him. At the end of two minutes his repertorial instincts got the better of him. He got out to reconnoiter.

They always seem to be runts, for some reason. Maybe it's the tight spaces they have to squeeze through, or the security radar they have to duck. This one was a little butterball nearly as wide as he was high, waddling across the street as fast as his chubby legs could pump. He had on a Lakers warm-up jacket and straws of greasy-looking hair stuck out from under his Dodgers cap all around. From three floors up I could tell he hadn't been in the same room with a razor in better than a week. A tan leather camera case hung from a strap around his neck and the way his pockets bulged told me there was more in them than just his hands. All those little aluminum film canisters would make him popular with the people standing behind him at airport security.

I gave him time to get inside the foyer, then went downstairs. I knew all the squeaky boards to avoid, and so I caught him standing on the slushy rubber mat inside the entrance, peering at the white snap-on letters on the building directory. I could almost hear his lips moving.

"I wouldn't go by it," I said. "Half those businesses turned toes up when the market took a header."

He actually jumped, just like a cartoon character, daylight showing under his Keds. But he had good reflexes. His camera came up before his feet touched down and the flashgun hit me full in the face. I was seeing purple-and-green spots while a pair of rubber-soled feet pounded the floor going away.

I caught the door while it was drifting shut, but there's no catching a little fat guy in the short stretch. I had to look both ways because I didn't trust my eyes yet, and by that time he had the door open on the driver's side. I sprinted the rest of the way and got my hand on the passenger's-side door just as he started rolling. I might have lost him then, but the street was slick with sodden snow and he spun his wheels at first. I got the door open just as he lunged across to lock it. I almost sat on his head. He lunged back the other way and opened the other door, bailing out of his own moving car. He was a born survivor. But I got hold of his jacket by the back and yanked him my direction. The tires had found traction; we slewed out into the street, hydroplaning on snow and slush with no hand on the wheel. I let go of him to grab it, and damn if he didn't try again to jump out. I swung up my elbow, barking him a good one on the temple, and as he slumped against me in a daze I spun the wheel into the skid, just the way they teach you in drivers' education, snaked a leg up over the console, and found the brake with one toe. The antilocking system paid for itself and we rocked to a stop in a diagonal across both lanes.

I looked up into a pale smear of face behind the windshield of a PT Cruiser stopped in the middle of the eastbound lane.

We'd missed colliding by the width of a hand. I waved, found reverse, and got out of the way. A full thirty seconds went past before the Cruiser started forward. By then the little butterball was stirring.

I reached across him, tugged his door shut, and locked it. I needed whatever advantage I could get over his reflexes. I withdrew my foot from his side of the car and got out the ID folder. The sheriff's star gave his eyes something to focus on.

He blinked at it. "That ain't real. You're the snooper from the top floor. I seen your name in the lobby."

"A lot of cops moonlight in this state. Steer this crate into the curb. If you try to run again I'll roll it right over you."

He pulled it almost squarely into the clear patch of pavement he'd been parked on top of before. This time we were pointed in the other direction. That made us legal for fifteen minutes. While he was straightening out I popped open the glove compartment and found his rental agreement among the empty McDonald's cartons jammed inside. His name was Fritz Fleeman—Fritz, not Frederick or Friedrich; it was probably on his birth certificate—and he was licensed to drive in Orange County, California. I put away the folder and shoved the hatch shut against the pressure from inside.

"Okay, Fritz. What makes me so important and who to?"

A pudgy hand went inside his jacket. I got hold of that arm high up and squeezed. That took all the grip out of his hand. His face twisted. "It's just a cell phone! I'm calling nine-one-one."

"Speaking."

"You ain't no cop."

I reached inside his jacket with my other hand, under the camera strap, found the little telephone in his shirt pocket, and brought it back out. I let go of his arm then. If he had a gun, he'd have gone for it instead. I laid the squawker on the dash. I was breathing through my mouth. He smelled like an elevator full of Frenchmen.

The whole car was as messy as the glove compartment. I was sitting on a pizza box and the backseat was covered with greasy paper sacks, crushed pop cans, Krispy Kreme cartons, and cameras. These included a Japanese digital job about the size of a cake of soap, vintage last week, and an old-fashioned drop-front Speed Graphic that belonged in a museum, among the scatter of Nikons, Polaroids, Kodak Instamatics, and those little throwaways people put on the tables at wedding receptions. Cans and cans of film. One or two of the better cameras would have retailed for more than the car he was driving.

"You ain't no cop," he said again. He actually stuck out his lower lip. He could pass for thirteen, even with the feathery growth of whiskers. He could have been my age. His face needed washing and dermatology.

"You ain't Ansel Adams," I said. "Start again. Who's paying for all this jazzy equipment?"

"I bought it myself, cash money. How much you make last year prowling motel parking lots? I bet I paid out more than that in quarterlies."

"Since when does a shakedown artist declare his income?"

He sneered. You need a putty pimpled face and green teeth to pull it off the way he did. "I'm with the Hollywood Press Corps, Jack. They may not want to admit it, but I make the parties they don't get invited to. Wander into any checkout lane, you see my byline. You catch that spread last week, Michael Jackson's taking injections to go back to being black?"

"I saw it. You don't have to push a button for a living to recognize an underexposed shot."

"Underexposed my ass! I caught him outside the hospital in Berne, sneaking out the door they use to wheel the corpses out of the morgue."

"What'd you do, stow away with the Swiss cheese?"

"Concorde, first class, smart guy. I made twenty-five grand on that one frame. That don't count what I expect to get from the Brits for the shot I took of Bonnie Prince Charlie scratching his ass at Heathrow when I was changing planes on the way back."

"What are you doing in my league, Flash? I can't sing or dance and steak-and-kidney pie gives me the trots."

"Brother, I can't see your league from the circles I spin around in. It's that bottle blond tamale up in your office brought me here to Skid Row. What's the squeeze? You catch her with Bill Ford in the backseat of an Explorer?"

"My office is empty, Fritz. Just me and the fixtures. Come on up. Bring your Brownie."

He wet his lips. They were plenty wet to begin with. Just thinking about getting a shot of this year's diva cooling her maraccas in the office of a private cop had all his glands going. Miranda Guzman's dogs had less of a drooling problem.

"Aw," he said. "She rabbited. I heard an old wheezebox chugging up the next street over. I should of went with my gut and hung a tail."

"You follow her around a lot, huh?"

He had shrewd little eyes the color of canned peas. "Now, who'd that be? Your office is empty."

"That was a haze. You get around, you know how it is in these union towns. We've got to give the new guy a going-over. Our work's not so different, yours and mine. I used to tiptoe around with a camera."

"It ain't the same thing."

"Of course not. You get paid to plaster your work in every A and P and Sam's Club from here to Nova Scotia. I got paid to bury mine. I bet you got shots of Gilia no one's ever seen, just waiting for the right headline to slug on top."

He leered, started to lean my direction. Then he sat back. His face shut. "I fill a lot of rolls. A lot of rolls. Most of it's shit. You got to be prepared to fill a lot of rolls with a lot of shit. Now and then you get something just by accident."

"As for instance?"

"Let's just say when a lady takes a sunbath on her bedroom balcony, putting screens all around ain't always enough. A fellow that knows his way around a long lens can get plenty out of the right angle and a full-length mirror on a closet door somebody left open."

"Oh, nudes. I thought maybe you had something. Anybody who hasn't seen her naked doesn't read enough magazines."

This time he got a handle on the leer without moving. "Shows how much you know. That's all I'm going to say."

"You saying she had company?"

"I ain't saying anything. But if I was to say something, a certain party that goes by the name of double-oh-seven would have him some explaining to do when he got home."

"So that's how she got the part. I wondered. Usually they have to prove they can get over a line without a grappling hook."

He looked smug. His nose needed wiping.

"Who's playing James Bond these days?" I asked. "I can't keep up."

"Christ, don't you know nothing? Go see a show, Grampa. They got sound now."

"I'm not interested in sex pictures," I said. "Not today. Ever take any of Gilia where she doesn't look like she just stepped off a cloud? You know, like one of us?"

"You mean like curlers and a ratty sweatshirt? No dice. She's too careful. These career broads spend too much time in the driver's seat to make that kind of mistake. Well, I did snatch one where she didn't exactly look all glammed up, more like a pretty you'd see on the street. Not *this* street; Jesus, this town looks like it was designed by the guy that did San Quentin. Say Wilshire, east of Santa Monica. The rest of the time, what you might see, that don't walk down any street you ever get to use."

"What, did a pigeon crap on her?"

"I wish. The *Globe* would of went ten thousand for a shot like that. I caught her squinting into the sun. You could still tell it was her, but you wouldn't believe it if somebody didn't tell you. The Gilia you see up on them big projection screens onstage, she just laughs at a little thing like the sun. I guess the mope she pays to lug around her dark glasses was home sick that day."

"Sell it?"

"Hell, no. Who'd shell out for it? It don't look like her. I mean it does, but it don't. How would you head it? 'Salsa Queen Looks Like Your Sister'?"

"I might buy it."

"You? Bullshit. You want to hang it in your bathroom, get yourself started every morning?"

"I'd have to see it first."

"You couldn't afford it."

"You don't look enough like Bill Gates to jump to that kind of conclusion," I said.

"What kind of crack's that?" He was more sensitive than he looked.

"I'm saying a clicker who makes up to twenty-five grand per snapshot doesn't usually drive a Geo and dress like a strike-breaker. Just like you wouldn't look at my neighborhood and guess I made fifteen grand this week. But I don't pull in that kind of coin only to risk it on what's behind Door Number Three. Let's have a look."

His little pea eyes jigged toward the backseat, then focused on me. "Tell me what she's paying you for and maybe I'll let you take a peek."

A stack of nine-by-twelve manila envelopes stuck out from under the pile of cameras and take-out containers on the back-seat. I reached across the front seat and scooped them into my lap. He made a grab for them. I stiff-armed him, cuffing him on the temple with the heel of my free hand, just about where I'd struck him before with my elbow. He fell back against the door on his side and stayed there. He wasn't out, just reluctant to invite more attention of that kind.

There were five envelopes. I went through the contents of the first two quickly. Mostly contact sheets, strips of film printed directly onto glossy black paper, with some finished eight-by-tens of the more commercial items. A lot of walking shots, movie and TV stars and singers and dancers and stand-up comics, a senator or two, striding down sidewalks and across hotel lobbies, some unaware of the camera, others reacting, seldom positively; a very nice pose in full color of the child star of a popular family sitcom giving Fritz the finger. It was a revelation how many millionaire entertainers picked their noses in public. They needed an old-time studio system to teach them how to behave and dress like the gods and goddesses they once were, but that ship had sailed along with Cohn and Selznick and the brothers Warner. I saw more dark roots and crooked toupees than a Beverly Hills hairdresser. The guy was an artist of a very particular type.

I found what I wanted in the third envelope. It was mostly Gilia, taken in some town other than Detroit, probably an earlier stopover on her national tour. Fritz had staked out a spot in front of a hotel with a revolving door and taken a couple of dozen shots in twelve or fifteen seconds of her walking out among her entourage, including Emmett and Felipe and Big Bad Benny, scowling bullets directly into the lens; if he'd printed them all on separate sheets I could have riffled them and gotten a moving picture. No sign of Matador, but then business managers stayed away from public occasions, and former Colombian drug lords were notoriously shy of cameras.

Fritz had printed only one picture of Gilia separately. It wasn't especially unflattering, just her screwing up her face against the morning or afternoon glare. She had on street clothes: an open-necked white blouse and loose pleated canary yellow pants. Her hair was twisted into a ponytail, still too blonde even for a Scandinavian, much less a *señorita*, but everyday as to style. While you'd probably look at her twice because she was an alarmingly attractive stranger to encounter on a public street, you wouldn't guess based on your first glimpse that she was who she was. She looked more like Mariposa than Gilia. I hoped.

I kept it out, put the rest back, then rolled up the eight-by-ten to prevent creasing and slid it into my inside breast pocket. I got out my wallet and laid the stack of envelopes on Fritz's lap with a hundred-dollar bill on top.

He looked at it as if it were a dead roach. "I wipe my lenses with hundreds."

"I'm just buying the print, not exclusive use. You can run up another and peddle it to the *Tattler* for a twelve-pack of lens wipers."

He reached for his cell phone. "I'm ordering up some law. You ain't no cop, don't try and kid me. I didn't agree to sell." He pecked out 911.

"Ask for Lieutenant Franklin. He heads up Vice."

"I don't want Vice. I want Robbery." But he paused with his thumb hovering over the SEND button.

"I helped ease Franklin out from under a bogus rape charge last year. A hooker claimed he traded a get-out-of-jail-free card for services. She missed some drug connections while I was tailing her. After forty-eight hours she went in voluntarily and took back her complaint."

"So you strung her out and she came clean. So what?"

"Franklin didn't say so what. He broke up a child-porn ring in January. I think he still has a couple of dozen pictures in the evidence room he won't need to make his case. They could've been taken by anyone."

He found his sneer, but his face got more pasty. I'd tapped into every photographer's nightmare.

"I never told a kid to drop his pants in my life. I never needed to to make a buck."

"Push the button then. You've probably got an army of character witnesses."

"Go boil your head. You can't tag me with that and make it stick."

"It doesn't have to stick. A thing like that follows you around. And if it should happen to stick, if say you crap out on stand-up citizens who'll vouch for your sterling character, you'll be registering as a convicted sex offender everywhere you go for the rest of your life."

"Son of a bitch." He opened and closed his fists. "Keep the goddamn picture, I don't need it. What you want it for anyway? It ain't nothing special."

"That's why I want it." I glanced at my watch. "She's probably back at the hotel by now. Maybe you can smuggle yourself into her suite under a tin cover with the prawns."

When I looked back up, the world went blazing white. It was the second time he'd used his flashgun on me.

"This time I tripped the shutter," he said. "I like to keep a record of all my friends."

It must have been quite a gallery. I grinned at him through the swimming spots and got out of his car. It started up and he tried to splash me as he took off.

He partially succeeded, but I was still grinning as I brushed at the snotty mess on my pant cuff. I didn't know any Lieutenant Franklin. Franklin's was the face on the hundred-dollar bill I'd left with him. I didn't figure the lie had bought me one more second in purgatory.

TWENTY-FOUR

Northwest was getting ready to open a new terminal midfield at Wayne County Metropolitan Airport, complete with an elevated tramway and more conveyor belts to lose one's luggage on than ever before, but for the time being the airline was operating its Midwestern hub out of the Davey Terminal, a crumbling old barn built square onto a hotel where a stewardess had been raped and strangled a dozen years earlier. From where I sat in a chain bar and grill on the sunny side of security, I could see the end of a line waiting to get through the metal detectors that was the line to end all lines, full of anxious faces, resigned faces, bored faces, angry faces—faces that did not belong to travelers looking forward to new sights and fresh adventures. Instead they were worrying about how much clothing they would have to remove and whether some turtlebrain in a uniform was going to let them carry their lucky two-inch nail file aboard. Overnight the friendly skies had gone from prodding them like cattle to lockstepping them through the system like felons.

I ordered a beer and a burger. I hadn't had breakfast that morning, which was usual, and I had skipped lunch, which wasn't, in order to get to the airport early in case the professor's plane caught some kind of tail wind. He was the cautious type, for good reasons, and if he found no one waiting he might return to his gate. I was still carrying around some lead splinters from an old argument, which took more explaining when bells started ringing than I cared to go into with strangers. Also I would have to buy a ticket before they let me prowl the gates. Anyway I'd skipped lunch.

He was fifteen minutes late, which according to the carriers is officially on time. He'd been right about my being able to pick him out of the crowd. Although he was built more along the lines of a Pamplona bull than I'd expected from an academic, wearing a well-cut gray worsted with a three-button jacket instead of baggy tweeds, you couldn't miss the eye patch, and just in case you could he'd gone with white instead of conventional black, a sharp contrast against medium brown skin and a swashbuckling choice in view of his careful temperament. Heads turned when that scrap of linen went past. The blasé passengers and well-wishers packing the bar probably thought he was Wiley Post reincarnated, or an immortal film director at the least.

"Professor Zubarán?"

He'd paused inside the entrance to scan the patrons. When I stood and called his name, he dropped his chin briskly and embroidered his way between the tables, towing a black nylon carry-on by its handle behind him. He had a handshake like a Teamster and very black thick hair brushed straight back that would be iron gray in a few years. There were already traces of it in his thick moustache. His good eye—the left one—was the true Spanish black, like Picasso's, and like Picasso's there was no sign of pacification in it.

"You look somewhat like what I would expect a private detective to look like," he said in his slow, careful English. "That is why I must ask to be shown identification."

I took my license out of the folder and handed it to him. He studied it a while, head cocked to make up for his lack of depth perception. He gave it back. "I suppose complete satisfaction is a chimera. One can do so much with computers and laser printers."

"If I thought I needed them I'd have brought X rays of my skull. How many concussions is the minimum?"

"I do not apologize. I'm told I may obtain permission to carry a concealed weapon, but so far I have refused to apply. I am afraid I would use it the first time a stranger addressed me in Spanish."

I thanked him for rearranging his schedule. He looked at his watch, a functional stainless-steel model strapped to the underside of his wrist. A pattern of ragged white scars showed there. I had similar marks on both wrists, but mine would fade. He looked up at the people waiting with their luggage.

"My plane was late. Naturally. If that's the security line, I can give you only a few minutes."

We sat down. A waitress trundled over. He shook his head and she picked up my plate and utensils and drifted away. He glanced with curiosity at the large square white envelope in front of me, but he was too polite to ask about it. I folded my arms on top of it so it wouldn't distract him.

"The Lincoln Question," I said. "What was it?"

He pursed his lips. "The method? I thought—"

"I know the method, Professor. What did they ask?"

"What do they always ask? Names, places of meetings, specific items discussed at those meetings. I denied any such knowledge. I did so out of ignorance, not valor. I am an educator, not a revolutionary. I taught literature. They accused me of inciting rebellion. They came to arrest me in the middle of my lecture on *Don Quixote*. Apparently the Knight of the Woeful Countenance was not a supporter of the state."

"I can see how far you got convincing them."

He touched two fingers to the patch. It would be a chronic mannerism. "Curiously enough, I think they believed me. That never stopped a man who truly enjoys his work from pursuing it. I do not complain. They left me with one eye. Others were not so fortunate."

"I'm surprised they didn't come back for the other one."

"I'm certain they would have gotten around to it eventually."

"Tell me about the escape."

He shrugged. He wasn't as good at it as Matador, but he had me beat. "There is little to tell. Dumas would not have bothered to use it. A guard was bribed; I never found out by whom. He unlocked my cell in the middle of the night and escorted me to the entrance the guards used when they reported to work. Outside a young woman was waiting. She led me down the path to a dock. There was a rowboat there with a man in it whose name I never learned and whose face I could not see in the darkness. He rowed me to a bigger boat, a cabin cruiser designed for the luxury of its owner. I sat in a cabin for two hours, at the end of which I was escorted out and onto another dock. That man I could describe to you, but I will not. I spent a very pleasant month as the guest of a family whose name I will not repeat. In the meantime an arrangement was made with your State Department and I entered this country on a faculty exchange program. That is my thrilling story, Mr. Walker. I doubt it will excite much interest in Hollywood."

"Did you know anyone with the revolution before you were arrested?"

"They tell me the leader had been a student in one of my classes. I wasn't familiar with the name, and when I saw his photograph I could not place him. I had had hundreds of students over the years. I'm afraid I remember very few of them."

"I heard he studied medicine."

"That is possible. Our university system, like yours—you see I do not yet consider it mine, even though I am employed by it—requires education in all the arts and sciences, regardless of the degree." He rolled his shoulders again. "If the government had come to me and demanded I eliminate tales of liberty from the syllabus, I would have refused. They did not ask. I was arrested anyway. Citizens of my country are incapable of revolting on their own. They must be led to it by subversive influences. That is the party line and there is no arguing with it. The odds are with the house, as you say here."

"So you never knew the names of your rescuers."

"I did not say that."

I unfolded my arms, drummed my fingers on the envelope. He glanced at it again, then raised his eye back to mine. "Mariposa Flores," I said.

He nodded. "A name scrawled on a scrap of paper, folded and

tossed between the bars of my cell while I slept. I suspect it was tossed there by the guard who took me out two nights later. I chewed it up and swallowed it. I had never seen or heard the name before, but I think it was given to me to provide me with hope."

He lifted his hand. I thought he was going to touch the eye patch again. He unbuttoned his collar and spread it, loosening his necktie in the process. The crease around his throat wasn't as vivid as the marks on his wrists, but it would be with him the rest of his life.

"I made the attempt the night after the Lincoln Question was put to me." He refastened the button and straightened his tie. "A guard found me and cut me down. After I recovered, I decided to wait until the next time they asked the question. That resolve faded, however. But for that name on a scrap of paper, I probably would not have waited."

I took a sip of my beer. It had gone warm and flat. Swallowing hurt my throat. "Any idea who decided to bootleg the name in to you?"

"None. I had no connection to the revolution. That was the fantasy of someone in the capital."

"What did you use for a rope, your bedsheets?"

"My trousers. We did not have bedsheets. It wasn't the Holiday Inn."

"The rebel leader hanged himself recently. They said he used bedsheets."

"I heard this too. He would not even have had his trousers. After my attempt, they stripped me and threw me back into the cell naked. The guard who let me out brought me an extra uniform to cover my nudity. Stripping became the standard practice after my experience. The young man was murdered."

A boarding announcement went out over the P.A. He cocked his head, listening. It was a New Orleans flight. His was California. He looked at his watch again.

"Did you get a look at Mariposa Flores?" I asked.

"I do not know if that was her name. She did not introduce herself." He nodded. "I saw her in the lights from the prison. A very pretty girl, even dressed as she was in man's clothes. Her face was dirty. I suppose she'd smeared it with something to blend with the shadows."

"Could you identify her from a picture?"

His eye went to the envelope. "You must understand this is difficult. I feel I am giving information I did not under torture."

"This time the information could help, not hurt. The young woman is accused of a murder that took place somewhere else at the moment someone was helping you escape."

"I remember you said something about that. Trust does not exist in me as once it did. Compared to that, what is an eye? I have another. My faith in human nature has been torn from me, and I have only suspicion and fear to fall back upon." His face twisted into a mask of pain. I knew the feeling.

"I saw her yesterday," I said. "She told me to ask you if you remember the problem of the birds."

He sat up straight, knocking over his carry-on case with his elbow. The bang stopped all conversation in the bar for a beat. Then the buzz resumed. Zubarán groped for the handle and set the case upright. His eye remained on me.

"She used these words?" he asked. " 'The problem of the birds'?"

"Yeah. I thought we had plenty without birds. I guess not, though. What did she mean?"

He shook his head. He was agitated. "I will look at the picture."

I opened the flap, drew out the eight-by-ten color photo Fritz Fleeman had taken, and smoothed it out on the table in front of him. It wanted to roll back up, but I anchored two opposite corners with the napkin dispenser and my beer glass. I'd shaded in the distracting blonde hair with the edge of a pencil. He studied the picture a long time. We'd spent longer than we'd originally set aside for our meeting, but when the P.A. system blared again he didn't appear to be listening. It was the same wrung-out voice announcing further boarding on the 3:36 to New Orleans. Have your picture IDs out and ready, also your vaccination records and your mother's maiden name. Turn your head and cough. I decided to use some of Gilia's fifteen thousand on new shocks and a rebuilt transmission for the Cutlass.

"I'm not certain." He was frowning. "It could be. So much has happened since that night."

I had a brainstorm. I should have thought of it before. I took a ballpoint pen out of my inside breast pocket, leaned across the table, and drew a bold dot to the right of the dimple above Gilia's upper lip. I sat back and waited. It was worse than waiting for Fritz to make his move back at the office, but on that occasion I'd been pretty sure of the outcome.

He pushed the picture away suddenly, dropping his chin the way he had when he'd spotted me in the bar. I caught the beer glass before it toppled. One more noise and we'd be up to our eyebrows in the National Guard. "It is she."

"Sure?" My heart was bumping like a square wheel.

"Yes. A bit older, and much less tomboyish. She's done something with her hair, and whoever she had remove that mole never practiced in our country. But this is the woman who led me down the path to the boat. If your murder was committed at that time, someone else committed it."

"Would you testify to that?"

The color slid from his face. The white patch lost some of its contrast.

"Not back home," I said. "Here, if it comes to that. Back home it's the rope either way."

"For both of us. There's no crime worse than demonstrating the fallibility of the government prison system." He looked at his watch a third time. "Yes, I'd swear to the authorities here that what I have told you is the truth. I really must get into line now."

I put the picture back in the envelope. We rose together and shook hands.

"What is the problem of the birds?"

He pulled up the handle of the carry-on. "It was a long walk. We knew we couldn't very well introduce ourselves, but the silence was oppressive. She asked me if I taught mathematics. I said no and she said that was a pity, because it was a mathematical story problem that she most remembered from her own education. It seems there were fifteen birds perched upon the wall of a mission. After a while three more birds joined them, then one flew away. The question was how many birds remained."

"Seventeen."

"That was the answer I suggested. She said it was the same answer her teacher gave when she asked why her answer had been marked incorrect. Her answer was zero."

He started toward the security line, pulling the case behind him. I laid some bills on the table and caught up. "Why zero?"

"When one bird flies away from a wall, all the others fly away with it. Everyone with eyes knows this. Even those with just one eye. Abstract knowledge does not apply to the world outside the classroom."

"Pretty smart for eighteen," I said.

"Is that how old she was? She has accomplished much in a short time."

We stopped at the end of the line. I looked at him.

He smiled broadly then, showing some goldwork in his molars he hadn't had done stateside. He never looked more like a buccaneer of the old Spanish Main. "Please tell the young lady I am a very big fan."

TWENTY-FIVE

Driving back into the city I couldn't keep a happy song from playing inside my head. It didn't matter that I was crawling through a white squall that had my fellow motorists crunched over their steering wheels, grinding their teeth and peering through one swipe of their wipers at a time. I had an innocent client who could afford my rates.

One murder down, sort of. I knew who *hadn't* done it, and I could prove it. It was up to a foreign government to find out who had. I thought I knew who it was, if they cared to ask me. They probably wouldn't. Cops are cops, no matter if they lecture their suspects on their rights or throw them in a leaky basement and forget about them until it's time to clean house with a handy suicide. Once they nail someone they like, they hang up the hammer until the next case. Their desks are piled just as high the world over. They can only afford to spend so much time and money on each item of business, and there's no budget for quality control, not like Ford or GM or Toyota. If it comes off the line with a faulty starter and doors that fly off every time someone taps the brake, it takes a lot more than Ralph Nader to fix what's wrong.

What I had on Angelo Suerto's killer wouldn't hold up in an American court. The monkeys who wore the robes in the place that held jurisdiction had built capital cases on shakier foundations, but even they wouldn't bother to build one on what I had to offer, because the perpetrator was beyond justice of the mortal variety.

One down. One to go.

Which was the point at which the song stopped playing.

The best coroner in America, armed with the latest equipment, couldn't pin down the hour when someone had pumped death into Jillian Rubio's veins. It could have happened anytime between the moment she left her mother's house and one of Miranda Guzman's dogs first caught a whiff of something that wasn't knotty pine seasoning under plastic on the other side of the fence across the street. Good sense said she'd died within minutes and that the lumberyard was handy, but the maximum-security wings are full of killers who wouldn't recognize good sense if it jingled in their pockets. Someone could have kept her prisoner for a week before working up the gumption to finish what he'd started, or driven around with her corpse in the trunk for days, then returned to the scene of the abduction and dumped the evidence. A suspect with Gilia's means and talent for disguising herself could have buzzed in on a red-eye, taken care of the business, and buzzed back to L.A. or Vegas or wherever, and no alibi would protect her. Or she might have hired it done. Some of her associates needed character witnesses in order to appear in court as a character witness for her. Hector Matador had scaled the Colombian corporate ladder by performing bloody errands for the guy on the next rung up.

The cops—my cops—wouldn't need much more than the Stelazine to make up their minds. Gilia was the only human link between two murders committed several thousand miles and two years apart, and that was worth running out, at least until they hit the wall. The same poison showing up in both cases was the kind of evidence that made walls disappear. Getting her off on the first murder wouldn't convince anyone whose business it was to run down the most obvious trail. He'd just say that's where she got the idea. When a blackmailer dies violently, the steps you have to follow practically glow in the dark, and lead only one direction.

I might have followed them myself, and would have, if they hadn't used Stelazine. Anyone smart enough to point out that birds seldom follow the rules of simple arithmetic is smart enough to come up with something that didn't spell out her name in lights.

Then again, maybe the cops were right. The teacher had been right about one from eighteen leaving seventeen. You can get too clever with an idea and fail the test.

It doesn't pay to think too much about cops when you're driving. They don't set much store by telepathic communication, but they can smell fear. I had exited the Lodge onto Jefferson when a DPD blue-and-white loomed up out of the flying snow in my rear-view mirror. When I made the turn onto Woodward, it turned behind me. Its lights struck firefly patterns off the swirling flakes, its siren growled. I drifted over in front of the Coleman A. Young Municipal Center and braked. The blue-and-white swung in behind, bouncing red and blue off the sad streaked face of the statue of the Spirit of Detroit.

They usually let you sit and stew while they run your plate number through the onboard computer. Not this time. Someone tapped on my window and when I ran it down I looked out at two hundred pounds in a glistening leather jacket and snow piling up on a plastic cap shield. The cop had his semiautomatic half out of its holster. I couldn't think of any of the fifteen traffic violations for which you can get pulled over while making a turn downtown that would make an officer draw his sidearm. I kept my hands on the wheel.

"You Amos Walker?" The voice was a tight tenor.

I said I was Amos Walker.

"Homicide's got a BOLO out on your car. You want to follow me or ride in back? You won't like the third choice."

I said I'd follow. It was only a few blocks. You're never more than a few blocks from a cop anywhere you go in this world.

TWENTY-SIX

The things you see sitting in a squad room at 1300 Beaubien, Detroit Police Headquarters:

—A homeless guy wearing a filthy red Santa Claus coat over a Nine-Inch Nails sweatshirt, possible witness to a drive-by, snoring and using a stack of arrest reports on the booking officer's desk for a pillow.

—A city worker on a stepladder, replacing a fluorescent tube in the ceiling, with his pants down around his hips and an object I swore was a crack pipe sticking up out of his back pocket.

—A very attractive detective third-grade with Domestic Disturbances, shucking out of insulated snow pants and smoothing the wrinkles out of a red skirt that caught her at mid-thigh. I figured she was drumming up business.

—A dinosaur from the old STRESS crackdown squad, last of his kind, evidence gloves on his hands, cleaning a twelve-gauge shotgun with what looked like antiseptic gauze and laying out the pieces on a newspaper spread over his desk, doing everything but powdering the butt with Johnson & Johnson's.

—A local Action Newswoman on a color TV no one seemed to be watching, interviewing a manic fan waiting for Gilia to emerge from a trailer on West Vernor, where the city had finally agreed to let her shoot her video, interviewer and interviewee both covered with snow and apparently seriously expecting her to step out into it.

—Gilia in the flesh, got up like Julie Christie in *Doctor Zhivago* in expensive fake furs, signing an autograph for one of the officers who had brought her in for questioning.

It's pretty much like that all the time, give or take a visiting superstar. I'm not there every day, but I'm not important enough for a floor show. For all I know they shoot pigeons off the window ledges Fridays.

Gilia didn't see me. There was a roomful of desks and chairs and computer consoles between us, and it's a big room, about the size of a 1950s high school gynmnasium and even smelling a little like Red Devil varnish and basketballs. After she handed back the pen, someone took her gently by the elbow and conducted her down a hall out of sight. Some of the magic went out with her. It was just a room after all, and detectives are just clerical workers with guns.

There was no sign of any of her people, not Benny and certainly not Matador, who was probably back at the Hyatt placing a call to Gilia's attorney in Beverly Hills, or wherever the better California lawyers were hanging their briefs these days. She wouldn't be under arrest, though, so there would be little the legal team could do, apart from making polite threats in Latin. They wouldn't know about the two years Inspector Alderdyce spent in prelaw at the University of Michigan before joining the academy in Detroit, and they might not be aware of them even after the conversation, unless they forgot their manners and called him a dumb flatfoot. Maybe not even then. He was the kind who didn't mind losing a hand or two as long as he cleared the table at the end of the evening.

I only knew for sure Alderdyce was involved because I was sitting in a plastic scoop chair outside his office, and I'd caught a glimpse of him looking my way briefly from near the windows, where he was in conversation with a detective sergeant I'd met before, but whose name had never stuck. One look, no more. I might have been a tile that needed replacing. After a moment he'd parted company with the sergeant and gone down the same hall the uniforms escorted Gilia down a few minutes later.

I got it. I was being shunned.

It's an old trick and may even predate good cop/bad cop and the Wedding at Cana. The theory was you ignored the victim until the knowledge of his own guilt got the better of him and he confessed. Don't laugh until you've been through it. Cops have squeezed full statements out of thugs with pickled hides just by drumming their fingers on a steel desk in a tiny room, bouncing random circles off a ceiling from a flashlight, chewing tinfoil. The first time the strategy worked had probably been an accident; one of Pilate's lieutenants on the Plain Toga Detail got stuck for a tactic and was working on the problem when the character sweating it out on the broken-down divan opposite him suddenly cracked. Two thousand years later they would have a Greek name for it and an explanation, along with the suspect's psychiatric profile in a folder and a table of figures predicting how long it would take. The table in my case being as long as the Bayeux Tapestry. The Long Wait hadn't a thing on the Lincoln Question. I balanced my checkbook in my head and when that got too depressing I looked at my nails.

The patrolie who had brought me in and plunked me down in the chair was long gone, back on the beat or down in the locker room changing into dry socks. I'd been sitting there about an hour and a half when the sergeant whose name I'd forgotten came up and kicked a leg of the chair.

"You're up, big fella."

He looked to be my size until I stood. He was a well-proportioned scale model of a full-grown man, no big head or short arms to give him away until you stood next to him. His burgundy shirt, olive drab safari necktie, and gray pinstripe pants could have been bought in the boys' department at Jacobson's. The Glock in his snap-on belt holster looked as big as a Frontier Colt sticking out behind his miniature hipbone. He must have lied about his height to join the department. He had red hair, freckles, and pale lashes. Maybe he was related to a token Irishman on the city council.

I followed him across the room. On the way past the worker

on the stepladder, he reached up and poked the crack pipe down below the edge of the pocket. I figured he was a pet.

We went down the hall to the same Bermuda Triangle that had claimed the others. I knew the hall, of course, just as I knew every other square inch of 1300 including the basement, where they used to conduct interrogations outside of Eleanor Roosevelt's earshot. The corridor was lined with framed photographs of dead police commissioners, dead retired football greats who had served on the Police Athletic League, dead Hollywood celebrities with tenuous connections to Detroit who'd had their pictures taken with police officials who may or may not be dead by now. Valleys had been worn in the marble floor by eighty years of wing tips, brogues, high heels, sneakers, and hobnails. The building has always been too elegant for the characters who work in it. No serious architect who wants to remain sane ever looks back at what became of his designs after the ribbon-cutting ceremony. There were tobacco stains on the Carrara that had seniority over the chief.

The sergeant went up on tiptoe to peer through a grated window in a door, then opened it, told me to have a seat, and closed it behind me. I couldn't tell if it was one of the rooms I'd been in before. Such rooms aren't planned. They spring up like mushrooms, indistinguishable from one another, from the two-way mirror to the heavy-duty plastic over the ceiling fixture to the furniture, three mismatched chairs and a particleboard table with one fuzzy rounded corner that looked as if it had been gnawed by rats. (Not a fanciful notion; when another Albert Kahn construction, the Packard plant, was imploded, an army of rodents the size of Chihuahuas swarmed across East Grand like British infantry.)

They're not interrogation rooms anymore. That term went out with cattle prods. Now they're interview rooms, a name that went about as deep as the new beige paint on the walls, the turpentine smell covering decades of sweat and cop spittle. As sterile as it looked, the room was as heavy with fear and misery as a hospital and as empty of hope as the walk from a morgue. Transferring me there was just the next chapter of the Wait. I'd skipped five circles of hell, all the way from limbo to the burning plain.

Only one new feature had appeared since my first acquaintance: an industrial-design camcorder on a tripod, aimed at the table area. It had replaced the old suitcase model reel-to-reel tape recorder, which in its turn had nudged out the stenographer, who for many years had been the only feminine presence in that entire seven-story monument to patriarchy. Even the most mannish-looking of the species had managed to introduce a note of hope into the whole bleak experience, like the first tentative birdsong heard at the end of a long winter. They took down your statement efficiently, with a show of disinterest, but if you wanted to hard enough you could hear sympathy in the scratching of their Eberhard Fabers. They were with the department but not of the department. I missed them the way I missed Checker cabs, cigarette billboards, and Captain Kangaroo.

Alderdyce came in right on cue in the middle of this maudlin muddle, followed closely by the miniature detective sergeant. Today the inspector wore a sharp blue pinstripe suit and polka-dot tie, white on red, on a shirt so white it hurt to look at it. He might have come straight there from a job interview at Fifth Third Bank. He strode straight to the other side of the table and smacked down a gray cardboard folder. The sergeant planted himself in front of the door like a toy bouncer.

"Angela Suerto," Alderdyce said.

I'd expected that. He'd given me too much time to sift through all the reasons I might have been tagged. I didn't mention before that the delaying tactic misfires as often as it works.

I said, "And a very Angela Suerto to you, too. Elena Verdugos all around."

"Nobody said you could talk."

I didn't look at the sergeant. It's always a mistake to make eye contact with little yappy dogs.

Alderdyce said, "Let him talk. Talking's what he's best at, didn't you know? This one can talk his way through rings of flame. It's a sight to see." He flipped open the folder. On top was a smudgy eight-by-ten photograph printed on fax paper. A professional like Fritz Fleeman wouldn't have bothered to reproduce it, but police photographers in the third world work on salary just like their brothers in the U.S. Their best work spends most of its life locked away in metal file cabinets.

The Suerto woman was a disappointment. From what I'd heard I'd expected a combination of Yvonne DeCarlo and Jennifer Lopez, one of those overripe Latina beauties with exotic lips and cheekbones and high arched brows, a mane of curly black hair and more curves than a bobsled run. The woman in the photograph looked like something you saw pushing a supermarket cart in an unfashionable suburb, a dumpy forty with a bulldog face and lank hair, gray along the part. But then the photographer hadn't caught her at her best. It was a morgue shot of her pale flaccid body lying naked on a steel table with a drain at the foot. A row of numbers written with chalk or a white grease pencil in one corner contained the date and the order of admittance.

"Stingy end to a gaudy life," Alderdyce said. "Amateur model, cantina dancer, pavement princess, mistress to a revolutionary, *Cadáver numero setentatres* in the mortuary in a city named for a virgin. You supply the irony, I'm fresh out." He peeled aside the picture. The sheet underneath was typewritten, another blurred fax. "Officer Gonzales is translating all this. I got the gist over the phone from a captain whose name I won't try to pronounce because I can't roll my *r*s the way he did. His English wasn't much better than my Spanish, but we worked it out."

"Cops are on the same page the world over," I said.

"See what I mean, Ohanian? You wouldn't want to have missed that."

Ohanian. No way would I have guessed Armenian.

Alderdyce went on. "Jillian Rubio came to this country as an infant. We got that from her mother, but nobody thought to ask if that was the name she went by in the old country. We checked with Immigration. They dug in the basement and came up with her birth name. You want to talk now, take a guess at what it was?"

"You're having too good a time telling it," I said. "I wouldn't want to step on your punch line."

Ohanian made a noise in his throat.

Alderdyce slapped the folder shut. A gust caught the faxed photo and it slid out between the covers, perched on the edge of the table for a second, then floated from there to the floor like the last leaf of autumn. I knew how it felt.

"Gilia Cristobal," he said. "Hell of a coincidence. We got a Gilia Cristobal down the hall. Which is one too many, but wait. Her name isn't Gilia Cristobal. But then the plot thickens, because both Gilias were born in the same country, which begs the question why did they come all the way to Detroit to fight over who gets to keep the name? What's the matter, lost your taste for conversation? You're making me out a liar in front of Sergeant Ohanian."

"How much of this did she tell you?"

"This is an interview room, Walker. You're the interview. I know what." He gripped the back of a chair, hard enough to bend the plastic. "Tell me a stretcher. It's your right. As I recall you were pretty specific about that yesterday. You want to give the speech again? Ohanian didn't hear it."

I got out a cigarette, to play with, not to smoke. I didn't know which one of them was supposed to slap it out of my mouth.

"If you know about Angela Suerto," I said, "you know about Mariposa Flores. Does Immigration know?"

"You heard the inspector. You're the interview, not us."

I was still looking at Alderdyce. "You're a dynamite team. Why don't you drink a glass of water while he talks?"

Ohanian took a step my direction, but his timing was off. He stopped before Alderdyce stuck out a hand.

"INS is busy sorting terrorists," Alderdyce said. "Here's how it plays out. Mariposa and Angela have a boyfriend in common, that hunky rebel type all the girls go for. Mariposa clears out the competition, using Stelazine, then jumps the rap using Gilia's identity. Gilia Number Two makes good stateside, Gilia Number One doesn't. So Gilia Number One sets out to level the field with blackmail. When that gets old, Gilia Number Two reverts to type. Stelazine again. But first she needs a finger, say a private badge who specializes in finding missing persons, to locate Number One so Number Two can slip her the needle. To repeat this information from the beginning, please press Three. No?" He turned his head. "I sure am sorry about this, Sergeant. He talks a blue streak when it's just us."

"Just like that frog in the cartoon."

"Go to hell, both of you," I said. "The Rubio woman's been dead since last November. If I fingered her then, why'd I wait three months and then call your attention to the corpse?"

Ohanian spoke up. "The client's in town, on a tour. She paid you off, probably, but you've had since Thanksgiving to go through it and start to think maybe you undersold yourself. So you go to her with a new deal, but she isn't having any. Presto, you find the stiff, right where you left it."

"Fingering myself while I'm at it."

"I didn't say you were smart. Just greedy."

"I'm lost. Who killed her, me or Gilia Two?"

"You tell us."

"This guy needs to take a walk," I told Alderdyce. "Pull his string, will you?"

"Go to the can, Sergeant." He spoke without looking at him.

"Sure, Inspector?"

"I can tell when a man needs to go to the can."

Ohanian opened the door. "I'll be around, big fella. You won't have to look for me."

I let him take that one on out. I didn't have anything half as good.

The ducts buzzed when the furnace in the basement kicked in. Apart from that the room was quiet. Then Alderdyce scraped out a chair and sat down opposite me, resting his hands in his lap. He looked like a grizzly waiting at the base of a tree with a camper in it.

I said, "The intercom switch used to be under the table. Where is it now?"

"It's off."

"Yeah. No law against lying to a suspect. What about that?" I tilted my head toward the video camera.

He got up, went over to it, studied it for a moment, then pushed a button. The tape cassette licked out into his hand. He put it on the table and sat back down.

I took the cigarette out of my mouth and started to put it back into the pack. The filter end was sodden. I flicked it into a corner. Ohanian would probably have had something to say about that. "She under arrest?"

The inspector shook his head. "Too early. You can't jump the gun with these celebrity cases. If the Simpson case taught us nothing else, it taught us that."

"Good. She's had a harder time than you know."

"Harder's coming."

"You don't know that until you know what's been."

"So tell me."

I did. When it came down to it I wasn't any stronger than the guy on Pilate's divan.

TWENTY-SEVEN

I hate mysteries," Alderdyce said. "You know how many trees have to die just for the paperwork?"

He was back in his seat. Shortly after I'd started talking, he'd gotten up and taken the scenic tour of all three blank walls, avoiding the one with the mirror set into it. No one likes looking at his reflection when there might be someone looking back. He'd stopped pacing only once, when I was telling him what had happened in the kitchen of the house on Adelaide. That story was going to get me free drinks for the rest of my life.

"I didn't know you liked trees. That why you became a cop instead of a forest ranger?"

"Damn straight. Most of the time the killer's sitting there with the body when the uniforms show up, or he steps in the blood on his way out and they just follow the footprints, the shoes are right there in his closet. Or he gets high and rats himself out to his buddies. My next favorite, he thinks he's cute and sprays some phony clues around to send us off in all directions at once. You can break a case in record time in a situation like that. Files we don't close, we know damn good and well whodunit; the witnesses won't cooperate. This Ellery Queen shit just gums up the works."

"DNA's supposed to do away with all that."

"It could, if the lab rats didn't brag it around. Fingerprints did the job until every sneak thief who could read Frank Merriwell figured out a ten-cent pair of gloves made him invisible. Couple of years ago some suburban cops found the body of a lady psychiatrist washed down with bleach, and they'd still be working it if someone hadn't talked. Nobody would've ever thought of bleach if some geek criminologist hadn't spilled his guts to *Popular Science*. The next generation of sex killers will wear radiation suits and pack douche bags."

"That ought to make them easy to spot."

"What we need here is an Official Secrets Act like they got in England. First time some sleazebag TV producer has an actor hold forth on blood patterns and oblique trajectories, the feds arrest him and shut down the show. Half the audience is criminals taking notes."

"Chill out, John. It's entertainment. If your idea catches on, all we'll have left is quilting shows and celebrity wrestling. We beat England twice. No one else has since 1066 and I like to think it's because of our leisurely arts."

"Who do you like for Rubio?" Change-up.

"Your boy Ohanian just about convinced me I did it."

He lifted a hand. "Ohanian's uncle's a philanthropist. The police lab got an electron microscope and we got Ohanian. We looked out the window when he walked under the 'You must be this tall' sign. He's short, but enthusiastic. He makes sure nobody nips a cup of coffee without feeding the kitty."

I tipped my head toward the mirror. "He's watching us right now, isn't he?"

"I don't think he reads lips. He has a point where you're concerned, you know. You're an obstructor of justice and damn near an accessory after the fact." He made it sound casual. Alderdyce was never more dangerous than when he was being your friend.

"You official types get me. You start out thinking you've got the corner on justice and wind up believing you're justice itself. That's how dictators get made."

"Listen to yourself, Che. Couple of hours with Barbara Fucking Fritchie and you're ready to strap on bandoliers and overthrow the system. Meanwhile you've got fifteen grand of hers in the bank. What else is she giving you?"

"Go boil your head."

He barked a laugh. "Where the hell'd you come up with that?"

"Fellow named Fleeman. He and Ohanian probably belong to the same chat room. I've had it in for the system ever since I found out Lassie was a boy, ditto the system for me. It happens I have a positive balance for a change. It's not against the law yet, Cromwell." I took out another cigarette, and this time I lit up. "The system's okay. I'm prepared to let it go on a while. It's just slow to start, and once it starts it's impossible to stop. You work for it, you're prejudiced in its favor. Most of the people I work for are prejudiced the other way. It rubs off. Where Gilia comes from, you don't go to the police. They make house calls, and if you know they're coming you try not to be at home."

"Which Gilia we talking about?"

"Legally speaking, Jillian Rubio wasn't Gilia Cristobal anymore. For the sake of this conversation, let's just let the one who's still using the name go on using it for now. You can always take it away later."

"That's fine. Assigning them numbers was the sergeant's idea."

I passed up another chance to club that dodo. "Okay, the police here aren't the police she's used to, but like I said, the system's the system. Proving she didn't kill the Suerto woman would get her off one hook back home and onto another. Coming out as Mariposa Flores, which she would have to do if she went to the police here, would put her on a hook with INS and probably the State Department, which has a long history of sticking to the rules. More so this year. What's waiting for her if she gets deported for bending those rules isn't their problem. Remembering that she makes five thousand dollars in the time it takes to floss every morning, if you were in her shoes and somebody offered not to involve the authorities in your tangled past for the price of five grand per month, what would you do?"

"I'd pay it. I'm not so sure I'd commit murder." He thought for a second. "No, I'm sure I wouldn't. That's what's wrong with your example. I'm not Gilia."

"You're forgetting Rubio's life insurance."

"That's almost always a bluff."

"You know it, I know it. Maybe even Gilia knows it. Calling it is another whole thing. But say she did. Wouldn't she use just about any method but the one that got her in trouble in the first place? Stelazine isn't that easy to come by. You need to be part of the medical community, or have a prescription. Why go to the trouble, any sort of trouble, if by doing it you'd just be signing your name to a second murder? Why not just crack Rubio over the head?"

"Amateurs commit most murders. They hardly ever change their methods the second time. Rubio had a prescription, by the way. The cops in Minnesota talked to her doctor. Her death broke the Hippocratic seal. She was bipolar and some other things. There was no bottle in her medicine cabinet, so she was probably traveling with it."

I smoked on that. I shook my head. "Mariposa wasn't just sleeping with a revolutionary. She helped him fight. She didn't leave her native smarts behind with her name. I don't see her painting herself into that corner."

"If she had it done, which is likely, using the same poison would be a terrific way for the hired help to jam her up. It would sweeten the pot later. People who outsource murders never seem to stop and think about the market they're creating for blackmail. Even the smart ones can be dumb. Go ahead, take a puff while I think about who the hire might have been."

"No puff's that short," I said. "Hector Matador."

"I like Matador. I like him a bushel and a peck. Don't tell me you don't."

"Matador's in love."

"Uh-uh. For that you've got to have the equipment."

"That's pretty much what I said when he told me. I was trying to make him snap at the bait. He'd already bought my faith for a penny."

"Oh, that. Another bluff. If he were serious, he'd have gone ahead and blinded you anyway. Those Colombians make bin Laden look like Count Chocula."

"Except why go to so much trouble to find out what Rubio did with the papers that made her case? Even if he lost his head and killed her before she could tell him? What could they be, a copy of her birth certificate, some newspaper clippings on the Suerto murder, maybe a bootlegged police report? You found out everything that was in them with one telephone call. They were only a threat because they might bring official attention to Gilia's immigration once Rubio was too dead to do it in person. If he wanted to go on bleeding Gilia, all he had to do was threaten to holler cop."

"In which case we'd burn him down right along with her."

"She wouldn't know that. He wouldn't tell her. You're not listening." I laid a column of ash in an old burn canal on the tabletop. There were no ashtrays. It struck me then that the place had probably gone no-smoking along with every other government building. I couldn't seem to avoid breaking the law that week. "But if you're Matador, and you *don't* want to jam her up, those papers are very valuable. You would blind a man, or anyway convince him you were going to, if you thought that would put them in your hands so you could set a match to them. The goon's in love. It happens. It happened to King Kong."

"He had to know we'd find out sooner or later. Even if Rubio was bluffing and there weren't any papers, we'd dig up her real name and go from there. Which is what we did."

"He's a freebooter. He'd lop off the first head as soon as it showed, then wait for the next and lop off that one. That's how he made it to the top the first time; ask Frankie Acardo. The only reason you got him is the heads outnumbered him in the end."

"It fits the facts," he said. "I hate that almost as much as I hate murder mysteries. There's usually a gap or two."

"That all you got?"

"That and the picture of Matador as Romeo. Macbeth, maybe." He got up again, and this time he walked right up to the mirror. With his back to me he said, "I don't owe Washington a damn thing except my taxes. What happens if I send them this information by way of the slow train to Newfoundland?"

"You might get that autographed CD for your kid on the *Theodore Roosevelt.*"

"*Ronald Reagan.* She already promised it. Your stories mesh, incidentally. Couple of gaps, like there ought to be in your theory. She's a tough little butterfly. And damn nice. You didn't hear me say that."

"Who'd believe me? You wouldn't tell me where the intercom switch is."

"I need a statement. On videotape."

"That go on the slow train?"

"Say it did. It's not a trade. I've already got enough to break your license and put you on twenty thousand hours of community service. You dropping the investigation?"

"You telling me to?"

"I would have, before my boy shipped out."

I didn't say anything. He didn't seem to be finished.

He said, "It would've seemed important then. It used to seem important to fish hookers out of the river and tie them around some pimp's neck and throw him in County. Plenty's changed."

"Things will get back to normal," I said. "The president says so. Your boy will come back from his hitch, get laid in San Diego, and marry some tramp. They'll come to visit with their whiny little brood and hit you up for money. When they do, they'll find you up to your ears in dead hookers, happy as Friday night."

"Someone's got to do it, right?"

"That's what they say."

"Why?"

"I don't know. They don't say."

"Who the hell are *they*, anyway?"

"Everybody who's not you or me."

"That what they teach you in toy detective school? Always have an answer?"

Again I didn't say anything. I didn't have an answer.

He turned from the mirror. He was as calm as a lagoon. "Who killed Jillian Rubio? Same person who killed Angela Suerto?"

"No."

"So you know who killed Rubio. You kind of left that out when you were talking."

"I don't know who killed Rubio. It wouldn't be the same person who killed Suerto. That person spent the last year in a cell and hanged himself there last week."

TWENTY-EIGHT

The lagoon rippled. "The rebel boyfriend? Why him?"

"He had a medical background, and being a passionate and dedicated leader, he'd know how to use it to obtain the medicines you need to fight a dirty war with lots of casualties. Many of them are poisonous if not diluted, Stelazine more than most."

"That's how. I asked why."

"Gilia said Suerto would betray him. She didn't mean sexually; she was talking about spying for the enemy. She thought he didn't know. Probably he was a better general than she gave him credit for. He identified the problem and eliminated it, with minimal loss." I held up one index finger.

"How much of that is guesswork?"

"As much as needed. The revolution's over, and so is Nico. Everything else is mop-up."

Alderdyce rewound the tape, popped it out of the camera, and slipped it into his side pocket. He said he'd shelve it with the training videos.

I got up from the table. I felt like I'd been sitting in the bleachers for twelve innings. "What about the happy Armenian?"

"He's been kissing his way up the chain of command since

he made plainclothes. Inspector's as far as he's gotten this year. Forget him."

"Now all we have to worry about is CNN, *Entertainment Tonight*, and *People*."

"We had security problems with her video. If they see through that, we'll tell 'em a bunch of new ones. Best way to keep a secret is tell a thousand lies. That way, whatever leaks out gets lost in the flood. You should understand that better than anyone." He opened the door. "She wants to see you."

I didn't ask who. "Where?"

"Her hotel, I guess. I left word to kick her an hour ago."

"I need to catch supper first."

"I hear the room service at the Hyatt doesn't suck."

"No good, John. I like 'em tall and brassy with tattoos."

"Try that on someone who hasn't known you since the sandbox."

"We still know each other?"

"Not just yet. You played this like a sucker from Day One."

"I know. It wouldn't have been my first choice if there were a way to play it smart."

"It's still happening. Matador knows you're here. What do you think he'll do now that Mariposa's police property?"

"He's tried to kill me before. The novelty's run out."

"I bet you said the same thing when he came at you with that hot penny. I'd have paid to see that."

On my way out I saw the little sergeant talking to the good-looking Domestic Disturbances detective in the red skirt. She was shaping her nails at her desk with a file attached to a key ring shaped like a miniature set of brass knuckles. He was in up to his neck and didn't seem to notice me.

The snow had stopped, leaving cottony fluff on the streetlamps and my car, which was parked legally this time. When I reached in for the brush, Gilia was sitting on the passenger's side in her costly counterfeit furs. The hat was a Russian shako type and she had the tall collar of her coat turned up for warmth. Her face looked small and almost calm. She smiled shyly.

"It looked like the car you would drive. I knew I'd find your name on the papers in the glove box. I expected a gun."

"It comes up out of the hood at rush hour. Didn't the cops offer you a ride?"

"I said I had one. Did I lie?"

"There's a brush on the floor on your side. I need it."

"Brush?" She looked down. The domelight didn't reach.

"It's like a big toothbrush. For the snow. In this zip code we need to see to drive."

She found it and passed it across the seat. She had on snug black leather gloves with fur trim, but she was shivering and her breath curled. I got in, started the engine, and showed her how to work the defroster. The snow pushed off about as easily as wet laundry and I had to use the scraper hard on the clotted ice on the windows, but by the time I got to the windshield the heat from inside had begun to melt it. The car was toasty when I tossed the brush into the back and slid under the wheel. She'd removed the gloves and opened her coat, underneath which was a long red knitted wool dress that clung to her like poured honey.

"I never saw snow in my life until the first time I played Denver," she said. "It's still kind of alien to me."

"That's the way it looks to me every December." I tugged on the headlamps. "Dearborn?"

"Where do you live?"

"Refrigerator carton on Livernois."

"Seriously."

"Someone lives in a refrigerator carton on Livernois. I bet he's serious about it."

"Are you mad at me?"

"Nothing personal. My guess is you don't invite yourself to addresses in Beverly Hills. You wait to be asked. Why you should think it's any different here is the point at issue."

"If you think I'm trying to take you to bed—"

"It's been done. Right now I'm hungry, and all I've got in the house is a box of Morton's salt."

"Where's a good restaurant?"

"Toledo."

"Where's that?"

"Ohio."

"There must be something closer."

"There's Greektown, but I don't feel like it. The waiters set fire to things and yell. In the old days they called that pillaging."

"Well, I don't want to go back to the Hyatt. We might run into Hector."

"You two fall out?"

"Not exactly. Hector's like—Greektown. Sometimes I don't feel like him. Where are we going?"

I'd pulled out into the street. "I live in a Polish neighborhood. There's a take-out place not far from me, if you don't mind garlic."

"You really don't want to go to bed, do you? What happened to not inviting myself to the castle keep?"

"I'm inviting you."

"You're an exasperating man."

"That's what you get when you've been kidnapped, tortured, threatened by cops, and had dogs set on you. Incidentally, you didn't kill Angela Suerto. Zubarán backed up your story. That bird thing brought him around."

She rode for a block in silence. "Does it matter?"

"It matters a hell of a lot to me. Whether it matters to Washington is between them and your attorney. Alderdyce is sitting on it for now, but too many know. Did you get in touch with your lawyer like I said?"

"He's aware of the situation. Do the police think I killed Jillian Rubio?"

"They're on the fence. They're not like the cops you're familiar with. They don't make up their minds until most of the precincts are heard from."

"What about you?"

"I think if you wanted her dead you'd use just about anything but what was used." I stopped for a light, pumping the brakes to avoid locking the wheels. "Zubarán said a friendly guard smuggled your name in to him before he was sprung. Who do you think arranged that?"

"I don't know," she said after a moment. "Nico's whore, possibly, to get me into trouble."

"Uh-uh. She'd have sent it to the warden or the police. The professor thought it was meant to encourage him. He was wrong too."

We watched a night-crawling diesel rig cut the corner off a left turn onto our street, missing the Cutlass' left front fender by inches. The light was green by the time it cleared. I started forward.

"Who, then?" asked Gilia.

"Nico. He sent it so Zubarán would be able to identify you later, to give you an alibi for the night of Suerto's murder. He'd planned it that far ahead. I guess he loved you in his fashion."

She thought about that for half a mile. "I underestimated him. Poor Nico."

"There are two ways to lose a war: trusting too much and not trusting at all. He was coming to the halfway point the night he sent you to rescue the professor. I don't know where he was when they caught him. Too far the other way, maybe. But he did what he could to protect you."

"I thought he was showing faith in me."

"He was. If an alibi was all he was offering, he could have sent you into town for cigarettes."

"You told the police all this?"

"If I hadn't, one of us would still be in custody. Don't undersell Washington the way you undersold Nico. They have entirely different protocols for foreign revolutionaries and murderers. The wheels turn more slowly. A smart lawyer ought to be able to jam a stick between the spokes."

"But not if I'm accused of killing Jillian Rubio."

"That's next on the list. But only after supper." I wheeled into the little cleared parking lot of the takeout place on Joseph Campau.

Gilia had the appetites of a proletariat. Peering through the thick glass in the ancient display case she chose kielbasa sandwiches with heavy slices of pumpernickel and cabbage soup from a massive crock. I threw in a container of turtle soup and a quart of milk, paid the counterman, an incongruous black in a white apron and hairnet, and carried the greasy sack out to the car. A few minutes later we pulled into my garage.

I helped her out of her coat and put it and her hat in a closet while she shook out her mane. She took the tour of the living room as I poured out the milk and transferred the food from paper and Styrofoam to crockery.

"Such a masculine house," she said when she returned. Silhouetted against the lamplight in the doorway, the knitted dress didn't give my imagination much to work with.

"I sweep out the hormones every day, but they keep coming back." I laid out napkins on the kitchen table.

"Was there ever a *Mrs.* Walker?"

"That was over before you were born."

"You're not so old."

"You're not so young. Sit."

She slid into the nook. "Are you Polish?"

"I'm not anything." I took a long drink of milk. I was thirstier than I was hungry. No one had offered me so much as a glass of water at 1300.

"I thought all Americans came from somewhere else, except of course the Indians."

"Them too. They came across the Bering Strait from Siberia. The only real natives were mammoths and midget horses, which they managed to wipe out long before Columbus. I never dug into the family history. I do enough of that kind of thing during working hours."

"And just what are your working hours?"

"Nineteen seventy-five to the present."

"There must be an easier way to make a living."

"Spoken like a true American. There must be an easier way than singing and dancing." I picked up my sandwich.

"You're one of the few outsiders who realize that. I am always up before dawn and seldom in bed before midnight. I have no social life."

"That's not what I hear."

"What you hear is carefully choreographed. When you see a

picture of me on the arm of a bankable movie star, it is the climax of a complicated business negotiation. I might add they are the only climaxes I experience." She stirred her soup. Then she let the spoon drift. "Before you take a bite of that sandwich."

The nook was a tighter fit for me than it was for her. I was still sitting when she slid out and draped herself awkwardly across my lap and kissed me. Whatever she was wearing won out against the garlic and cabbage.

When we separated I put down the sandwich. "This how you worked the balcony scene?"

Her dark eyes were puzzled. Then she nodded. "I thought I saw something moving in the bushes that day. Did you see the picture?"

"I couldn't afford it."

"That, too, was a business deal."

"What's this?"

"Recreation." She kissed me again.

"This won't work here," I said when we came up.

She undraped herself, but only long enough for me to stand up. This time I had leverage on my side. Her teeth scraped at my tongue. Then the kitchen went white.

"Amos!" It was a gasp.

I was already moving. The flash was fading from the window. I went out the back door and ran around the corner. His Geo was parked in the street and he might have made it except he turned and aimed his flashgun at me and I deflected my vision to the ground without slowing up. The bulb flared and I lunged and snatched the camera out of his hands. It was strapped around his neck. I twisted the camera and threw my weight against him, pinning him against the car and choking him. His Dodgers cap slid off. His greasy hair stuck down all around like Beetle Bailey's, only a lot less tidy, and he was bald at the crown like a monk. He still needed a bath. In the light from the corner streetlamp his face was dark with congestion, the whites of his eyes glittering. I untwisted the strap, snaked it up and over his head in one movement, groped until I found the catch on the back of the camera, and yanked out the film like glistening entrails.

"I got Jeff Daniels on that roll!" He sounded more squeaky than usual. He was still filling his lungs.

I hit him hard in the chest with the camera. He expelled what he had and hugged it as if I might take it away again. I leaned my face close to his. "Get back in this roller skate and go. If I see it or you again I'll have you up on a morals charge before you can say Woody Allen."

"There ain't no Lieutentant Franklin with the Detroit cops! I checked."

"I mean for window peeping. Some of my neighbors have visiting grandchildren. There's no telling what you had on that roll. It won't convict you, but the complaint will follow you from here to the Riviera. Go back to Hollywood. All you have to worry about there is private security and Sean Penn with a snootful."

I gave him some space. He looked around, found his cap, and slapped it onto his head along with a fistful of slush. It was still running down his face when he scrambled into the driver's seat and spun his wheels. This time I stepped back far enough to avoid getting splashed.

Fritz Fleeman. The next time I heard the name, the L.A. cops had him in custody for trespassing on Alec Baldwin's estate.

Gilia was standing at the back door when I waded back through the snow on the lawn. Her face was tight. "Did you get the film?"

"I trashed it. Let's eat."

She didn't argue. The mood was as dead as Jillian Rubio.

TWENTY-NINE

I slid into the curb around the corner from the Hyatt. With most of the windows lit up it looked like cut crystal against a sky swiped clean of stars. There was more snow coming, or one of those spitty February rains if the temperature went up.

She opened her door. "I'm sorry. A boy should be able to see his girl home."

"I'm not a boy, and you're not my girl. Apart from that you're right. I still say I can use the publicity."

"It isn't that. We might run into Hector. He is a dangerous man."

"I told you that. You didn't believe me."

"I did not know then he was in love with me."

She let go of the door and leaned over and kissed me. Then she slid her glove down my cheek. "I cannot help thinking we have missed an opportunity, *hombre*."

"We'll always have Hamtramck."

She laughed the way she sang, with all of her life behind it. The joke wasn't that good. She got out then and swung the door shut. I watched her under the streetlamps, small and elegant in her furs, until she vanished around the corner. Then I let out the clutch and coasted away. The street shone like oil, with clumps of plowed snow piled like runes in the gutters.

I didn't want to go home. I bought a copy of the *News* from a sidewalk stand and found a Denny's and read the paper front to back, sipping coffee someone had drained from a radiator with the night help vacuuming up crumbs around my feet. There was nothing new on the Rubio investigation, and dead Nico had dropped right out of the columns, replaced by suicide bombers in the Middle East. Even a shaky self-hanging was no competition for a nineteen-year-old fanatic with a vest made of C-4. But they found ten inches on the front page for the video Gilia was shooting in Mexicantown. Half of metropolitan Detroit had blown off a day's wage hoping for a shot as an extra. After that I couldn't find a thing to laugh at in the comics.

When I'd had my fill of black coffee and yellow press I paid my bill and drove around the suburbs, listening to an all-night truckers' station selling broken hearts and Thermo King refrigeration units. There wasn't much traffic, most of the houses were dark, and the store windows spilled the ghostly blue glow of security lights.

I wasn't pining for lost love. I had boxes of .38 cartridges older than she was, and people who took up with stars who weren't themselves stars always wound up looking like empties along the freeway. I had a skinful of caffeine and garlic and a bellyful of cops and crooks and university professors and a murder no one much cared about except the ones whose job it was to care about it and a middle-aged woman who bred large dogs, *muy fiero*. Except if it wasn't solved before the feds mixed in, a lot of people would care on the double.

A small car almost clipped me as I turned into my street. It was going twice the limit and I wouldn't have paid it any more attention than the close call with the truck earlier except it's a quiet neighborhood. Not that many people drive through it that late, and when they do they aren't hurrying. It was moving too fast and the block was too dark for me to make it out in detail. It might have been a Chevy Corsica. It might have been brown.

I parked half a block from the house, popped open the booby hatch, checked the load in the Luger, and stuck it under my belt on the left side where I could get to it fast using a cross draw. I flicked off the domelight and got out and eased the door into the frame without latching it. I made very little noise, but it sounded like explosions in the stillness.

Most of the houses on the street were dark. Silver-blue light throbbed in the ground-floor window of the saltbox two doors down from mine where the old woman who took the Polish-language newspaper sat up watching infomercials on her black-and-white set. It went out suddenly as I was walking. That made it a little after 1:00 A.M. She was as reliable as the nuclear clock in the U.S. Naval Observatory for keeping time.

It took me ten minutes to get from my car to my front door. I kept as much as I could to the shadows and tried not to hurry through the lighter patches from one to the next. There was something on the door that might have been a leaf from last autumn, carried by a gust and stuck there with frost. There is always one house that attracts debris from the street and on that block it's mine. I ignored the object and tried the knob. It was locked, just the way I'd left it. I hadn't expected anyone waiting inside to give himself away by leaving it open, but whatever I had that passed for instinct and experience told me the house was empty.

I looked closer at the thing on the door. I found my pencil flash in my pocket and snapped it on. The thing was black, with fragile-looking membranous wings, which stretched out as they were didn't extend any farther than a man's spread hand. A tiny, bunched, ugly face, almost eyeless, but whose ears were nearly as large as a cat's. Someone had nailed it to the center panel with a three-inch galvanized spike through the thorax. I didn't know if it had been dead at the time, but if it hadn't, that would have done it.

A bat. That was something new.

THIRTY

"*Vampyrum spectrum*," Barry Stackpole said. "More commonly known as the vampire bat; the false vampire, actually, with a big range throughout South America. The true vampire is Central American, and kind of disappointing, growing no larger than our little friend here. This one's a baby. Easier to smuggle through Customs, I imagine."

We were looking at a screen-size closeup on his seventeen-inch monitor. The squashed face, big ears, and exposed nasal cavity were identical to the face of the dead specimen spread out on a sheet of Xerox paper on the computer desk. I'd put on gloves to remove it from my front door and dump it into a Ziploc bag, which he'd opened and taken by the corners to slide the carcass out onto the sheet. We'd both heard too much about rabies in bats to handle it. Not to mention how many Bela Lugosi movies we'd watched.

It was Saturday morning. I'd left my little visitor in the garage overnight, slept James Bond–style with one hand on the Smith & Wesson under a second pillow, and made an appointment with Barry over the telephone after coffee. He was living in Highland Park that year, in a rented ranch style with a spare bedroom that looked like the control room of the Starship *Enterprise*; back when he was still working for other people, he'd had the reputation of never leaving a job without taking some of the equipment with him. Apart from the technology, it was a modest little place in a suburb that was struggling against the gravitational pull of Detroit. That black hole was hungry for population and would annex hell to have it. When it comes to maintaining a low profile, Barry makes Salman Rushdie look like Madonna.

"How come you know so much about bats?" I said.

"Degrees of separation."

Having thus enlightened me, he boogied his keyboard and brought up a file slugged SLEEPING WITH FISH. Without pausing, he scrolled through a glossary of underworld terms and plinked up rapid-fire explosions of color-coded sidebars, most of which lingered barely long enough for me to form an impression of what they contained. Some came with graphics. I spotted the comic valentine in Machine Gun Jack McGurn's dead hand, several Mafia *coups de grace* (loose translation: bullet holes in heads), severed Yakuza fingers, a black hand traced on a scrap of paper, orchards of flaming crosses, a nightmare shot of a dead stool pigeon with his own genitals crammed into his mouth; other images that meant nothing to me, but had obviously meant a great deal to someone else. Whoever said crooks lacked imagination had never stopped to contemplate the many colorful ways the criminal class in every society has thought up to sign its work and warn nonbelievers of the wages of sin. Sin being whatever the local gang lord, warrior chief, shogun, Grand Wizard, or head accountant defined it to be.

"Black Panthers used to mail a crow to suspected FBI informers," Barry muttered, possibly to himself. "They called it 'slipping 'em the Jim.' Clever."

I made no comment. My back was sore from bending over his shoulder and the MTV activity on-screen made my eyes smart. For a lot of people, the Internet is a doorway to the universe. For me, it's a boon to the aspirin industry.

"*Voilà!* Or, I should say, *olé!*" He'd made one final tap and sat back with a flourish.

I looked at a newspaper page with a blurred black-and-white photo of a thickset, bearded Hispanic in a storm trooper cap and

Sam Browne belt, stretching a small bat between his hands. The text was in Spanish.

"Holy what?" I said. "I left my Berlitz at home."

"Oh, sorry." He tapped five keys in the time it would take me to strike one on my old Underwood. The page disappeared and a translation took its place, in bold yellow letters against royal blue.

"But why wear out your eyes?" he said. "This story hit the fan several years ago. Seven or eight stiffs turned up in Medellin one week—hardly front-page material there, that's a slow Monday—but they were all employed in the transportation business: taxi drivers, streetcar conductors, tour boat captains, commuter pilots, of which the city has more than Alaska. Mules, naturally; still not Section A. Except according to friends and relatives of the deceased, in every case the victim had received a dead bat by way of private messenger services. There was some confusion for a while about whether the bats were true vampires of the variety found in Nicaragua and Panama or the false type I mentioned at the start of my lecture. Not important. Finally someone thought to bring in a sociologist from the university in Bógota, who traced the practice back to the Chibchan Indians near Cartagena in the sixteenth century, who believed that stray bats only visited the dwellings of those who were about to die. Could be coincidence. Modern drug lords are not known to test high in anthropology. But after those corpses showed, the government started having difficulty finding paid informants at any price."

"They identify the drug lord behind it?"

"ID's never a problem down there; they list in the Yellow Pages." He scrolled down two paragraphs. "Jose Cipriano Nuñez, an avuncular character called Papa Joe by those who dealt with him directly. There wasn't a waiting list. They tended to outgrow their usefulness inside six weeks and float picturesquely down the Rio Cauca."

"What would a Medellin Cartel big shot be doing in Detroit? L.A.'s their big market."

"Papa Joe's not anywhere, except all over the central Cordilleras. Someone scored a direct hit on his classic '34 Bentley with an artillery shell in a mountain pass four years ago. Criminal waste of a beautiful automobile. Bógota suspects his brother-in-law, Francisco. He moved up five slots on the *Fortune* Five Hundred list of scumbags, scalawags, and highbinders the next week. There's a footnote."

He crossed his artificial leg over his good one and grinned at me. I waited. My back spasmed. I leaned forward then and tapped a couple of keys, any old couple of keys. A list of names appeared on the screen and a box with a snippy little legend asked if the user wanted to delete this file, yes/no. Barry spat a stream of invective, uncrossed his legs, and manipulated his mouse. A tiny blue pistol poked its muzzle at "no." He waited, then exhaled, brought up his screen saver. This was a montage of tommy guns, armored sedans, and fedoraed plug-uglies from the golden age of the gangster film. I could never figure out if he hated racketeers or revered them, even as he was exposing them. Maybe he'd wanted to be one and his father wouldn't buy him a blackjack.

"Where'd you learn to do that?" he said. "I thought you didn't know a control key from a bottle cap."

"I don't. Let's hear the footnote."

"To be called Papa, it helps to be one. Hector Matador was the first one to call him that."

I nodded. "I always thought Matador was a guerrilla name."

"A show of surprise might be expected," he said. "It might even be appreciated. When you play a friend for a numbskull, one might consider it the least you could do."

His face was as flat as paint. It only got that way when he was close to blowing. The only thing separating his brain from the open air was a sheet of steel not much thicker than foil.

I said, "Boo frigging hoo. Sometimes the friend's an enemy."

"How many stories have I sat on for you?"

"Matador is one of those things you're not objective about. If I'd told you he was in it, you'd have been on him like a bumper sticker. There's a whole generation of would-be newshawks around town who make their time following you from lead to lead. This one's hotter than hot. It's fission."

"You said the other day this was a quid pro quo to be named later. Later's now."

"More than ever."

I gave it to him, starting with Gilia at Cobo and finishing with the bat nailed to my front door. I had to lay it out in order; otherwise the two things didn't belong to one story. Listening, he closed his eyes a couple of times, to commit a name or an address to memory. He'd gotten out of the habit of taking notes when the Supreme Court decided they were public property. The Adelaide episode made no visible impression. He went through worse every time the climate changed.

"Alderdyce had a hard-on against Matador," he said when I'd wrapped. "Always has. I don't see him for this. A slug in the brain's more his style. And he could be in love, why not? Cops forget these guys have glands and follicles and a circulatory system just like them. If they were machines they'd never get caught."

I leaned my back against the only section of wall not covered with electronics. He had the only chair. "That's how I see it. I didn't want to. The guy's a coatrack. You want to hang something on him even if you didn't bring a coat."

"That's how conviction records get broken. The Rubio woman had a partner. Either he surprised her on her way to the bus stop or she arranged with him for the ride and the bus story was just a blind so her mother wouldn't know she was part of a double act. If there's anything at all to that 'in the event of my death' dodge, it suggests a partner, someone to hold the evidence and deliver it."

"Banks have safe-deposit boxes and hardly ever cut themselves in on blackmail," I said. "Also she wasn't greedy enough for two. Gilia tips her hairdresser more than five grand a month."

"Winos kill each other over a slug of Boone's Farm. Half of five grand's a fortune when you're working for minimum wage. Some people spend their lives too close to the ground to aim high. There had to be a partner. People get abducted and killed every day by strangers. Some of them may be extortionists. One or two might be poisoned. Not with this poison, though, and not this victim."

"Alderdyce said Stelazine was used to tie in Gilia and hike the ante."

"Even a cop gets a bright idea now and then." Barry had lost his police credentials when a packet of cash dropped out of a chief's ceiling during remodeling and Barry broke the story on his cable show. The chief had gone to prison but the whistle-blower's privileges weren't restored. These days he didn't even read *Dick Tracy*.

"He also thought Gilia hired Matador to do the job," I said.

"I wouldn't mind tying it around his neck myself. It would be one way to balance out the karma for all the knots he's slipped. But you have to have a client."

"Yeah. Sorry about that. Next time I get the urge I'll stick a fork in a wall socket. After this job it'll be a vacation."

"I didn't mean it like that."

"Sure you did." I raised two fingers in absolution. "I still don't like Rubio breaking a family reunion in half to keep an appointment she'd had standing for months. I think I'll go down to Mexicantown tomorrow and have another look around."

"Why tomorrow?"

"It's Sunday. Miranda Guzman takes her favorite pooch with her when she goes to church. She keeps the rest locked up in the kennel out back."

"You're a little old to be crawling through transoms."

"I'm no older than anyone who knows what a transom is. Being able to get into a movie on a student ID doesn't make you Peter Pan."

"Okay, so we're both old. When did that happen?"

"I'm jinxed enough without this discussion. So you want the bat?"

"If you didn't, I thought I'd put it in Lucite, stick it on the shelf next to the change purse they made out of Willie Santacetti's scrotum. Want me to watch your back? These *mestizos* play for marbles."

I shook my head. "When Matador comes at me, it'll be from the front. He'll want me to know who's killing me."

"At least let me get you a tranquilizer gun," he said. "For the dogs, not Matador. For him you need a wooden stake."

"Where would you get a tranquilizer gun? All your contacts use bullets."

"The Malevolenza brothers ran a horse parlor out of a big-game preserve up in Midland until the feds kicked it in last summer. I was with the second team. If I'd gone in with the first, I could have brought back a water buffalo."

"I'd have more use for the buffalo. These dogs sprinkle tranquilizer guns on their kibble." I took my coat off a table stacked high with computer manuals and shrugged into it. "Do you ever get to thinking all these popcorn machines might edge you out of your job?"

"Never. They can hack into a file, but they can't peek through a keyhole. What about you?"

"Same answer. So how come I need a license and you don't?"

"First Amendment, pal. I serve the public all of a piece, not one at a time like you."

I started to button the coat, then remembered to leave it open. I was wearing the .38 all the time now and needed access. "We okay?"

He drummed his fingers on the arm of his ergonomic chair. "If Channel Seven breaks this before me, we may not ever be okay again."

"I'll call you right after nine-one-one."

"By then you may get my voice mail. Ever since they installed cordless phones I can monitor all the emergency calls in the greater metropolitan area."

"That's just about the most illegal thing I ever heard."

"No more illegal than crawling through transoms. Word of advice? Don't go down there wearing a pork chop around your neck."

I had a good answer, but he was already back at the keyboard, playing the underworld fugue. I let myself out. No one shot at me in the thirty-foot stretch from the house to the car, but that didn't stop the skin between my shoulder blades from crawling. Matador would come from the front, but I wasn't so sure about his squad of irregulars.

THIRTY-ONE

A. Walker Investigations."

"I wasn't sure if I would catch you in. Back home I was told Americans never worked weekends."

An overmodulated TV voice was speaking in the background on his end, but I recognized the accent.

"The streets aren't paved with gold, either," I said. "How are you, Professor?"

"Exhausted and irritated. My internal clock is three hours fast. I was expected to retire last night at what was for me seven P.M. so that I would be fresh to address a breakfast meeting at lunchtime. Why does man fly?"

"Why do birds walk? How's the weather?"

"Predictable and bland, with a forty percent chance of earthquakes. I was wondering if our little talk had borne fruit."

"Some. It's a little green right now, but I expect it to get ripe in a day or two." I stopped myself there for the sake of metaphors everywhere. "Do you know anything about bats?"

The TV droned on about a fire in Laurel Canyon. The sun wouldn't be up yet outside his hotel room. "Do they all leave a mission wall at the same time?"

"I don't know."

"Then my answer is very little. Is it important?"

"Only to bats and Indians. I was just making conversation. I don't have much in common with educators."

"Nor do I. They are self-important bores. But I can neither lay brick nor repair an automobile engine." The TV went silent. "I wanted you to know that the young woman we discussed is an individual of character. I define character as a capacity to acknowledge and atone for the wrongs one has committed. It is a quality not uncommon among my fellow countrymen, though you would not know this by observing the behavior of our government. We do not look upon expiation as a birthright."

I went silent myself for a moment. "Excuse me one second, Professor. Someone's at the door." I laid the telephone on the blotter, got out a handkerchief and mopped both palms. I picked the receiver back up. "False alarm, sorry. Would you repeat what you just said?"

He did, word for word. I thanked him and wished him a safe trip. He said something equally courteous, and we passed out of each other's life. You never hear about academics and detectives again once the gods have stopped mucking around with the smooth steady line of your life. I hung up and looked at my palms. Epiphanies always bring out the stigmata in me.

The telephone rang again. Alderdyce didn't seem surprised to have caught me in the office. He asked if anything was new.

"Vampire bats are Central American, false vampires range wider and farther south," I said. "That's about it."

"I'll take your word for it. The only bats I know anything about are Louisville Sluggers." That ended that line of conversation. For a detective, he wasn't very curious. "I thought you'd want to know we lost Matador."

"Uh-huh. Lost as in bereavement or lost as in you're reassigning another surveillance team to Dumpster detail?"

"The little son of a bitch is slipperier than a snotty nickel. Checked out of the Hyatt this morning and dropped his tail like a tadpole inside a dozen blocks. His boy Benito's still in the hotel, for what that's worth. I'm guessing not much. Benny never was much of a challenge for a red-blooded type like you."

"Thanks, John."

"That's it? Thanks?"

"Are you offering police protection?"

"No."

"Then yeah."

"If we see him, we'll pull him in. If he's packing, he'll finish out his sentence."

"He'll be packing. This one's personal."

"We probably won't see him," he said. "He'll be slowing down at yellow lights and signaling his turns. For a murdering bastard he's a cautious sort. How long's it been since you took time off to go fishing?"

"What year is it?"

"I hear the fishing's good off Maui."

"I hear everything's good off Maui. I may go there someday, when no one's chasing me."

"You know what the mortality rate is for heroes?"

"Cowards die too."

"I know. A thousand times, Wilde said. He was wrong about just about everything else, so it shouldn't come as a surprise he was wrong about that."

"I didn't know you read the classics."

"It was either that or a Tigers game, and I knew how that would come out." It was quiet at 1300 for a moment. "You're not good enough, Amos. I memorized his rap sheet. He left a longer one in Colombia and they both read like *The Seven Samurai*."

That gave me pause, but only because I couldn't remember his ever calling me Amos before. "You know his name isn't Matador."

"What's the difference? Ivan the Terrible's parents didn't name him Ivan the Terrible. You have to earn a name like that. They're literal folks down there. They don't call a big man Tiny or a fat man Slim."

"I know. I was just keeping you on the line."

"What are you carrying these days?"

"Chief's Special." I didn't mention the spare Luger in the car. He knew about that, but not officially.

"No one carries those anymore. Get yourself a stopper. Only I wouldn't get one where I had to wait three days to pick it up. That last part's not advice, understand. We're very high on gun control in my line."

"I'm used to the thirty-eight."

"You're one stubborn son of a bitch."

"I love you, too."

I went home at dusk. I'd only gone to the office because that's where I did my best thinking. The thermometer had edged up above freezing but the ground was still cold and the man on the radio who couldn't pronounce "meteorologist" spent most of his two minutes explaining why that meant an ice storm was coming. I picked up supper at a drive-through and ate it driving. I couldn't remember tasting any of it.

The Pistons were playing on TV. I watched most of two quarters, but I got tired of watching grown men swinging from hoops for seven figures and turned it off. I wanted a drink but I didn't pour one. Home isn't home when you can't lower your shield. I was reading a magazine and not taking any of it in when the telephone rang. It was Gilia.

"When I didn't hear from you I thought I'd better call." She sounded high-strung. She was doing a benefit at Cobo Hall that night, a trade-off with the city for permission to shoot her video. I figured she was getting into warrior mode.

"I'm okay. How'd you get this number?"

"I'm famous. Don't tell the people in charge at Ameritech. I wouldn't want to get a fan in trouble. Are you upset?"

"It's okay as long as it's you. I guess you heard Matador checked out."

"That's why I called. I didn't know until just now, when I tried to reach him in his suite. I think he may be coming after you."

"Maybe he's just on a bat." I started to laugh. I shut my mouth. I'm not normally hysterical.

"Why don't you come down and see the show? I'll leave two tickets at the box office. You can bring a friend."

"Thanks. I think I'll stay home. I'm a little tired from doing nothing all day."

A woman was speaking rapid Spanish in the background. I guessed it was Caterina Muñoz, the wardrobe mistress, cursing a crooked seam.

"You're not safe there," Gilia said.

"I wouldn't be any safer at Cobo. It's a good show, but I've seen it. I'll call you tomorrow."

"You should call the police."

"These days the police call me. It's a service they provide for customers who are frequently threatened. It comes with a gold whistle and a plot in Mt. Elliott Cemetery."

"Amos, I'm—"

"Don't say it," I said. "People pay me to find things out. Often the things you have to pay people to find out are things other people don't want found out. It's the reason I charge more than a search engine."

"You don't need to show off to impress me."

"I'm not. I'm doing it to impress me. I got the don't-be-a-hero speech once already today. It was the wrong thing to say for the right reasons. I've put too much time into the first two acts to walk out on the third. That's not heroism, just common curiosity."

"Nico felt the same way. He didn't make it to the curtain."

"Okay, point out the only flaw. But he had an army to fight, and look how long it took them. All I've got is Hector, and he telegraphs his punches. Incidentally, I talked to the professor today."

That derailed her for a beat. "What did he say?"

"He said you have a capacity to atone for past wrongs. He said it's a common characteristic where you both come from. Was he off base?"

"Off base?"

"Full of crap."

"No. I never thought about it, but I wouldn't argue. It's a Catholic country, after all. What has that to do with what we were talking about?"

"Everything and nothing. Good luck tonight. I'm supposed to say break a leg. The guy that started that tradition probably never broke one."

"I'm shooting in Mexicantown tomorrow. Will you come?"

"It so happens I'll be in the neighborhood."

"Just give your name at the barricade. I'll tell them to expect you."

The conversation was over, but I didn't want to let her go. "Can you tell me why you ever decided to film a music video in Detroit in February?"

She laughed. Except when she sang it was the only time she seemed to forget she had ever fought in a revolution. "I don't like my people to become too soft. How can you expect to feel the music when you do not know what it is like to be tired and hungry and cold?"

"If you can't lie any better than that, you should turn down the acting job."

"Once again you see through the butterfly's wings. The hotel rates are cheaper in winter. I have a very large company, and I prefer to finish a tour in the black. Did you know you can fill stadiums from New York to San Francisco and still lose money?"

"Sell T-shirts."

"I do. T-shirts, coffee mugs, my head bobbing on top of a twenty-dollar doll. That pays for the gasoline for the property truck. Sometimes it's all show and no business."

I had no frame of reference for comment. The Muñoz jabbered uninterrupted for thirty seconds. No other sounds, not even the band tuning up in the auditorium. Cobo's an old barn but the walls are as thick as bunkers.

"I have to get into character," she said finally; and as she said it the accent broadened. "Take care, Amos. You're least safe at the moment you feel safest. Nico taught me that."

"In that case I'm safe."

I probably should have told her good luck again. Maybe you should always tell a performer good luck at the beginning and end of a conversation. Then again maybe they just cancel each other out. What I said was good-bye.

The next time the telephone rang I was in bed. I wasn't asleep, and when I padded out into the living room I took along the revolver and didn't turn on any lights. When I said hello, the word wobbled into a hollow silence. I didn't even hear breathing.

I breathed for both of us. "Just for my own curiosity," I said, "where'd you get the bat?"

No one answered. No one hung up, either, and we were like that for a minute, two characters on opposite ends of the greatest invention in the history of communications, saying nothing. Then I remembered Matador's men had been in the house and knew where the telephone was, and consequently where I was at that moment. I cradled the receiver and got away from the spot.

It could have been a wrong number, or someone who'd called to sell storm doors and lost his nerve. I needed caller ID.

After a few minutes I walked through the house carrying the .38, checking windows and all three doors by the little bit of moonlight that kept me from bumping into furniture. Then I went back to bed. I got up three more times, twice to investigate noises I'd never noticed before in the quiet of the house, a third time to investigate why there were no noises at all. That time I poured a slug of Old Smuggler into a tumbler of water and put it all down in one easy deposit, like Bromo.

I may have dozed off once or twice, never deeply enough to lose awareness. Just before I went to sleep for real I could make out the features of the bedroom in the leaden light of predawn. I dreamt I was in the old Detroit General Hospital, sitting on a chair listening to my mother's respirator pumping and sighing.

When I woke up with a jump, full daylight pounded me in the face.

I'd survived the night. Now I had to make it through the day, which is the most dangerous time of all, because that's when you feel safe.

THIRTY-TWO

Church bells were ringing, reverberating with the heavy solid self-assured thrum of old-time coinmetal, a sound that can't be duplicated on a mixing board. They were swinging all over town, Detroit having nearly as many places to worship as it has bars and Pizza Huts. Religion runs deep into the pavement of industrial cities, built as they were on the strong backs of survivors of pogroms, purges, holocausts, and ethnic cleansings. Mosques, temples, cathedrals, kingdom halls, reading rooms, and cult coffeehouses sprout within blocks of one another like a theme park for the devout.

I couldn't pick out Most Holy Redeemer from Most Blessed Sacrament from Most Holy Trinity in the chorus, or for that matter make up my mind about how all three can claim to be the most; but then I'd sinned too much, blasphemed not a little, and seen too many saved and too many sacrificed to be sure of anything beyond question. Everybody is reaching out for something: God, a glass, a dog-eared dollar, a grope in a sweaty doorway—I'd given up the moral authority to pass judgment. Every hourly rate motel room has a Bible, and every set of pews its share of cheats and pedophiles. Today I was hoping one of the pews had Miranda Guzman.

I'd had to detour around Vernor ten blocks and circle back to park near the house. The police had barricaded off four blocks for Gilia's video and an additional six to make room for gawkers. I could hear electric guitars blanging up and down the scales from half a mile away, and the TV trucks whose crews were covering the event for the local news were parked nearly as far down as I was. I hadn't seen so many EMS vans and blue-and-whites gathered in one place since the riots. They couldn't all have been assigned to security. Cops are no more immune to rubbernecking than the rest of us. Ten stories up, a helicopter with the FOX-2 logo painted on its fuselage pummeled the air, which was heavy with rain or snow or ice, or something anyway that smelled like copper. One good lick on a bass and the low clouds would split open like a piñata.

The narrow yellow house was still sandwiched between the tire shop and the Mexican restaurant. *La Casa del Rubio.* I was almost surprised to see it. So much had happened since the last time, I'd half expected to find it razed and a forty-story casino sprung up in its place. Behind it, the yellow police tape would still be fluttering in a square around the section of the lumberyard where Isabella, the canario bitch, had sniffed out what was left of Jillian Rubio. It had only been four days.

I climbed the three painted wooden steps. The sign was still in the window advertising that the resident was an authorized presa canario breeder, CHD Free Guaranteed. I couldn't believe that a little over half a week before I'd never heard of the breed. I pressed the buzzer, keeping an eye on the wicker shade behind the sign. If a squat black snout pushed it aside I was out of there.

The buzz echoed emptily, followed by barking. The barking wasn't coming from inside the house, but from the kennel in back. The bull wasn't home. That meant Miranda Guzman wasn't either.

The lock was a dead bolt. I'm clumsy with a sliplatch and can't pick my nose with a jimmy. I looked around. God and Gilia had cleared the street of witnesses. I punched in the window with the butt of the .38, reholstered it, reached through and around and found the latch and twisted it. The bolt shot back. I retrieved my arm and let myself in.

No alarm sounded. More to the point, nothing jumped me to

tear out my throat. I was standing in the living room with the worn sofa-and-love-seat set, the magazines on the wicker coffee table, the carved crucifix on the wall, and the Spanish Bible on the side table with the rattan mat. A new votive candle stood on the little shelf under the crucifix, not burning. Mrs. Guzman was too practical not to extinguish it before she went out. Apart from that the room was as unchanged as a closed movie set.

I wasn't sure where to start. I didn't know what I was looking for. All I had was the knowledge that this was the house in which Jillian Rubio had spent her last hours. If I had any psychic powers I might have been vibrating like a tuning fork, but as it was the only sensation I got from things unseen was the smell of lemon wax, and underneath it dog. All I had to work with were my hands and my eyes and a small gnawed hunk of brain.

I went to the back of the house and worked my way to the front. A small kitchen looked out on the kennel, where a couple of the dogs were sleeping on the bare earth and a couple more were conducting personal self-inspections, including Isabella. A spare bedroom that had been a den had probably been Jillian's during her visit, but it had been cleaned since and the bed made, and if there'd been any clothes in the closet or personal items in the little dresser and nightstand, the cops had taken them along with her luggage. The rest of the ground floor told me little about Miranda that I hadn't already known or suspected and nothing about her daughter.

The house was a one-and-a-half-story construction, with a narrow steep staircase grandfathered in before code and sloping walls upstairs. Miranda had to stoop to approach her bed in order to avoid cracking her head on a joist. A paperback Spanish translation of a novel by an American author with a half-naked Saxon on the cover lay open facedown on the nightstand. Nothing in there.

The only other room upstairs besides the bathroom wasn't much bigger than a walk-in closet and was used for storage. Boxes that had contained cans of dog food were filled with the picture magazines Miranda liked, odd scraps of material, junk too broken to use but not worth lugging downstairs and out to the curb. Spavined umbrellas, out-of-style clothing, spare lightbulbs, a big old scuffed suitcase of foreign manufacture, shoved clear to the back and wearing a two-inch coat of dust. It would have been the first thing she put in storage after moving in, had probably contained whatever she had brought with her from the old country, and had been taking up the same space for as many years as she'd lived in the house; when you keep dogs, you don't do much traveling unless you're prepared to go to the trouble to find someone you trust to take care of the feeding and related chores. I wondered if the tapestry overnight bag she'd lent Jillian for the emergency trip had come from that same closet. I wondered what use Miranda had had for an overnight bag at all.

A thought sprouted in that close space. It didn't promise to end up big or even good. Hunches are like dates, and you have to kiss a lot of frogs if you're serious about pursuing the game. No judge would waste tax money on the one I had. Lack of evidence isn't evidence. She might have bought the bag for a trip to inspect breeding stock. But it got me to thinking about suitcases and what they might contain.

I had to move a heavy box out of the way and turn sideways to wriggle to the back of the closet, and then I had to lean across a stack of department-store catalogues and move a pile of heavy moth-eaten coats and dog manuals from on top of the suitcase to get to it. I got a lungful of house dust and when I sprang the green brass latches the inside of an empty suitcase.

When I turned away I bumped into the pile of junk I'd moved. Something slid out and landed on one end on the only clear patch of floor with a clank. It had a black tip with a flanged base. I dropped the pile back onto the suitcase, took hold of that end, and extricated the other from the tangle. It gave me some trouble because it was hooked at that end. It was an aluminum cane with a black composition handle.

The police were looking for that, without much hope of finding it. The killer who had picked Jillian Rubio up in his car while she was headed for the bus stop would surely have discovered it after he'd disposed of the body and gotten rid of it as well. It hadn't been found with her corpse. A woman whose legs had been weakened by a crippling disease early in life would have needed it to walk several blocks to catch a bus. She'd have needed it to leave her mother's house.

I left the suitcase as it was and started downstairs, carrying the cane by the middle, where I was least likely to smear fingerprints. Halfway down I stopped. Miranda Guzman was standing at the base of the stairs. She had the big male presa canario with her, and judging by the sounds that were rippling from its throat it didn't like what it was looking at any more than she did.

THIRTY-THREE

"You broke into my house."

She wore the cloth coat with the cheap fur collar she'd worn to church the other day. The black lace scarf was loose around her neck, no longer necessary to conceal her vanity from God. The dark hot eyes in that maturely beautiful face, flushed but not from the cold, were fixed on mine. She'd seen the cane in my hand. If she didn't look at it, perhaps it didn't exist. The big muscular bull only had eyes for the vein pulsing in my throat.

I nodded carefully. Dogs don't like jerky movements. "I rang the bell. No one answered, so I broke in. You should call the police."

If I'd expected that to rattle her, I was disappointed. She was as calm as a dormant volcano. There's no such thing as an extinct one.

"Lupo."

She spoke the name quietly, with absolute assurance that the meaning was understood; the same way Matador had said, "Felipe," just before the red-hot penny made its appearance. The dog's short stubby ears swiveled forward, like twin cocked hammers. The muscles across its chest bunched. The leash was off its collar, coiled up in its mistress' hand. I wondered if Lupo could clear the stairs in one spring. I decided he could, with fuel to spare.

"Young women confide in their mothers," I said. "Even an estranged daughter needs someone she can talk to, particularly when she's having a crisis of conscience. How much did she tell you about her arrangement?"

"Lupo?"

Slightly different inflection. The dog licked its chops, waggled its hips. No congenital hip displacement there. It was digging its rear paws into the floor for the pushoff.

"I'm guessing everything. There never was any cache of papers. You knew her story better than anyone. You would have the original of her birth certificate, if it was necessary. You were her ace in the hole, all set to step in just in case Gilia realized the only way to stop blackmail is to stop the blackmailer. You were the partner."

"Put down the cane and leave this house."

Lupo made a little whimpering noise of impatience, without going off point. My reaction was different. I figured there was only one way left to pronounce the dog's name.

I shook my head slowly. With my gun undrawn the cane was the only weapon handy. I wasn't turning my back on either of them.

Silence crackled. It made me think of Lupo crunching a hambone.

"Lupo, sit."

The hairs stood out on the backs of my hands when she said "Lupo"; but the dog grunted and sank onto its haunches. I took advantage of the reprieve to change hands on the cane and free my right. The distance between it and the .38 was still seven times farther than a canine bound up nine steps.

"We spoke of this before," Miranda said. "I am not a blackmailer."

"Just a murderer."

Lupo's ears twitched. Maybe the dog understood the word.

She said, "The cane means nothing. Two years ago I twisted my ankle, breaking up a fight between Isabella and one of her whelps. The cane is from then."

"In that case, you won't mind if they take a look at it in a police lab." Bluff. She might have wiped it off, and if any of Jillian's DNA was left it would be too close to her mother's to prosecute.

"You spoke of a crisis of conscience." She had a little trouble with the unfamiliar phrase. "I thought then perhaps you understood. My daughter was a good woman. Her life was difficult. She lost her way, but she found it again. We are none of us perfect under God."

My palms were damp. They'd been damp when Professor Zubarán had said the people of his country were capable of making up for past wrongs.

I said, "She never had any intention of keeping that appointment in Milwaukee. That's why she came here, to tell you what she'd been doing and that she'd decided to quit. Maybe she was going to return the money she'd extorted from Gilia. You fell out over it."

She said nothing. I opened and closed my free hand a couple of times, drying it in the air. A fast draw is useless when your palm is slippery.

I went on. "The cops thought—me, too—that the killer snatched Jillian off the street, probably in a car, and dumped the body a street over after injecting her with Stelazine. It had to be injected to work that fast. The only thing wrong with that theory was it was based on your statement that she broke off her visit to keep an appointment. Since that jibed with the date she'd had with Hector Matador, we bought it. It didn't have to make sense that she would come all this way to spend Thanksgiving with you, then reverse directions to make a pickup she'd been making once a month for a year. Everything doesn't have to match up in a homicide investigation as long as most of the facts fit. But if you run it so it does, she had no reason to be on the street the day she was killed. That means you made it up. She made this trip so she wouldn't be tempted to keep that appointment at all. So there was no car, and if there was no car there didn't have to be a needle. You could have emptied her prescription bottle into her cornflakes and let her take her own time about dying. Then you waited until after dark and lugged the corpse next door.

That wouldn't have been too much physical effort for a woman who's used to dragging a hundred-and-fifty-pound dog around on a leash."

"That is what you say."

"That's what the cane says. You should've dumped it with the body."

"I could not go back."

She wasn't talking to me. Her voice was so low that the dog, expecting a scratch behind the ears to go with what it thought was a murmured endearment, turned its huge square head to look up at her. No affection there. It returned its attention to me and smacked its loose lips, making a sound like a shovel scooping up wet cement.

"The cane was in the corner where she'd leaned it," Miranda said in that same almost inaudible tone. "I didn't see it until I came in from the lumberyard. I couldn't go back. Nothing could make me go back. I put it where I would not have to look at it."

Something had broken through in that stairwell. Zubarán had been dead right about the character of his countrymen. I said, "It had to be the money. She gave you a glimpse of how much could be made from the situation, then took it away in the same breath. So you got rid of her. How long were you planning to wait before you made your own arrangement with Gilia?"

"*¡Hijo del perro!*"

Her voice rang out the way it had in church when she'd called me a pig. Lupo leapt up on all fours, the ruff around his shoulders standing. I didn't know if it was because of her tone or the fact she'd called me a son of a dog.

Miranda's face was a primitive mask, something carved out by her ancestors before Christ to frighten away demons.

"*¡Culebra! ¡Mofeta!* I did not sin to follow it with sin. *La Casa del Rubio* was founded by *conquistadores*. Nobles and conquerors. There is not a parasite in the line. I told her this. She would not listen. She wanted to confess to a priest. I said all the priests in this city are of common stock, that she would disgrace the family by degrading herself before *jíbaros*. She laughed. She asked what honor I brought to the family when I cleaned dog filth. I had heard this before. It was why I banished her from my house the first time. But this time I held my temper. I waited until dinner, and then I did the thing I knew I must do to preserve the House of Rubio. It is as it is with dogs: The bloodline must be kept pure at all costs."

"You never forgave her for getting sick, did you?"

She took that in with an insane kind of self-discovery. "No. In dogs, several generations are required, and you must destroy those that are tainted. Had I known then what I now know, I would have taken this action then."

I waited until her voice stopped ringing off the stairway walls.

"Lady," I said, "you're loco."

Her face smoothed out. I knew what was coming. I drew the .38 and pointed it at the dog. Its name died in her throat. Lupo, whining frustration, looked up at his mistress, then back to me.

"Sit," she said.

Lupo sat. When all was said and done the dog meant more than the daughter; but then she'd put more work into it. I owed Noah Guzman an apology for what I'd been thinking about him all week.

I tightened my grip on the cane and walked downstairs. Neither dog nor woman moved, although as I backed around it the dog followed me with its head, growling on a rising note as if pleading. Miranda paid it no attention. Her head didn't turn. She was staring at something in the middle ground between her and the sixteenth century.

I wanted to use a telephone, but not the one in that house. I opened the door and backed through it and didn't turn around until I'd pulled it shut behind me.

A blue Bonneville was parked against the curb in front of the house. As I stepped onto the sidewalk the door opened on the driver's side and Hector Matador bounded out, raising a chromed semiautomatic too big for his slender hand.

I was still holding the revolver. We fired at the same time. He spun halfway around as if he'd been sideswiped. I'd aimed for his middle, but just as I'd squeezed the trigger something piled into me from behind, a runaway piano or a big log rolling off the back of a truck, making a noise halfway between a roar and a scream, and I stumbled and fell beneath its weight. I half rolled to keep from landing on my face and my elbow struck the sidewalk, but before the pain made its way up my arm I pushed the weight off me. It slid to the grass without bouncing, all dead heft like a sack of meat. My hand was soaked with blood, not mine. Lupo, the great canario bull, sprawled beside me with his tongue on the ground and his eyes already beginning to glaze. The bullet had pierced his heart in midpounce. A hell of a snap shot on the part of someone who hadn't fired a pistol since before he went to prison for firing it the last time.

I heard howling. I thought the dogs in the kennel had sensed what had happened and gone into mourning. Then I saw Miranda Guzman standing on the top step in front of her house, both hands balled into fists at her sides with the leash still coiled in one. Her mouth was wide open and the sound that came out was more canine than human.

Matador lay on his side with one foot hanging over the curb. He had on a three-button beige suit that went well with his brown skin. One side of the coat was stained almost black. He was breathing heavily.

I pushed myself up with one hand. The other arm was dead from the elbow down, but when it moved someone stuck an ice pick into the bone, and a wave of nausea washed over me. I was pretty sure I'd cracked something when I hit the sidewalk. I clamped the arm tight to my side and picked up my gun with the other hand but didn't put it in the holster. Matador was still Matador and I couldn't see what had become of his.

Someone, probably a returning churchgoer, had called 911. I heard the first gulp of a siren coming up out of the ground a hundred blocks away. The police units and emergency vans parked near the video set would be just catching the same squal. In another minute we were going to be up to our necks in authority. I went over, saw the shiny pistol lying next to Matador's hip, and used my toe to nudge it out of his reach. I felt a little faint then, and to keep from falling I sat on the grass next to him. His one visible eye was open and it moved my direction.

"Help's on its way, amigo," I said. "You picked the best time and the best place in town to get shot."

"I am a fortunate man, Anglo." He sounded hoarse.

"Where'd I get you?"

"The ribs, I think. You are one bad shot."

"I was distracted."

"I wish the woman would be quiet. Such display is not sympathetic."

"She'll quiet down when her P.D. tells her to." The arm had begun to ache like a tooth. "You surprised me there. I thought you were shooting at me."

"That was the intention when you came out."

"What happened?"

"I do not like dogs. A dog chewed up the first good pair of shoes I bought when I came to this country."

"I thought it was something else."

He laughed hoarsely. A siren whooped startlingly close by and I had to lean over to hear him.

"Everything here is something else, Anglo. That is the draw."

THIRTY-FOUR

Big Bad Benny had his marching orders. He had on a red leather suit today and looked like a monster tomato bowling a path through the printhawks and *Eyewitness News* wonks stacked twelve deep outside Gilia's suite with me trailing behind. They dressed and smelled better than Fritz Fleeman. They were probably different in other ways as well, but when they herded up like that, squawking and flapping their feathers, you wanted to drop a safe on them just the same.

When we were inside, he put a shoulder to the door and leaned it shut, nearly breaking a microphone and the set of fingers holding it, and told me to wait there while he tapped his knuckles on the door to the bedroom.

"*¿Quién es?*"

Déjà vu flashed through me and settled in my chipped elbow. I hadn't liked the exchange the first time I'd heard it outside Gilia's dressing room at Cobo Hall.

This time I got in without a "hokay." Benny stayed outside. She looked up from an oyster-colored writing desk in the corner opposite the king-size bed. She had on a sky-blue traveling suit with natural shoulders, no blouse, and those little rectangular reading glasses that look like twin microscope slides. Her hair was loose. She took off the glasses, put down her pen, and stood, all in one movement.

"I know now why you didn't show up yesterday. Is it as bad as it looks?"

"Nothing's ever as bad as it looks." My arm was in a blue nylon sling padded with foam rubber, with an elastic strap that went around my chest to keep the arm immobile. "It would get me a seat on the subway, if we had a subway. I can play tennis in four to six weeks. If I played tennis." We said the last part together. She laughed. Then she stopped.

"Hector?" she said.

"He'll be strapped up tighter for a little longer. They took out a rib and pinned two others back together. That's not the worst of it. Having that pistol sends him back to Jackson."

"Life?"

"Alderdyce thinks a nickel bit. That's American for five years. Out in two if he minds his manners inside. If there are any animal rightists on the jury he may get the chair." I started to shrug, thought better of it. "This is all contingent on what the judge thinks of my testimony. The cops gave it a three-point-five, with most of the loss on the dismount." I'd sketched in the broad strokes by telephone from the emergency room at Detroit Receiving. By then I'd been over the finer points several times with the officers in the waiting room.

"He saved your life."

"Yeah. He let me down there at the end. Matador being Matador was the one thing I thought I could count on in this town. He called me *un postizo* when they were loading him into the ambulance. What's that?"

"It is not flattering."

"I didn't think it was. He was probably in pain. He won't be sending anyone any bats for a while."

"That's the second time you've mentioned bats. I don't know what it means."

"Private joke between enemies. Miranda Guzman put the punch line on it."

"What about her?"

"Man One, if she's competent to stand trial. They tend to take it easy on you when it's your own flesh and blood, no one seems to know why. Say, ten to fifteen. That's seventy to a hundred and five in dog years. She ought to spend them in an upholstered room."

"She confessed."

"She confessed. It came natural. It was Sunday." I was tired of discussing Miranda Guzman. She'd been the sole topic of conversation for twenty-four hours. "Shouldn't you be packing?"

"Packed. Caterina sees to that. My flight leaves in three hours, just time enough to get through security and the jackals out in the hall. And write a song." She laughed, gesturing at the desk-top.

"I didn't know you composed your own stuff."

"Today I'm inspired. It's called 'Penance.' "

"A national characteristic, I'm told. How are you with Immigration?"

"As we speak, a firm of overpriced attorneys is working on that very thing. With luck, the government at home may change hands between delays and extensions. I may return a hero. In which case I will endow an infantile disease research center there in Jillian Rubio's name."

"Penance?"

"Redemption, I hope. What is this?"

I'd slid an envelope out of my inside breast pocket and placed it on the desk. "There's a check inside. The medical expenses ran high on this one, but most of it's there, not counting my *per diem*."

"You earned the entire fifteen thousand."

"Maybe. Endow me a drinking fountain at the Rubio Center."

The equatorial sun came out when she smiled.

A blatty little horn sounded when I stepped out under the canopy. A red Geo was parked in the turnaround in front of the lobby. I went over to it. Fritz Fleeman's war with hygiene rolled out when he cranked down his window. His reporter's instincts kicked in when he read my expression.

"Cool your jets," he said. "I'm headed out. When Gilia goes, so go I."

"Grammar. I thought it was some intern's job to put that in back at the paper."

"I ain't just a shutterbug, pal. I'm a photojournalist." He stuck something outside the window.

I took it. It was a grainy shot printed on cheap paper of a couple kissing.

I said, "That's my bad side. How'd you switch the film?"

"You learn to load on the run. I can make you famous."

"How much you charge not to?"

"I don't work that street. Anyway, if I did, you'd just shove it up my ass, am I right?" He twisted his head to look up at me from under the bill of his cap.

"Down your throat. But you're right in principle."

"Then I'd get sore and sell the shot, and then I'd have to come back to this shithole and take your picture again some other time, because you'd be a fucking celebrity. This town's best feature is it's got nothing and nobody worth a frame of Fuji standard stock."

"That's what it says in Michelin. So why show me the picture?"

"Call it a souvenir. Just at a guess I'd say you don't kiss many superstars."

"Kiss, no. I shot one once. That count?"

"Only if I peddled to the *Police Gazette*." He started the tickity engine. "Get your business straightened out?"

"What business?"

He showed his bad teeth and cranked up the window. This time he took off easily. The pavement was sheeted with ice.

The Gilia Cristobal/Jillian Rubio story hit big. Alderdyce got his fifteen seconds of fame on *Nightline* and an offer from NBC to air his life story over two nights. He declined without disappointing anyone beyond consolation; by then another household name was in custody for forgetting to leave his gun behind when he went through security at LAX and the story got stale. It flared up again when Gilia's new video came out, and again when someone in the U.S. State Department issued a statement that the government had decided not to deport her in return for some patriotic TV public-service spots she'd agreed to appear in. After that she moved back to the entertainment section.

I didn't get a photo op, not even a line. Professor Miguel Zubarán took my spot among *People*'s 100 Most Intriguing People. It had to be the eye patch.

Miranda Guzman was declared mentally unfit to stand trial and admitted to the criminal ward at whatever institution had replaced the old State Forensics Hospital in Ypsilanti. Hector Matador pleaded guilty to parole violation and served twenty-six months in the Southern Michigan State Penitentiary in Jackson. I spoke briefly at the sentencing.

Several months after the story broke I received a FedEx package with the return address of a talent agency in Los Angeles. I took out the videotape and popped it into my VCR. The Detroit footage was brief and showed Gilia in a long white communion-style dress with her hair tied back, kneeling in the middle of West Vernor before a digitally inserted life-size sculpture of the Virgin and Child. It had a nice stark cold Ingmar Bergman look. Whatever she'd shot on the riverfront didn't make the final cut. The rest was the usual frantic montage of her in various costumes against various backdrops, exotic and tawdry, lip-synching a song of her own composition. No letter had accompanied the cassette and I didn't write back. The song shot up the Top Forty list and lingered at No. 1 for four weeks until it was replaced by Eminem. I think it won some kind of award.

From time to time I get out the photograph Fritz Fleeman took and look at it. More and more it looks like a picture of two people I recognize vaguely, without remembering their names or the circumstances of our meeting. Anyway it's fading now, and in a year or so it will be nothing but a white rectangle of cheap photo paper, as blank as a wiped slate. It's called Redemption, and it never comes without a stiff tag.

ABOUT THE AUTHOR

Loren D. Estleman, author of the acclaimed Amos Walker private detective novels and the Detroit series, has won three Shamus Awards from the Private Eye Writers of America, four Golden Spur Awards from the Western Writers of America, and three Western Heritage Awards from the National Cowboy Hall of Fame. He has been nominated for the Edgar Allan Poe Award, the National Book Award, and the Pulitzer Prize. His other novels include the western historical classics *Billy Gashade*, *Journey of the Dead*, and *The Master Executioner*. Detroit hit man Peter Macklin made his return in *Something Borrowed, Something Black* (2002), having previously appeared in three novels: *Kill Zone*, *Roses Are Dead,* and *Any Man's Death. Poison Blonde* is the sixteenth Amos Walker novel, his first for Forge Books. Estleman lives in Michigan with his wife, author Deborah Morgan.